MIXED BLOOD

MIXED
BLOOD

A Thriller

ROGER SMITH

HENRY HOLT AND COMPANY
NEW YORK

Henry Holt and Company, LLC
Publishers since 1866
175 Fifth Avenue
New York, New York 10010
www.henryholt.com

Henry Holt® and ® are registered trademarks of Henry Holt and Company, LLC.

Library of Congress Cataloging-in-Publication Data

Smith, Roger, 1960–
    Mixed blood : a thriller / Roger Smith.—1st ed.
        p.   cm.
    ISBN-13: 978-0-8050-8875-5
    ISBN-10: 0-8050-8875-X
1. Fugitives from justice—Fiction.   2. Americans—South Africa—Fiction.
3. Cape Town (South Africa)—Fiction.   I. Title.
    PR9369.4.S65M59   2009
    823'.92—dc22   2008008842

Henry Holt books are available for special promotions and premiums.
For details contact: Director, Special Markets.

First Edition 2009

Designed by Linda Kosarin

Printed in the United States of America

1   3   5   7   9   10   8   6   4   2

For Sumaya

MIXED BLOOD

CHAPTER 1

Jack Burn stood on the deck of the house high above Cape Town watching the sun drown itself in the ocean. The wind was coming up again, the southeaster that reminded Burn of the Santa Anas back home. A wind that made a furnace of the night, set nerves jangling, and got the cops and emergency teams caught up in people's bad choices.

Burn heard the growl of the car without mufflers as it came to a sliding stop. The percussive whump of bass bins bulging out gangsta rap. Not the usual soundtrack of this elite white neighborhood on the slopes of Signal Hill. The car reversed at high speed and stopped again, close by. The engine died, and the rap was silenced in mid-*muthahfuckah*. Burn looked down at the street, but he couldn't see the car from this angle.

Susan watched him from inside the house, the glass doors open onto the deck.

"Come and eat." She turned and disappeared into the gloom.

Burn went inside and switched on the lights. The house was clean, hard-edged, and modern. Very much like the German rich kid who had rented it to them for six months while he went home to Stuttgart to watch his father die.

Susan carried the fillet from the kitchen, moving with that backward-leaning, splay-footed waddle of the heavily pregnant. She was beautiful. Small, blonde, with a face that stubbornly refused to admit to being twenty-eight. Aside from the huge belly, she looked exactly as she had seven years ago. He remembered the instant he first saw her, the feeling of the breath being squeezed from his lungs, his head dizzy with the knowledge that he was going to marry her. And he did, not six months later, laughing off the difference in their ages.

Susan looked the same, but she wasn't. Her lightness was gone, her easy laugh a memory. Lately she'd seemed to be in constant communion with her unborn child. That's how she referred to it, as her child. Her daughter. As if Burn and Matt were another species, outside of this exclusive club of two.

Burn sliced into the fillet with a carving knife, and blood pooled on the cutting board. Perfect. Rare, the way they all liked it. Matt lay on his belly in front of the plasma TV watching the Cartoon Network. Just like home.

"Hey, get over here and eat," Burn said.

Matt was about to protest; then he thought better of it and came across to the table, dressed only in a pair of baggy shorts. He was four, blond like his mother but with some early trace of his father's frame.

Susan was seated, piling salad onto their plates. She didn't look at Matt. "Go and wash your hands."

"They're not dirty," he said as he clambered up onto a chair. He held his hands out for her to inspect. She ignored him. It wasn't intentional; it was just as if she wasn't tuned to his frequency anymore. As if her son reminded her too much of his father.

Burn tried to get Susan's eye, to somehow draw her back to them. But she stared down at her plate.

"Listen to your mother," he said gently, and Matt took off for the bathroom, sliding on his bare feet.

Burn was carving the fillet when the two brown men came in off the deck. They both carried guns, pointed action-movie style at right angles. From the way they were laughing, he knew they were cooked on speed.

The night the trouble came, Benny Mongrel was watching them, the American family, out on the deck of the house next door. The guy drinking wine, glimpses of the blonde woman, the kid running between the deck and the house, the sliding door open onto the hot summer night. A snapshot of a world Benny Mongrel had never known.

He had been in and out of jail since he was fourteen. He wasn't sure, but he guessed he was turning forty. That's what his ID said, anyway. When he was paroled from Pollsmoor Prison last year after serving a sixteen-year stretch, he swore he wasn't going back. No matter what.

So that's why he was pulling the night shift on the building site as a watchman. The pay was a joke, but with his face and the crude prison tattoos carved into his gaunt brown body he was lucky to get a job. They gave him a rubber baton and a black uniform that was too big. And they gave him a dog. Bessie. A mongrel like him, part rottweiler, part German shepherd. She was old, she stank, her hips were finished, and she slept most of the time, but she was the only thing that Benny Mongrel had ever loved.

Benny Mongrel and Bessie were up on the top floor of the new house, the roof open to the stars, when he heard the car. It was tuned loud the way they did out on the Cape Flats. He walked to the edge of the balcony and looked down. A red early-nineties BMW-3 series sped down the road toward him, way too fast. The driver hit the brakes just below where Benny Mongrel stood, and the fat tires found builder's sand and the car fishtailed before stopping. The BMW reversed until it was level with the entrance to the building site. The wheelman cut the engine and the hip-hop died.

Everything went very quiet. Benny Mongrel could hear Bessie wheezing as she slept. He could hear the pinging of the BMW's cooling engine. He was tense. He was aware of that old feeling he knew so well.

Benny Mongrel stood watching, invisible, as the two men got out of the car. He saw enough of them in the streetlight, caps on backward, baggy clothes, the Stars and Stripes on the back of the tall man's jacket, to recognize members of the Americans gang, the biggest on the Cape Flats.

His natural enemy.

He was ready for them. He put the baton aside and slid the knife from where it waited in his pocket. He eased the blade open. If they came up here, they would see their mothers.

But they were going toward the house next door. Benny Mongrel watched as the tall one boosted his buddy up, the shorty pulling himself onto the deck like a monkey. Then he was reaching a hand down to the other guy. Benny Mongrel couldn't see them from where he stood, but he knew the American family would be eating at the table, the sliding door open to the night.

He closed the knife and slipped it back into his pocket.

Welcome to Cape Town.

━━━◆━━━

Susan had her back to the men. She saw the look on Burn's face and turned. She didn't have time to scream. The one closest to her, the short one, got a hand over her mouth and a gun to her head.

"S'trues fuck, bitch, you shut up, or I'll fucken shoot you." The hard, guttural accent. The man's skinny arms were covered in gang tattoos.

The tall man was round the table, waving his gun at Burn.

Burn put the carving knife down and lifted his hands off the table, in plain view. He tried to keep his voice calm. "Okay, we don't want any trouble. We'll give you whatever you want."

"You got that right. Where you from?" asked the man coming at Burn. He was as lanky as a basketball player.

"We're American," said Burn.

The short one was laughing. "So are we."

"Ja, we all Americans here. Like a big flipping happy family, hey?" The tall man nudged Burn with the muzzle of the gun, positioning himself behind the chair to Burn's right.

The short one pulled Susan to her feet. "Oh, we got a mommy here."

Burn watched as the man slid his hand under Susan's dress, grabbing at her crotch and squeezing. He saw her eyes close.

It was coincidence, pure and simple.

Somebody had told Faried Adams that his girlfriend, Bonita, was selling her ass in Sea Point, when she was supposed to be visiting her mommy in the hospital. Faried hadn't minded that she was hooking again, but he'd absolutely minded that she wasn't giving him any of the money. He wanted to catch the bitch on the job.

So lanky Faried went and banged on the door of his short-ass buddy Ricardo Fortune. Rikki lived in one of those ghetto blocks in Paradise Park where washing sagged from lines strung across walkways and the stairways stank of piss. Rikki had a car. But he also had a wife, Carmen, who moaned like a pig about everything. Which is why Rikki smacked her all the time. Faried would do the same; in fact that bitch Bonita was gonna get a black eye tonight, too. If she was lucky.

Faried and Rikki took the BMW to Sea Point after Faried put a couple of bucks in Rikki's hand. They cruised up and down the hookers' strip, slumped low in the car, bouncing to Tupac as they drove. There were a few brown girls working the street, all thick makeup and dresses that just about covered their plumbing, but no Bonita.

"I fucken had enough of this, man," said Rikki. "Let's go."

"Okay, tell you what. Drive over to Bo-Kaap. My cousin Achmat is there. We can come back later, and maybe I catch Bonnie swallowing some whitey's dick."

Rikki was shaking his head. "I don't want to go to Bo-Kaap, man. I rather go home."

"We can smoke a globe. And then we come back later."

"Achmat going to have a globe?"

"No, I got it by me."

"Why the fuck you only tell me now?" Rikki was throwing the car into a U-turn, ignoring the minibus taxi that had to slam on its brakes.

Rikki shot up Glengariff Road, wanting to hang a left into High Level, the quickest way to Bo-Kaap. But his cell phone, a tiny Nokia he had recently stolen from a tourist at the Waterfront, blared out the opening bars of Tupac's "Me Against the World." Rikki fished it out of his cargo pants, saw who was calling, and sent it to voice mail. Fucken Gatsby. The fat cop wanted money. Money that Rikki didn't have no more.

Distracted, he overshot the turn and ended up on the slopes of Signal Hill.

"You missed High Level," said Faried.

"I know. I'll cut through."

Rikki was speeding the car down a narrow road, fancy houses hugging the slope. Then he hit the brakes and the car skidded to a stop.

"What the fuck?" asked beanpole Faried, his head banging the roof.

Rikki was reversing back up the road. "You got your gat?"

"Your mommy wearing a panty?" Faried patted the Colt shoved in his waistband. "Why?"

Rikki stopped the car and cut the music. "Let's go into that house." He pointed to a house with a deck built over the garage.

Faried was staring at him. "You fucken crazy, brother?"

"Quick, in and out. Those places is full of stuff. Maybe we have some fun, too." Rikki smiled, showing his rotten teeth. "Let's smoke that globe, and we do it."

Faried thought for a moment; then he shrugged. "Why the fuck not?"

He took the stash of crystal meth and the unthreaded lightbulb from his jacket pocket. With practiced ease he fed the meth into the bulb and held it out. Rikki applied his lighter to the base, and within seconds Faried was sucking up a big chesty of meth. It made a *tik-tik* sound in the globe, the sound that gave meth its Cape Flats name. He held the tik smoke in his lungs and passed the globe to Rikki, who sucked at it. Rikki blew out a plume of smoke.

Nothing like Hitler's drug to put you in a party mood.

⟍⟋

The short man, the one with his hand under Susan's dress, gyrated obscenely, moving his hips against her. His mouth gaped, and Burn could see the blackened front teeth. Susan opened her eyes and looked straight at Burn.

The guy behind Burn laughed. "We gonna have us some nice fun tonight."

And that was when Matt came running back into the room. The eyes of the two men were drawn to the boy, who skidded to a stop, staring at them.

This gave Burn the moment he needed. As he twisted in his chair, he grabbed the carving knife from the table and buried it to its haft in the tall man's chest. Blood geysered from his ruptured heart. Burn stood, grabbed him before he fell, and used his body as a shield. He felt the lanky man take the bullet fired by the short one. Then Burn shoved him away, launched himself, and grabbed the short guy by his gun arm. His weight took both of them to the floor. Burn twisted the man's arm and heard it break. The gun clattered to the tiles.

Susan backed away. Burn kneed the short guy in the balls, and he curled like a worm into a fetal position. Burn looked over his shoulder. The tall one was dead, his spreading blood almost reaching Matt's bare toes. His son was frozen, staring.

Burn reached back onto the table for a steak knife.

"Take Matt out of here," he told Susan.

"Jack . . ."

"Take him out of here!"

Susan rushed across the tiles, grabbed the boy, and disappeared down the corridor toward the bedrooms.

Gripping the steak knife, Burn kneeled over the short man, who was staring up at him, wide-eyed. "Mister, we wasn't gonna do nothing . . ."

Burn hesitated for only a moment; then he reached down and cut the short man's throat.

CHAPTER 2

Carmen Fortune fed her four-year-old son, Sheldon. He lay in a small crib, his withered limbs jerking and his sightless eyes moving in their sockets. The food dribbled from his mouth.

He had been born three months premature, blind and deformed, with massive brain damage. Nobody knew how or why he'd survived. Except Carmen. She knew God had cursed her. Made sure that every time she looked at her son she remembered all the tik she had smoked while she carried him inside her. He was a constant reminder of the hell that waited for her one day.

If it wasn't for the grant the state paid every month for Sheldon, she would put a pillow over his face and no one could blame her. But her useless bastard husband, Rikki, smoked away whatever money he scammed or stole.

What the fuck, she was already in hell. Could it, honest to God, get worse?

Carmen was twenty but looked thirty. Her faced was bruised and swollen from the latest beating. Rikki hit her because she wasn't giving him a normal child, one that he could show off to his buddies to prove that he didn't father only mutants. That's what he called Sheldon: a fucken mutant.

The doctors told her that her womb was finished; she couldn't have no more kids. She didn't tell Rikki. He would have killed her. Better just to take the beatings.

When she heard the banging on the door, she knew there was only one fat white bastard who would hammer like that.

"Uncle Fatty!" She yelled across to where an ancient rail-thin man, wearing only a pair of dirty briefs, slumped in front of the TV. He drank from a bag of wine, his toothless mouth sucking at it like it was a tit. "Uncle Fatty, open the fucken door!" He mumbled something but stayed where he was.

The banging continued. Carmen drew her nightgown around her body, crossed to the door, and pulled it open. Gatsby filled the doorway, fat and stinking.

"He's not here," said Carmen.

The white plainclothes cop pushed her aside and walked in. Without a word he crossed the small living room, stuck a head into the kitchen, and then went into the only bedroom. She heard the closet doors banging and the sound of breaking glass. Then he came back out, wheezing like a cheap concertina.

Carmen stood with her hands on her hips. "I tole you."

"Where is he?" Gatsby came right up to her, and she could feel his foul breath on her face. He had food in his mustache.

"How the fuck must I know? He went out with Faried. In the car."

"Where to?"

"I dunno."

Gatsby had her against the wall. Jesus, he stank. "Talk to me."

"They said something about Faried's girl whoring in Sea Point."

"That's all?"

"Yes, that's all. And what is this? The Weakest fucken Link?"

Gatsby stared down at her. "No wonder he smacks you. You've got a mouth like a shit-house."

"And you stink like one."

Gatsby's fist came up. She didn't flinch. "Hit me, you bastard. I'm used to it."

He wheezed and dropped his hand. "Tell that fucker Rikki I want my money. Tonight still."

She shook her head. "Good luck."

Gatsby slammed out, and she locked the door. Uncle Fatty had passed out in a spreading pool of piss. Carmen went into the bedroom and saw that the fat boer had broken her mirror.

"Men," she said to herself as she sat down on the bed. "I wish they would all fucken die."

＞

Burn washed the blood from his hands at the kitchen sink. As he wiped his hands he stood and listened intently. Nothing. No shouts, no sirens, no concerned neighbor ringing the buzzer. He walked past the bodies toward the bedrooms, closing the passage door behind him. Burn found Susan and Matt in the main bedroom, huddled on the bed. Susan cradled their son.

Matt looked at him over Susan's shoulder. "Daddy . . ."

"Daddy's here, Matty." Burn sat down on the bed. "Everything's fine." He reached out a hand and touched Matt's hair. He knew he couldn't avoid looking at his wife's eyes any longer. "You okay?"

Susan stared at him. "What do you think?"

Burn reached a hand toward her face. She pulled back. "Don't."

He dropped the hand. She looked at him with haunted eyes. "So what happens now?"

"I clean up. Get rid of the . . . them."

"Just like that? And what, we just forget this happened? Go to the beach in the morning?" Her eyes were locked to his.

"I did what I had to do," he said.

"That's your mantra, isn't it, Jack? And you're sticking to it." She was still staring at him, hating him.

He stood. "I'm sorry."

"Sorry for what? That we're not at home? That you brought us to a place where animals like that . . ." She stopped, shaking her head, her eyes pinning him. "Or are you sorry that you've become one of them?"

He dragged his eyes away, unable to offer her any words. He had cleaning up to do. As he reached the door she spoke.

"Jack." There was something urgent in her voice. A different kind of fear.

He turned to her. She was watching a pool of blood spreading from between her legs onto the white duvet. "Jesus, Jack, I'm losing her . . ."

Benny Mongrel, squatting on his haunches, took Rizla papers and a bag of Dinglers cherry tobacco from his uniform pocket and rolled a cigarette, his fingers deft and practiced. His eyes hadn't moved from the American's house since the two men had crossed the deck and disappeared inside. He'd seen nothing more. All he'd heard was the single gunshot.

Bessie had reared up at the sound of the shot and started to whine softly. Benny Mongrel had put a hand on her head to calm her. "Shhhhhh, Bessie. Still."

The old dog had keened once more, then collapsed onto the concrete with a sigh and lay there with one eye open.

Benny Mongrel had sat and watched, waiting. Waiting to see the gangsters come out of the house and drive off into the night in that red BMW. But there was no sign of the men. Or the American and his family.

The guy who had called him *sir*.

Benny Mongrel had been called many things. He had been called bastard, bushman, rubbish, and, for many years, Prisoner 1989657. White men in suits had called him a menace to society. Brown men bleeding from his knife had called him brother as they begged for mercy. He had none to show them. Cape Flats gutter curses had been spat at him since he was ripped from the womb of a woman he never knew. But nobody had ever called him *sir*.

Not until the American.

Benny Mongrel and Bessie were walking the front of the site one evening, the old dog dragging her back legs, when the little white kid had come running up to them. He only had eyes for Bessie and reached out to pet her. Benny Mongrel wasn't sure how Bessie would react and he pulled back on her chain, but she wagged her tail and stood there docile as you please, the kid stroking her matted fur.

Then the white man came over. He'd been unlocking the street door to the neighboring house, a high-walled fortress like all the others in the street, when the kid scooted over.

"Hey, Matt. Take it easy."

The guy spoke like the people on those TV shows the other prisoners had watched in Pollsmoor Prison. American. He looked a bit like somebody from those shows too, biggish with a clean face and some gray in his dark hair.

Even though it was nearly 7:00 p.m., the sun was still high, so when the kid looked up at Benny Mongrel for the first time, he could see his face clearly. And that was when the kid let go of Bessie and jumped back, like he had seen about the worst thing imaginable. He stood and stared up at Benny Mongrel, unable to tear his eyes away. He opened his mouth to scream, but all he could find was a whimper.

The big guy scooped the kid up and held him, face into his shoulder. Then he looked Benny Mongrel straight in his good eye. "I'm sorry, sir. Excuse my son."

Benny Mongrel said nothing. Just stood there looking at the white guy who never reacted, never even blinked as he took in the horror that was the left side of his face. Benny Mongrel had lived inside this mess of misshapen bones and keloid scar tissue for more than twenty years. He didn't care. His face had served him well. It had been an asset in the life he had lived.

Most people reacted the way the kid did when they saw his face, but the American guy stuck out his hand. "My name's Jack. I live next door."

Benny Mongrel had never shaken hands with a white man, and he wasn't about to start now. He hauled at Bessie's chain, whistled sharply to get her moving, and headed back onto the site.

But something about the American had got his interest. He would watch them from the top floor of the building site, the big guy and his small blonde wife and the kid. In their house or driving away in their fancy Jeep.

Benny Mongrel finished rolling his cigarette. He lit it, his ruined face visible in the flaring match. He sucked the warm smoke deep into his lungs, and as he exhaled he heard the siren.

The ambulance screamed up to the house and two medics got out. The door in the garden wall buzzed open, and Benny Mongrel watched as they hurried inside. The medics carried the white woman out on a stretcher. They put her in the back of the ambulance and drove away. The light flashed, but the siren was mute.

Benny Mongrel waited. Puzzled. Where were the gangsters? And where were the cops?

Then the garage door rolled up and the big guy reversed out in the Jeep. The door rolled shut. As the Jeep passed beneath him, Benny could see the child strapped into the car seat in the back.

Benny unfolded himself from his squatting position and walked to the edge of the balcony. He looked down at the red BMW, then back at the house next door. Bessie appeared beside him and licked his hand.

He patted her head and spoke in a whisper. "I think they seen their mothers, Bessie."

Inspector Rudi Barnard, known on the Flats as Gatsby, drove his white Toyota through the rape and murder capital of the world, the dark flip side of the Cape Town tourist postcard. The night was full of the usual music of the Cape Flats: sirens, snatches of screams and laughter, gunshots, and pumping hip-hop. The Flats were where anybody who wasn't white had got dumped back in the days of apartheid, far from the privileged suburbs slung like jewels around Table Mountain. A desolate, bleak sheet of land persecuted by wind and dust.

Even when it wasn't hot, Barnard sweated, but on this January night the water dripped from his jowls, gluing the shirt to his sumo-sized gut. All the windows of the Toyota were open as he drove, but the air lay heavy as a dead whore across the Cape Flats.

Rudi Barnard loved Jesus Christ, gatsbys, and killing people. And out here on the Flats he could feel that love the most.

The bumper-sticker simplicity of reborn Christianity suited Barnard well. He would get up each morning and pray. Then he would part his air bag–sized butt cheeks and smear Preparation H on his hemorrhoids, clothe himself in jeans and check shirts from the Big 'n Tall shop, strap on his Z88 9 mm service pistol, and go forth and dispense frontier justice in the name of the Lord Jesus Christ.

Unbidden, an image of Carmen Fortune's body came to him, her breasts and thighs barely covered by the short nightgown. He pushed it away. Barnard couldn't remember when last he'd had sex with a woman. Sometime before his bitch of a wife had finally left him. He didn't miss her or the screwing. He had always found the process disgusting. When the urge grew too great for prayer to subdue, he spent a few guilt-stricken minutes in communion with his hand and a *Hustler* magazine.

To distract himself from that image of the half-breed's brown thighs, he grabbed the mike of the car radio, barking out an APB on Rikki Fortune's red BMW. Saying it might be in the Sea Point area. He wasn't desperate for the five grand Rikki owed him. His web of vice and corruption generated a constant source of income that met his modest needs. But he couldn't let a little cunt like Rikki get away with anything.

Fear was his God-fueled power. Any sign of weakness and it would be his body found dumped in an open strip of veld.

The law of the jungle.

⤙

Burn paced the waiting room of a private hospital in a leafy suburb of Cape Town, his son sleeping on a chair, his young wife and her de-tached placenta somewhere behind swinging doors, and two dead bodies going cold in his dining room.

When they'd fled the United States three months before, he'd had little time to decide on a destination. Not Asia, because they would be too visible and he had wanted to be sure of medical care for his pregnant wife. Not Europe, too much of a colony of the States. It would be harder to disappear. It was a toss-up between Sydney or Cape Town. Australia, despite its huge landmass, had a tiny population, and Burn had felt claustrophobic just thinking about it. South Africa sounded good, with a Western infrastructure if you could afford it, but chaotic enough for a man to fall through the cracks.

But that chaos had reached out and grabbed hold of his life by the throat.

"Sir?" A pale-skinned young nurse in a crisp uniform appeared before him. "You can see your wife now."

Burn stood and reached down for Matt. The nurse shook her head. "I'm sorry, but the little boy can't go in with you." She smiled. "Don't worry, I'll sit with him."

Burn managed a smile in return. "Thank you."

Susan was in a private ward that looked like a hotel room. She lay in bed, wan and beautiful. She opened her eyes when Burn came in.

He hesitated, then took her hand. She let him. "How are you feeling?"

"Everything's okay, Jack. My baby is fine."

He nodded. "I know."

"I just need to stay in here for a couple of days."

"Good. Let them take care of you."

She took her hand back. "You go now."

"Are you okay?"

"I just want to sleep."

"I'll see you tomorrow."

She nodded, closing her eyes, already withdrawing from him as he walked away.

CHAPTER 3

It was just past 10:00 p.m. when Burn slowed the Jeep Cherokee outside his house. He was tense, expecting police cars and security patrol vehicles. There were cars, all right, more than usual, lining both sides of the road. But they were the luxury vehicles common to these streets of plenty: convertibles and SUVs.

The night, now that the wind had died, was still and hot, and he caught the tang of animal fat cooking on a wood fire. He had to fight back a sudden feeling of nausea, knowing what waited for him in his dining room.

He pressed the garage remote, and as the door rolled up he heard snatches of an overorchestrated version of a Beatles song he couldn't place, and the trill of genteel laughter wafting across from the party at a neighboring house. He nosed the car into the garage and released the door. He sat for a minute, listening to the sound of his son sleeping on the rear seat, before he opened the car door.

Burn carried Matt into the living room and lay him down on the sofa. The sliding doors to the dining room were closed. He had shut them so the paramedics who came to attend to Susan wouldn't see the carnage within.

Burn went into the kitchen and took heavy-duty black garbage bags from the drawer by the sink. He found a roll of duct tape and a retractable carpet knife and pulled on a pair of plastic kitchen gloves.

He checked that Matt was still sleeping and quietly opened the sliding doors. Burn had killed men in Iraq, but it had been nothing like what had happened in his home that night. Combat during Desert Storm had the surreal feel of a PlayStation game, the high-tech weaponry keeping death at a distance.

Not like this.

The tall man lay on his back, the carving knife still buried in his chest. The bullet he had taken from the short man's gun had entered his abdomen below the ribs. He'd bled out. Burn could take some refuge in the knowledge that stabbing the man had been a reflex, a primitive impulse to protect his family.

There could be no such comfort taken from the death of the short man, who lay in his own blood, milky eyes fixed on the ceiling, the gaping wound in his throat like an accusing mouth. To call him a man was an exaggeration; he looked no older than twenty, and his smallness made Burn's actions seem all the more brutal. Burn had disarmed him, rendered him harmless. In a normal world Burn would have called the cops and let the law enforcement machinery do what it was meant to do.

But Jack Burn no longer lived in a normal world, and the police had not been an option. So he had murdered the scrawny man. And telling himself that he'd had no choice didn't make him feel any better.

❯

Benny Mongrel watched the house next door.

He heard the slap of car doors and a man laughing. The party up the road was still going strong. Bessie had been on edge all night, what with that gunshot and the music and the white people laughing like horses. But mostly because of the food; that smell of meat cooking on the fire had driven her nearly crazy. She sat next to him, shifting on her aching hips, her snout still searching the air for the smell of lamb on the spit.

He stroked her coarse fur. "Don't worry, old girl," he whispered. "There'll be pickings for us in the bins tomorrow."

Benny Mongrel was on edge, too. He pondered, over and over again, the significance of the gangsters disappearing into that house.

The Americans.

When Benny Mongrel was eighteen, a member of the Americans gang called Bowtie April had chopped him with an ax, taking his left eye and caving his face in from brow to chin. He had killed Bowtie, torn his throat out with his bare hands, before he allowed the cops to drag him off to the hospital. The doctors hadn't cared a fuck about another gangster punk. On the Cape Flats reconstructive surgery wasn't on the menu. They had stitched him up and sent him to prison.

He was a blood Mongrel. His name and the tattoos that scarred his body were testament to that. So when he went to prison for the first time, he knew which of the number gangs he was destined to join. The prison number gangs: the 26s, the 27s, and the 28s. They rule the prisons. Anyone stupid enough to resist the law of the number ends up dead.

Or worse.

The Americans are always 26s. The Mongrels are always 28s. No one asks why. It is just so. And they hate each other. So those men who had seen their mothers tonight would get no sympathy from Benny Mongrel.

He watched as the garage door rolled up again. Nearly midnight. The Jeep reversed out and the doors closed. The guy and his son passed beneath him again as they drove away.

"Ja what, they got a mess to clean up, Bessie."

Barnard was still eating his gatsby as he drove through Paradise Park, ready to take care of the last of the night's business. A half-breed tik cooker who paid Barnard protection money was selling to suburban schoolkids. Barnard didn't give a shit about the schoolkids, but the situation was attracting heat. Other dealers were getting pissed off. Local politicians were asking questions about the tik suppliers. And the protection they got.

After the visit to Carmen Fortune, he'd hauled his fat into the Golden Spoon, home of the best gatsby in Cape Town. Which meant the whole fucken world.

As soon as the Muslim woman behind the counter had seen him, she'd shouted into the back, "Masala steak full house for the inspector." Without him asking, she passed him a pine nut Double O from the fridge, keeping as far away from his stink as she could.

He grunted and tipped the bottle, glugging back most of the fake pineapple brew in one swallow. Then he lit a cigarette beneath the NO SMOKING sign. Let the bitch say a word.

The woman put his gatsby down on the counter without comment.

The gatsby is to Cape Town what a hot dog is to New York, and the full house was Barnard's feast of choice: a football-sized French loaf stuffed with chunks of steak, eggs, melted cheese, and fries, all drenched in mayonnaise and industrial-strength chili.

Barnard shoved half of the gatsby into his mouth, sauce oozing down his jowls. He spoke as he chewed. "Gimme a pine nut for the car."

The woman had handed him another bottle, and he'd left without a word or an offer of payment.

Barnard was still chewing as he approached the tik cooker's place. He saw a patrol van pulled up outside, blue light flashing across the front of the squat house.

Fuck, what now?

When Barnard levered his massive bulk from the Toyota, the suspension lifted with a groan, as if relieved to be free of him. Two uniforms were standing beside a knot of people surrounding a dark shape lying on the road. The cops tensed at his arrival. They were afraid of him. He liked that.

"What's going on?" He spoke around the last mouthful of food.

"Drive-by, Inspector."

A half-breed girl no more than ten lay on the road. She was dying. A wailing woman was on her knees beside the child, people trying to pull her away.

Barnard looked on impassively. "Who were they targeting?"

The other cop pointed into the house. "There's a gangster inside. They got him as he ran in. The kid was crossing the road."

"The guy, he dead?"

"No. Wounded."

Pity. Barnard walked into the house. In the front room a skinny half-breed in his twenties sat slumped on the floor, bleeding onto the worn carpet, shaking with fear. He was shirtless, his body a scribble of gang tattoos. He had taken a bullet to the leg. Barnard knew it wasn't life-threatening. He would have to sort this out before they hauled this punk off to the hospital and he started to talk his mouth off.

The boy looked up at Barnard. If he had been scared before, he was terrified now.

A woman in her fifties, crying, mopped the boy's head. She kept on repeating, over and over, "Stay awake."

"Go outside," Barnard said, dismissing her with a flick of his pink paw. She hesitated, saw the look on his face, and decided she better do as he said. "Close the door."

Barnard grabbed the kid by his jaw and jerked his head up. "Look at me, you bastard." The kid looked at him. "Jerome, why the fuck you don't listen to me? I told you not to sell to that school."

"I didn't. They lie."

Barnard held up a hand. "Shut it, okay? Why you think they shooting at you? You got everybody pissed off."

"Inspector, I'll stop. I swear, on my mommy's life."

Gatsby shook his huge head. "Too late, Jerome."

He unholstered his Z88 and shot the kid point-blank in the right eye. He had enough time to take the throw-down, a snub-nosed .32, from his waistband and wrap the kid's fingers around it before the door slammed open and the uniforms came in.

"He drew on me," Barnard said, holstering his Z88.

The uniforms looked at him, unspoken questions in their eyes. The half-breed's mother burst past them and cradled her son's bleeding head in her hands. Weeping.

Something wet from the kid's face had landed on Barnard's gun hand. He wiped it on the back of a sofa that sagged like a swaybacked dog.

As he walked out to his car, lighting a cigarette, he struggled to get a tiny cell phone out of his jeans and thumbed a number. No signal. He'd have to wait to call that little bastard Rikki and lean on him some more.

Barnard heard the ambulance siren in the distance. The paramedics were wasting their time. He could see the half-breed in the street was dead, too.

>

Burn drove along High Level Road, his eyes drawn to his rearview mirror. The two dead men, wrapped in the garbage bags, were under a tarpaulin at the very rear of the Jeep. The short guy had been easy to wrap and carry down to the car, but the tall man had left Burn sweating with exertion. Then he'd had to fold him double to fit him into the Jeep. The last body he had carried down had been that of his sleeping son. Burn prayed that Matt slept on; he'd already seen too much that night.

What Burn wanted to do was run again. Pack up and disappear like they had three months ago. But he couldn't. Not yet. Not until Susan was stable.

He turned into Sea Point Main Road, on his way to the freeway. Before he could change his route he found himself in a roadblock, orange cones narrowing the road to one lane, uniformed cops with flashlights flagging down vehicles. A roadblock to flush out the stolen cars, the unlicensed drivers, and the drunks.

A car slowed behind him. There was no way he could reverse. He was trapped.

There were two cars in front of him. The cops were talking to the drivers, shining flashlights into the car interiors. They had pulled one man aside and were checking inside his car and in the trunk.

Burn started to sweat.

At last a flashlight waved him forward. A black cop in uniform shone the light into his face as Burn eased the driver's window down. "Good evening, sir. Please turn off the car."

"Good evening." Burn killed the engine.

The accent immediately attracted the cop's attention. "Are you on holiday, sir?"

"I'm out here visiting for a while."

The cop directed the light onto the backseat and saw Matt asleep in the car seat.

"Your ID and license, please."

Burn handed them over. The cop checked his passport photograph against his face. As always at these moments over the last few months, Burn prayed that they would stand up to scrutiny. Then the cop checked his international driver's license and handed both documents back to him.

"Thank you, Mr. Hill."

He seemed ready to wave Burn on when a cell phone rang, from the very rear of the car. Shit, Burn thought, it must be in the short guy's trousers. The cargo pants with the endless pockets. The cell phone ring was loud, strident, the opening bars of some hip-hop song. Incongruous in this Jeep.

The cop heard it, looked at Burn, then started to walk toward the rear of the car, his flashlight held ahead of him.

Burn waited.

CHAPTER 4

It seemed as if the cell phone would never stop ringing. Then it did. Sudden, abrupt silence. Burn watched in his side mirror as the cop moved toward the back of the Jeep. Burn knew that if he was going to act, it would have to be now. The car in front of him was being waved away; the road was open. Either he was going to risk letting the cop find the bodies or he was going to take his chances and run. Floor the Jeep and get the hell out of there, hoping he had the jump on any pursuers.

And then? Ditch the car. Get back to the house, get rid of anything incriminating, open the safe, and access the backup passports he kept in case of just this kind of emergency. He knew the drill. He and Susan had done it before. He had the documents. He had the cash.

He watched the cop, who was about to shine his light into the rear of the Jeep. Burn found his hand moving toward the ignition key.

It would have to be now.

"Fuck you, you black bastard!" The voice was loud, angry, and drunk.

Burn spun around in his seat. A big Mercedes, brand-new, was parked behind him. The driver, a beefy white man in his fifties, was out of the vehicle. He had just shoved a uniformed cop away from him. "Keep your fucking hands off me!"

Cops were converging on the drunk, battling to subdue him.

The cop who had stopped Burn waved a hand, gesturing for Burn to drive on, before he ran over to join his colleagues in the brawl.

Burn's hands were shaking as he started the car. He drove away slowly. The last glimpse he had of the drunk was as the big man was thrown to the ground, three cops wrestling him into handcuffs.

"I owe you a drink, pal," Burn said quietly as he headed down to the freeway.

Burn drove along the N2 toward the airport. Even though it was way past midnight, the road was busy, taillights streaming away like fireflies in the dark. He kept to the speed limit as kamikaze taxi drivers from the Flats rattled past him in their battered minibuses, jammed full of faceless workers on their way home from the late shift.

Burn checked on Matt in the rearview mirror. His son was asleep, strapped into his car seat, his blond hair a halo in passing headlights.

Mean houses and shacks sprawled on either side of the freeway as Burn left Table Mountain behind. The Cape Flats. Where more people died of violence every day than in your average war zone. Where children disappeared and their violated bodies were found in boxes under neighbor's beds. Where the dispossessed had their hungry eyes fixed on the rich man's playground around the mountain.

Burn understood enough about Cape Town to know that the dead men in the back of his Jeep were coloreds from out here on the Flats.

When he had arrived in Cape Town, Burn, like most foreigners, had assumed that it was all black and white in South Africa. But things were more complex, of course, in the country that invented apartheid. He had learned that more than half the population of the city, mostly living out on the desolate Flats, were colored. And *colored* in South Africa didn't mean what it did in the States. These were brown people of mixed race, a blend of tribal Africans, European settlers, and their slaves from Asia.

So he had killed two colored men. The tattoos he'd seen on their bodies branded them as gangsters. He knew that dead bodies out on the Flats were commonplace, not even rating a mention in the newspapers. He was going to drive out past the airport and dump them in the veld and hope that if they were found, they would be seen as the by-product of a gangland killing.

Just another night in Cape Town.

Burn took the airport exit and almost immediately swung onto a back road, leaving other cars behind. Within minutes he was driving along a dark and deserted road beside the far runways, a stretch of open ground between him and the nearest small houses.

He checked his mirrors. No cars. He turned the Jeep off the road, bumping his way along until a patch of windswept scrub hid his car from both road and houses. This would have to do.

Burn killed his headlights and got out, carrying a flashlight.

The veld was deserted, littered with junk blown in by the wind, but there was no sign of any human presence. Burn checked that Matt was still asleep before he swung up the rear door of the Jeep.

He lifted the tarpaulin and reached down and grabbed the bigger of the two bodies, letting it fall to the sand like a mummy wrapped in black garbage bags. He dragged the body until it was partly hidden by a clump of bushes. He came back for the second one and left the small man lying a distance away from his dead friend.

Burn checked that the only signs of his presence were the faint tracks the Jeep had left in the dust. The southeaster was picking up again and would wipe the sand clean by the time he was back on the road.

Matt woke up as Burn climbed back into the car. "Daddy?"

Burn leaned between the seats and took his son's small hand. "I'm here, Matty."

"When we going home?"

"Right now."

"Home to Barney?"

Barney was the Labrador they had left behind when they fled their home in Los Angeles. Matt had loved that dog.

"No, not to Barney," Burn said. "We'll get you another dog, I promise."

"I want Barney." Now Matt was crying.

The tears of his son, coming after all that had happened that night, pushed Burn close to his edge. He had to fight to stay focused and withdraw his hand, start the car, and head back to the road.

Matt cried himself to sleep as they drove.

—————

Most nights Benny Mongrel dozed on the top floor of the house, sitting beside Bessie under the stars. But that night he couldn't. He kept on playing the scene over in his head, the American gangsters climbing up into that house like monkeys. And not coming back.

For the first time he looked forward to being picked up at dawn.

When the Sniper Security truck rattled up just before 6:00 a.m., Benny Mongrel waited downstairs with Bessie. He helped her up onto the back and sat down on the bench, Bessie beside him. The truck bumped down the mountain and skirted downtown Cape Town. It was too early for rush hour, so the driver sped through the city streets, away from Table Mountain and its fleecy cloth of cloud. Soon they were in an area of run-down factories and cramped houses that hunched against the railway line.

There were four other night watchmen in the truck. Benny Mongrel ignored them. He had made no friends at Sniper Security. Life had taught him that if you worry about other people, you forget to look after yourself.

Benny Mongrel had lived by his wits since he was an hour old, thrown onto a garbage dump and left to die, his tiny naked body still covered in afterbirth. Some survival instinct had forced him to cry out into the night, and to carry on crying into the gray and drizzly dawn as a ragged band of homeless people mined the acres of garbage for anything of use.

He cried until a homeless woman reached down and pulled him from a pile of rotting bones and fish heads and lifted him to her breast. And then he never cried again. Ever.

So began Benny Mongrel's procession through orphanages and poorhouses. Some unknown petty official had given him the name Benjamin Niemand. Benjamin Nobody.

By the time he was ten Benny Niemand lived on the streets. He was twelve when he approached a group of Mongrels who were hanging outside a shebeen in Lotus River, eyeing a band of Americans chatting up girls across the road. Benny Niemand walked straight up to the Mongrel leader, Chippies, and told him he wanted to join their gang.

They all laughed at him, and Chippies, half in jest, handed him a long-bladed knife and pointed toward the group of Americans. "See that one with the hat on?"

Benny Niemand saw a thickset man of thirty, heavily tattooed, leaning against a building as he pulled a girl toward him. Benny nodded.

"Show him his mother and you can be a Mongrel." Chippies laughed, exposing his missing front teeth, expecting the boy to hand the knife back.

Instead Benny Niemand walked across the road, the knife held close against his leg. The tattooed American had walked the girl into a doorway, and his hand was moving between her legs. Benny Niemand tapped him on the back with the hand that wasn't holding the knife.

The American spun on him. "What you want?"

"To show you your mother," Benny said, and slipped the knife between the American's ribs. He pulled the knife out, watched the dying man slump to his knees, heard the screams of the girl, and calmly walked back to where the Mongrels stood. He handed the knife to the leader.

From then on he was Benny Mongrel. He lived by his wits, and he developed an almost infallible sixth sense. He knew when trouble was coming.

He and his knife were always ready.

The truck slammed to a halt in the Sniper Security yard in Salt River. Bessie lost her footing and skidded in the back of the truck, her nails fighting for a grip on the slick metal. One of the other guards laughed but quickly shut up when he saw Benny Mongrel looking at him. Benny Mongrel helped Bessie down. Her hips were always much worse in the morning, and she limped when he led her off toward the kennel enclosure.

"Hey, Niemand." Ishmael Isaacs, the shift foreman, stood across the yard. He waited for Benny Mongrel to come across to him. The epaulettes on the shoulders of his crisp uniform were a sign of his seniority.

Isaacs, a brown man like Benny Mongrel, had done prison time, and the fading tattoos on his arms proved that. He had been out for years and had made a better life for himself. Benny Mongrel knew that Isaacs had taken against him from the start, probably because he was an ex-con, an uncomfortable reminder of the foreman's own past.

"What's up with that dog?" Isaacs watched Bessie's painful progress as they neared him.

"Nothing, Mr. Isaacs."

"She always walk like so?"

"No, she just a bit stiff. From being in the truck."

Isaacs grunted, his eyes scanning Benny Mongrel. He sniffed the air. "When last you wash?"

"Yesterday. Before work."

"Your ass stinks." Isaacs stretched out an arm and flicked a dismissive finger at Benny Mongrel's sleeve. "And don't they teach you to iron in Pollsmoor?"

Benny Mongrel said nothing, not showing anything on his face. Like this fucker was a warder back in prison.

"Tomorrow, one hour before shift, you report to me for inspection."

"Yes, Mr. Isaacs."

"And make sure your ass is clean and your kit looks proper. Or I dock your pay. Got me?"

"Yes."

Benny Mongrel watched as Isaacs turned on his heel and walked away. He wanted to show that bastard the epaulettes tattooed on his own shoulders, real rank, earned the hard way. Then he wanted to show him his knife.

But he whistled softly and led Bessie off toward the kennels.

———————————

Burn woke up with a wet body against his. For a crazy, nightmarish moment he was sure the dead men were in the bed with him. This was enough to jolt him upright like he'd been tasered, and he flung the covers aside. Matt was sleeping next to him, and he had wet the bed. For the first time in nearly two years.

Burn lay back, calming his racing pulse. He cradled his sleeping son and stroked his head. Then an image came into his mind. A red BMW parked next door, outside the building site. He'd glimpsed it when he'd followed the ambulance to the clinic and wondered if it had brought the dead men to his street.

When he'd come home after dumping the bodies, the party next door had still been going strong, the BMW lost among the other cars. He'd forgotten about the red car. All he'd wanted was to wash the stink of death from his hands and body.

He looked at the bedside clock. It was after seven.

Burn pulled on jeans and a T-shirt and left his son sleeping on the damp double bed. He unlocked the front door of the house and went down through the small front garden to the door set into the high wall. He opened it, peering out cautiously.

The BMW was still there, but so were the building crew. There was no way he was going to be able to move the car unobserved. Burn cursed himself. This was a loose end he shouldn't have allowed. But the decision was forced on him: he would have to leave the car until that evening, when the builders were done for the day.

Burn shut the door.

CHAPTER 5

Benny Mongrel climbed from the minibus taxi that had dropped him in Lavender Hill. He slung his small kit bag over his shoulder and set off, walking like he was hugging the wall of an invisible prison corridor.

Apartheid's faceless bureaucrats had displayed a macabre sense of humor when, with a pen stroke, they banished thousands of people to ghettos on the Cape Flats with sweet names like Surrey Estate, Blue Downs, and Ravensmead. This was no more apparent than in Lavender Hill, where there was no lavender and not a single hill, just an endless sprawl of cramped houses built on windswept scrubland.

Benny Mongrel passed a straggle of pedestrians and dodged side-walk vendors selling fruit, vegetables, cigarettes, and cheap sweets that tasted like piss. Even though he wore a cap, the hard morning light threw his livid scar into stark relief. His ruined face was like an icebreaker on the prow of a ship, parting people in his wake. They whispered behind his back, and only the half-naked children with snot-caked faces stared openly. He didn't care what people said as long as they left him alone.

Benny Mongrel lived in a shack behind a narrow house. He unlocked the padlock on the makeshift door and stepped inside, his eyes adjusting to the windowless gloom. A stained mattress, a blanket scarred by cigarette burns, a three-legged chair, a primus stove, and a rusted tub to wash in. The corrugated iron room was barely big enough for him to spread his arms wide, and he couldn't stand upright without his head touching the roof.

Once a day he was allowed into the bathroom of the main house to empty his slop bucket. A frayed extension cable snaked from the house, giving power to the naked lightbulb that dangled from a hook in the roof of his shack.

The place was a furnace in summer and flooded during the winter rains, but Benny Mongrel didn't mind. After spending decades sharing prison cells designed for ten men with fifty others, the shack felt luxurious.

When he was released from prison, he had made a decision not to return to Lotus River, where he'd spent his brief youth. He had no family and nobody to call a friend, but he could have fallen in with the older Mongrels, who sat in taverns, drinking, smoking marijuana and tik, reminiscing, and planning the action that would send them back to the security of prison.

He never wanted to go back. Somehow he knew that a different sort of life was possible outside prison, even though he wasn't sure exactly what that was. The only clue was Bessie. He missed the old dog during the empty, endless days. He couldn't wait to see her at night, feel the reassuring sandpapery rasp of her tongue on his hand.

Benny Mongrel lay on the mattress in his trousers, his torso alive with crude prison tattoos: epaulettes indicating his officer rank on his shoulders, the words *I dig my grave* and *evil one* scrawled across his chest. Dollar signs, knives, and pistols. A Zulu shield, the emblem of the 28s.

It was too hot to sleep, and the relentless southeaster sandblasted Lavender Hill.

He thought about what had happened the night before. About those men who went into the house and never came back. The Americans. The 26s.

Benny Mongrel had killed more Americans than he could remember, in prison and out. The Mongrels and the Americans were kept apart in Pollsmoor. They watched each other uneasily in the corridors and across the exercise yard. Every now and then a new prisoner would come in, and one of the older gangsters would order him to kill one of the enemy, as an initiation rite. If he balked, he was gang-raped and made a wife.

Benny Mongrel had passed his initiation without blinking.

The last man he had killed had been an American, a 26, a year before he was paroled. There had been a half-heard word, an insult muttered as he passed. In prison this could not go unanswered. Benny Mongrel could have ordered a junior to do what needed to be done. But he preferred to do the work himself.

In the showers he slid the prison shank between the American's tattooed ribs. He held the man close as he died, and as the light faded from his eyes he whispered what he always whispered, "Benny Mongrel say goodnight."

He was back in his cell by lockdown.

The Americans and the other 26s were very quiet in the exercise yard the next day. Warders came and spoke to Benny Mongrel. He shook his head, shrugged. He knew nothing. They had tried to pry information from other lips, but men lived in fear of Benny Mongrel and knew it was better to stay silent or they, too, would hear a whispered goodnight.

What had happened last night wouldn't just end there. No. He could sense invisible lines reaching out to the Flats, connecting to that house on the mountain. And to him, a Mongrel, a 28, who guarded the next-door house, just trying to lead a peaceful life.

Shit.

He sat up and took the knife from his pocket. He opened the blade and inspected it for imperfections. Then he reached under the mattress and found a scrap of sandpaper wrapped around a wooden block. With patient precision he honed the blade against the sandpaper.

After a few minutes he ran an index finger very softly down the blade. Beads of blood broke the surface of his skin. He wiped the blade, closed the knife, and slid it into his pocket.

Benny Mongrel lay back on the mattress in his shack and stared up at the tin roof, listening to the wind as it howled. Grit and dust blew in through gaps in the tin, and the corrugated iron rattled like gangs of manacled prisoners marching through Pollsmoor.

The southeaster blew itself out with a last violent gust, and then all was still. The city, purged of smog and filth by the wind they called the Cape Doctor, took on an almost hallucinogenic beauty. A cappuccino froth of white cloud floated on top of Table Mountain, and cars carrying tanned bodies and surfboards streamed down to the beaches.

Burn and Matt drove along the beachfront, past the tourist mecca of Camps Bay until they came to a small beach known only to the locals. Burn, Susan, and Matt had stumbled onto it during a walk, and it had become their favorite place to swim.

The beach was accessed by a steep path from the road above, too steep for most people's liking. Burn and Matt walked down, holding hands, Burn lifting the boy when the path fell away too sharply for him to keep his footing. Burn was dressed in shorts and a cotton shirt, his feet in sandals. He carried a cooler and a beach umbrella. Matt was wearing his baggy swimming trunks, a bright T-shirt, and rubber flip-flops. They emerged through the bush onto a small beach surrounded by boulders, the azure ocean washing the sand. They were alone.

Burn jammed the umbrella into the sand and opened it, arranging towels in its shade. He stripped down to his swimming trunks. "You want to go in for a swim?" he asked Matt.

The boy was playing with a toy truck in the sand, absorbed. He shook his head.

Burn took a plastic bag from the cooler and went down to the water. He waded in, feeling the sharp bite of the icy Atlantic. No matter how hot the day, the water in Cape Town was always cold. At first, used to the temperate Pacific, he hadn't ventured beyond his knees. Then he had grown to like the chilling sting, followed by the thawing when he went back into the sun.

Burn kicked out and headed toward a clump of rocks, towing the plastic bag with him. He untied the bag and took out the knives he had used to kill the two men. One by one he allowed the knives to sink between the rocks into the deep water. He paddled a little farther and released the gun he had taken off the short man's body, watching it slowly tumble out of view.

He had kept the tall man's weapon: a snub-nosed Colt. He knew it was a risk, keeping the gun, hiding it in the closet in the bedroom, but it made him feel secure somehow. Like he would be able to fight back.

Against what, he didn't know.

The water was starting to chill him, stinging his head and balls, but he forced himself to stay in a while longer, diving down until he touched the undulating kelp on the bottom. Then he floated to the surface and swam back to the sand. He waded out, gasping from the cold, feeling the sun on his body. Matt was under the umbrella, playing.

Burn dried himself. He took a plastic bottle from the cooler and started to smear high-protection sunblock into his son's skin.

"Matt?"

"Yes." The boy was still playing with his truck, not looking at Burn.

"Look at me."

Matt dragged his eyes from the toy to his father.

"Last night, those men . . ." Burn was finding this as difficult as he knew he would. "They wanted to hurt Mommy."

Matt stared at him. "Why?"

"They were bad men. And I had to do what I did to stop them hurting Mommy, or you or me, do you understand?" Burn held his son's gaze, the clear blue eyes that reminded him so much of Susan's. But without the shadow of mistrust that had entered hers.

"Yes. I was scared."

"So was I."

Matt hesitated. "Those men . . . they're not coming back?"

Burn shook his head. "No. They're not coming back."

Matt nodded. "Are they dead?"

Burn stared at his son. "Yes," he answered. "They're dead."

The boy nodded. "Okay."

Burn rubbed the sunscreen into Matt's face, avoiding his eyes. Matt was wriggling, anxious to escape. "Matt, it's okay if you feel scared. If you need to talk to me or Mommy."

"No, I won't be scared again. Not if they're not coming back."

"Matty, look at me." The boy squinted up at him. "You know you can't talk about what happened last night to anybody but Mommy and me. You understand?"

Matt nodded. "Yes, Daddy."

Burn felt sick, making his son an accomplice. He rubbed in the last of the sunscreen and took his hands away from his son's body. Matt found a sudden burst of energy and sped off to the water, running in until his toes were chilled, then running out again, laughing.

Burn lay on his back, propped up on his elbows, watching his son play on this idyllic beach. Still battling to process the violent detour his life had taken.

A detour that began two years back when Tommy Ryan knocked on his door.

He and Susan had just moved into a new house in the Valley when Tommy arrived, carrying a kit bag and wearing his killer smile only slightly dimmed by years of hard living and dubious dentistry. It was more than ten years since Burn had seen him.

After Desert Storm Burn had taken his discharge and moved to L.A., where he'd found work in the booming security industry. Tommy stayed on in the marines for another couple of years, then drifted into a series of jobs that never lasted, judging from the infrequent cards, always with different postmarks.

Susan hadn't taken to Tommy Ryan. Burn sensed that when she looked at Tommy, Susan saw a fun-house reflection of her husband. The Jack Burn who might have been if things had worked out badly for him. But she'd done her best to hide her feelings, and made up a bed in the guest room for Tommy without asking how long he intended to stay. She laughed at Tommy's jokes and pretended to enjoy the war stories. But Burn noticed that Susan avoided Tommy, spending her time with Matt, who was hitting the terrible twos head on.

Tommy had a gift. Bragged that his bullshit detector was more accurate than any polygraph. One night over a couple of beers, he asked Burn if he was happy and didn't buy the answer. After a few more beers, Burn told him the truth: he was strapped for cash. His security business was less than a year old and not yet showing a profit. Renovations on the house had cost more than he'd planned, and Susan hadn't worked since they were married.

His old buddy smiled that famous smile and offered a solution that was typically Tommy. Why didn't they go down to Gardena and play poker? Tommy reminded Burn of the handle he'd worn back in the marines: Lucky. Earned because he'd cleaned up at every poker game he'd played.

"Jesus, Tommy," Burn said. "We were playing for beer and smokes."

"The cards are still the same, bro. 'Cept now you'll take dollars from the suckers."

And he did. He'd walked into the casino with two hundred dollars and was up two thousand by the time they quit.

Tommy laughed as they drove home, dawn already touching the San Gabriels. "What did I tell you? You haven't lost your magic, man."

The next day was Susan's birthday, and Burn was able to buy her the pair of Italian shoes he knew she secretly coveted and take her to dinner at a fancy restaurant. They drank wine and laughed, almost like when they were dating. Then she paused a moment, her face suddenly serious in the candlelight, and asked if he could afford this. Susan was the daughter of an alcoholic gambler who had disappeared when she was ten, and Burn knew how she would react if he told her where he'd got the money. So he looked her in the eye and lied to her for the first time. Said business was good.

What else could he do?

He and Tommy went down to Gardena a couple more times. Tommy, of course, had introduced Burn to the other players as *Lucky*, and the name stuck. Each time he played, Burn lived up to the name. Sometimes he won big, and sometimes his winnings were modest, but he always left with cash in his pocket.

Cash that made things that little bit easier around the house.

After two weeks Tommy started looking restless, and he packed his kit bag and hit the road, leaving a trail of postcards from San Diego, Baja California, Fort Lauderdale, and then Chicago, where he had family.

Over the next two years Burn had carried on making those secret trips down to Gardena. Where he was Lucky.

Until his luck ran out.

Carmen Fortune woke alone in her bed. As she always did, she kept her eyes closed as if she was still asleep, listening for any sound of her husband. The way Ricardo Fortune started the day was an indicator of the treatment she could expect. If he was still passed out when she awoke, his body stinking of booze, tik, and other women's juices, she knew she had time to put some distance between herself and him. He would drag his body from the bed after midday, demanding food. If he didn't have any tik, he would be irritable and his fists would talk.

On the rare occasions he was up before her, it meant he had a job to do. Gang- or drug-related business, which meant that he was too pre-occupied to bother with her. He would dress, clean and load his pistol, then slam out of the apartment.

But there was no sound when she woke up. All she could hear was the rasp of Uncle Fatty snoring on the sofa. Carmen got out of bed and parted the frayed curtain on the window in the bedroom. The glass was broken, shattered by a rock thrown by one of Rikki's many enemies, and half the window was boarded up with a Castle Lager box. She looked out into the street, at the spot where he usually parked his red BMW. There was no sign of it. Carmen relaxed.

She went through to the living room and kicked Uncle Fatty in the ribs with her bare foot. He grunted and rolled over, his scrawny frame covered by a filthy blanket. Fatty, whose real name was Errol, was the brother of Rikki's mother. He had worked for the council for years until he was pensioned off with lung problems. He'd always been a drinker, but when he retired he went from gifted amateur to pro. He gladly handed over his pension to Carmen, wanting only a constant supply of cheap wine and a roof over his head.

Carmen checked on Sheldon. He was in his cot next to the TV, sightless eyes open, hands moving. He had survived another night. She smelled that he needed to be changed. She would deal with that later.

Carmen had three abortions before Sheldon was born. Two were babies from her own father. He'd started coming into the room she shared with her two baby brothers when she was seven. There was no way, in the tiny house, that her mother could not have known. Carmen had fallen pregnant the first time when she was eleven.

Her mother had beaten her, called her a whore, and taken her to the clinic. Her mother had never said a word to her father; she had just quietly hated Carmen. When Carmen got pregnant again a year later, her mother threw her out of the house and Carmen went alone to the clinic.

By the time she was fifteen, she was carrying the child of some guy from the neighborhood, Bobby Herold. The Mongrels kicked Bobby to death in front of her eyes, the day she went to the clinic for the third termination.

Then she met Ricardo Fortune, and it happened again.

Amazingly, he had married her. The skinny little bastard strutted around like a king, Carmen and her swollen belly like a trophy at his side. Then Sheldon had arrived, and the beatings had followed not long after.

Carmen made breakfast. Uncle Fatty dragged himself from the sofa, walking around the apartment in stained briefs. She slapped a plate of baked beans and egg in front of him.

"You better wash today. Your ass stinks."

He said nothing, pecked at the food. His toxic engine could only be kick-started by his postbreakfast drink.

Carmen fed Sheldon. She couldn't face changing him now. He wouldn't know the fucken difference. The downside of Rikki not being there was that there was no tik to take the edge off the day. She would have to go and score.

She washed herself and dressed in her best jeans and blouse. She tried to discipline her coarse hair with a clogged brush, cursing Gatsby for breaking her mirror. Fat fucken boer.

When she heard the knock at the door, she assumed it was one of Rikki's useless connections. She yanked the door open, ready to give them a mouthful, when she saw Belinda Titus, the social worker who dealt with Sheldon's case. They usually met at Social Services when Carmen went in once a month to collect Sheldon's grant.

"I've come to check on your son, Mrs. Fortune."

"You didn't phone, nothing." Carmen blocked the door.

"That's the point of an unscheduled inspection, Mrs. Fortune. Please let me in."

Carmen stepped back.

Belinda Titus was only a couple of years older than Carmen, also from the Flats, but she carried herself with an air of superiority.

"She thinks she shits ice cream" was how Carmen described her to Rikki in one of their rare conversations. The social worker, by her manner and the way she looked at Carmen, made her feel like trash.

Belinda Titus stood looking around the dingy apartment, wearing a pinched expression on her face. Uncle Fatty chose that moment to emerge from the bathroom, still wearing nothing but his filthy underwear. He looked at the two women, stayed mute, just sat down on the sofa and stared into space.

The social worker walked across to the cot where Sheldon lay. She moved aside the sheet covering him, and her nose twitched. She looked up at Carmen.

"Mrs. Fortune, this child is in a disgusting condition."

"I was about to change him."

"That's the least of it. Without even examining him, I can see he has bedsores. And look at this bedding; it is shocking."

Carmen felt herself coloring, felt the anger rising. She battled to control herself. "I tole you. I was gonna clean him and change him."

"I can't let this child stay here in these disgusting conditions." Belinda Titus was reaching for her phone.

"What are you saying?" asked Carmen.

"I'm saying that colleagues of mine will come and collect him and take him to a place of safety. Where he will be properly cared for."

"You can't do that!"

"I can, Mrs. Fortune. And if you try to stop us, I will call the police."

"You can't just take my child away from me!"

Belinda Titus ignored her and spoke rapidly into her phone, giving the address of the apartment. Then she slipped her fancy little phone into her pocket and fixed a withering look on Carmen. "I have to do what is best for the child."

The social worker busied herself with filling out an official form she had taken from her attaché case.

Carmen sat down. She felt like puking. If Sheldon went, so did his grant. And her tik money with it.

The half-breed spun on his head like a top; then he sprang up into a kind of handstand, the muscles on his naked torso popping. He landed in the splits and seemed to pull himself up to standing by the hand that grabbed his balls. He thrust his hips back and forth into the face of a teenage girl who laughed like a bitch in heat. There was a group of them, dancing like monkeys in the yard of a faded-blue house.

Just watching them made Rudi Barnard tired. He had a headache, and the animal music that thumped out of the boom box hit him like a jackhammer. He was parked in one of Paradise Park's cramped side streets, the sun turning his car into an oven, even with all the windows open. Sweat pumped from Barnard, burned his eyes, got the rash between his thighs going.

He was feeling edgier than normal since he had wasted the tik cooker. He'd had to hand in his weapon at Bellwood South Police HQ, go through the usual rigmarole of filling out forms and making statements. Meaningless bullshit that would come to nothing. Still, it drew attention to him, and he didn't like that.

The fucken racket was driving him crazy. He was about to exit the car, go into the yard, and smack the gyrating half-breeds with the boom box, when a new Pajero SUV cruised past him. It was top-of-the-line, with shining mags and windows tinted darker than was legal. The Pajero stopped outside a house that was in marked contrast to its squat neighbors. A new two-story, surrounded by a high wall and razor wire. The gate slid open and the Pajero drove into the yard. Barnard started the Toyota and followed. The gate closed after him.

Three men got out of the Pajero. Two were Cape Flats muscle, all hair gel and tattoos. The third was older, midthirties, not big but with the look of a man who wasn't scared of the sight of blood. Manson. Head of the Paradise Park Americans.

Barnard, wet and wheezing, levered himself out of his car. "You fucken late."

Manson shrugged. "Business. What you got?"

Barnard went around to the rear of his car, popped the trunk, and gestured toward a kit bag. One of Manson's guys opened the bag, revealing a stash of handguns.

"How many?" Manson asked.

"Twenny-seven." Barnard was lighting a smoke, shielding the match from the wind. He watched as Manson checked out the merchandise. Weapons confiscated by patrol cops on the Flats. They brought the guns to Barnard, and he paid them a pittance or agreed to turn a blind eye to their extracurricular activities. Long as they didn't threaten his own.

Manson was cocking a 9 mm, sighting along the barrel, aiming at the sky. "How much?"

"Gimme three grand."

"You crazy, man." Manson pulled the trigger of the unloaded gun, and the falling hammer clicked. Anybody else talking to Barnard this way would have been spitting teeth by now, but he allowed Manson some leeway. The American had a network that Barnard tapped into, and he always paid on time.

"Okay, make it two-five."

"Two."

Barnard coughed and spat. "Fuck, it's too hot to argue. Two-two. Take it or leave it."

Manson nodded and gestured for his guy to take the bag from the trunk. Manson slipped a wad of notes from his designer jeans and peeled off a bunch for Barnard.

The fat cop didn't count them, shoved them into his wet pocket. "You seen Rikki Fortune?"

Manson shook his head. "I'm looking for him too. He owe you?"

"Ja, but I can't find his ass nowhere."

"He's taken some liberties. Maybe he's lying low."

"Do me a favor, you find him, lemme talk to him before you sort him. Okay?"

Manson nodded. Barnard lowered himself into the protesting car and shut the door. Manson leaned into the open driver's window. "You heard anything about this new anticorruption task force?"

"No. Fuck all. What's up?"

"Just heard bits here and there. Gonna be a cleanup. Targeting cops."

Barnard laughed. "Must be election time." He started the car.

Manson stepped back. "Keep your eyes open, anyways."

"I was born with my eyes open." The gate slid open and Barnard drove out. His headache was worse. He needed a gatsby.

Susan Burn was a prisoner of fear.

She lay in the sunny private ward feeling dread like a poison heavy in her body. She'd always known, of course, that after what Jack had done back in the States, retribution was inevitable. But she had gone along with his plans. Allowed him, as always, to convince her.

It was as if she had been waiting for those men to step into their lives, with their guns and their rapists' eyes. When they'd appeared, she had recognized them even though she'd never seen them before. She had known who they were and why they were there. They had been sent to even a score, to settle a karmic debt.

And it would not end with them. She knew that with absolute certainty.

So when her husband walked into the ward carrying a bunch of arum lilies—her favorite—she had to resist the temptation to do what she always did: forgive him. Believe in him. Believe in this handsome, smiling man. The man she loved.

She forced herself to see him crouched over the skinny brown thug, ready to cut his throat. She needed to keep that image close, to fuel her resolve.

"Hi, baby."

When he leaned down to kiss her, she turned her head away, feeling his lips brush her cheek. He stepped back, uncomfortable for a moment as he lay the flowers on the cabinet beside her bed. She could see signs of strain on his face, a jaundiced tint beneath his tan.

"How're you feeling?" He took a chair beside the bed.

"I'm fine." She looked at him, still seeing the man with the knife. "Where's Matt?"

"He's sitting outside."

"How is he?"

"He's okay. We went to the beach today, for a while."

She was staring at him intently, and she could see it made him uncomfortable. He tried to find a smile. It wasn't convincing.

"What?" he asked.

"You went to the beach?"

"Well, it's a great day. And I thought it might, you know, take his mind off things."

"So the sun and the ocean will cure everything? It'll all be okay?" She could feel the color rising in her cheeks.

"Baby, take it easy." He reached for her hand, confident that he could placate her. She took her hand away.

"Jack, it's not going to be okay. Not this time."

"All this will pass."

She shook her head. "No, Jack. No. You're not going to stroke and soothe me into submission, not now." She saw his eyes grow wary. "Lying here after what happened, it's forced me to confront things."

"Like?"

"Like when I met you I was twenty-one. A kid. You were nearly forty. I was in awe of you. I let you run my life."

"Susan . . ."

She held up a hand. "Let me finish, Jack. When you did what you did, back home, I was shocked. Stunned really. I was in freefall. What I should've done was taken Matt and got the hell out. With my baby."

He was staring at her. He'd seen her angry before, but never this certain. This determined.

"I regret not doing that. I regret listening to you, buying into your promises about the better life we were going to have. I want out, Jack."

She saw something come into his expression, like the play had become way less predictable. "What do you mean?"

"I want to go back home. I want my children to grow up having a normal life."

"You know what that means?"

She nodded, her eyes not moving from his. "It may mean that I spend time in prison. I'm prepared for that. One of us has to stop being selfish and think of our children, Jack. And clearly you're not going to be that one."

"You know that going back is not an option for me?"

"Yes, I know that. The stakes are much higher for you."

"Jesus, Susan, I'd be put away for life."

"I understand." She almost reached across and took his hand. But she forced herself not to. "But do *you* understand that you've imprisoned us? What happened last night shows how far you've gone. That man with the knife in his hand wasn't the man I married, Jack."

She watched him sag, like all the strength was draining from his body. "So what are you saying exactly?"

"When I get out of here, I'm going to contact the U.S. Consulate. I'm going to do whatever it takes to get Matt and me and my baby back to the States. If I have to do jail time, my sister will take the kids."

He stared at her. "You've spoken to her?"

She shook her head. "Of course not. I don't need to speak to her."

"So where does this leave me?"

"I don't know, Jack. That's for you to decide."

CHAPTER 6

When the Sniper Security truck pulled up at the site, the builders were leaving, talking loudly in Xhosa, laughing as they walked down the road to the taxis. Benny Mongrel jumped down from the truck and helped Bessie to the ground. The truck drove off, and Bessie squatted against a pile of builder's sand, her back legs unsteady as she pissed. Benny Mongrel looked away, giving her the time to do her business.

He had arrived at Sniper Security an hour earlier than his usual reporting time of 5:00 p.m. He had looked around for Ishmael Isaacs, the shift foreman, ready to report for inspection. Before getting the taxi to town, Benny Mongrel had stood in the tin bath in his shack and scrubbed his body with Sunlight soap. Then he had been forced to ask the fat bitch in the next-door shack if he could use her iron. Even though she nearly shit herself when she saw his face, she was greedy enough to demand money. Back in the day he would have smacked her and walked with the iron. But he paid up, pressed his uniform, and took the iron back to her. She had grabbed it and slammed the door in his face without a word.

Anyway, there he was smelling of soap, with creases like knife edges in his uniform.

But another guard had told Benny Mongrel that Isaacs had already gone for the day. He wouldn't be back. Fucken asshole.

While Bessie pissed, Benny Mongrel took in the view from high up on the slope. All was still. Honey-colored sunlight washed Table Mountain, Lion's Head, and Signal Hill. Toylike yachts caught the breeze on the placid ocean far below.

He saw the red BMW still straddling the yellow line. A pink parking ticket was glued to the driver's window, flapping in the soft breeze.

Bessie appeared at Benny Mongrel's side and licked his hand. He took hold of her chain, and the two of them headed into the unfinished house.

$\rightarrowtail$

Burn felt like he had been sucker punched. He was relieved that Matt, tired out after the time on the beach, was asleep in his car seat as they drove home.

Burn knew that Susan was serious. He also knew that she was right. That didn't stop him from feeling as if his entire universe had fragmented and been sucked into a black hole. Being without his wife and son was something he couldn't process. Not being there to father his daughter was too painful to imagine.

He knew he had brought this upon himself.

As he drove over the Neck and down toward Sea Point, the panorama of mountain and ocean was invisible to him. What he was seeing was the ease with which he had been set up back in the States, and how willingly he had slipped his head into the trap and let it spring shut.

After Tommy Ryan left, Burn had become a regular down at Gardena, sitting at poker tables with strangers who were prepared to wager more than most of them could afford. Burn hadn't let sympathy get in the way of him taking their money. Money that helped him grow his business and make things more comfortable for Susan and Matt.

And Burn couldn't deny it: he'd enjoyed the rush gambling gave him.

So he started betting on sports. A guy he met at the poker table put him onto a bookie named Pepe Vargas, who drove an old Eldorado and wore pinkie rings. Vargas amused Burn with his cheesy suits and easy humor. He was a character, and somehow having him around made Burn feel that he was leading a more interesting life. Vargas seemed to like Burn and extended him credit. He never acted bothered if Burn was late in paying.

Then the slide began. Horses stumbled on the homestretch, quarterbacks fired bum passes, and hockey pucks followed paths that defied any reasonable logic. Suddenly Burn owed Pepe Vargas nearly twenty grand, and Vargas started calling the house, looking for his money.

These calls, and Burn's absences, made Susan suspicious. After a particularly heavy confrontation when she accused him of being unfaithful, he told her about the gambling. She was shocked and angry. Was he going to do what her father did: fade away from his family, leaving a trail of bad debt, lies, and heartache?

Burn swore to her that he'd stop. He'd pay Vargas off, and that would be that.

He kept his word until his biggest contract went south.

Burn had installed a security system in a new mall out on the fringes of the Valley. It was state-of-the-art stuff—security cameras, motion-triggered alarms, smoke detectors—all wired into an operations room that looked like something out of mission control at Houston. He had to hire more staff and front for expensive gear to deliver on the contract. The developers of the mall had given him only a first payment, a quarter of the billable total—long spent—when they ran out of money. The mall, agonizingly close to completion, was mothballed while bloody legal battles were fought.

Burn's name was just one on a long list of contractors looking at getting ten cents on the dollar at best.

Meanwhile Burn's employees needed to be paid, and his suppliers were screaming for money. Money he didn't have. He was in danger of losing the house, mortgaged to cash-flow his business.

Which was when he did the thing that totally fucked up his life.

And the lives of his family.

Burn called Pepe Vargas and asked him to take a phone bet, eighty large on a tough middleweight out of Jersey City named Leroy Coombs, an ex-champion who was making a comeback against a no-hoper as part of the undercard of a Vegas title fight.

He heard the bookie go quiet on the other end of the line, probably thinking about the money Burn still owed him. But Vargas took the bet.

Burn was running a crazy risk, betting money he didn't have. But it was a sure thing. The opponent was a glorified sparring partner; there was no way Coombs could lose.

Burn sat at home and watched the fight on HBO. It went according to plan for ten of the scheduled twelve rounds. Coombs toyed with his opponent, and though he couldn't knock him out, he left him looking like hamburger by the end of the tenth. Burn was starting to feel good, convinced his recent run of bad luck was over.

Then in the eleventh Coombs got complacent, started clowning, and took a blow that should never have landed. A looping right that caught him on the chin and sent him to the canvas. He didn't get up before the ref waved his arms over his prone body.

The fight was over.

Burn watched, stunned, as Coombs was helped to his stool, his legs like cooked spaghetti. He knew that if he tried to stand, he'd feel the same.

His cell phone rang. It was Vargas, wanting to know when he was coming down to Gardena to make good the damage. Burn muttered a promise and killed the call.

After this loss, with the unpaid bets still on his tab, Burn owed Pepe Vargas nearly a hundred thousand dollars. An amount of money that he had absolutely no way of getting his hands on.

The bookie called again the next day, and his easy manner was gone. He told Burn to meet him down in the casino parking lot that afternoon.

Vargas cruised up next to Burn in his Eldorado and asked him to step into his office. A man sat beside Vargas, a man Burn had never seen before. Burn slid into the backseat and Pepe pulled away. Vargas stopped the Cadillac near a diner, and with a brief, almost apologetic glance in the rearview mirror, he left the car.

The man in the front seat turned to Burn. He was quiet, self-contained, carrying with him an air of understated menace. "You can call me Nolan."

"Why would I call you anything?" Burn was reaching for the door handle.

"Don't get out, Jack." The way the man used his name grated on Burn's nerves.

"Why not?"

"Because you don't want me coming to your house. Believe me."

Burn stared at Nolan. "What do you want?"

"I'm going to do you a favor. The hundred grand you owe Pepe is going to go away."

"How?"

"You're going to do a job for me."

"I don't think so." Burn opened the car door.

"If you leave this car, please understand that I will kill your wife and your son."

Burn stared at him, half out of the car. "What did you just say?"

"You heard me. Now close the door and listen very carefully."

Burn had closed the door. And it had begun. It had ended with a cop lying dead in the snow in Milwaukee and Burn and his family on the run.

Burn had got them to Cape Town and found them the house on the slopes of Signal Hill. They had more money than they would ever need. All they needed was a life. They were busy inventing one for themselves, day by day, when the brown men with the guns came in off the patio and sent it all to hell.

And now Susan was going to leave him.

As he slowed outside the house, Burn activated the garage door remote. He was nosing the Jeep inside when he noticed a police car parked behind the red BMW. A uniformed cop walked around the vehicle, speaking into his radio.

Burn drove into the garage, and the door dropped like a slow guillotine.

———➤———

It was still light when Rudi Barnard pulled up behind the red BMW. There was no sign of the cop who found the car. Probably getting pissed in some Sea Point whorehouse. Suited Barnard fine.

Barnard sat in his car a moment, surveying the scene. This wasn't his turf, this wealthy suburb clinging to the side of Signal Hill, with the sweeping view of Cape Town and the Waterfront below. And it sure as fuck wasn't Ricardo Fortune's. No, something was wrong here.

That morning Barnard had woken with a nameless sense of foreboding. He couldn't shake the feeling that trouble was coming his way. So, on bended knee, Barnard had asked his God for reassurance. For protection. For a sign.

And like Moses, God had sent Rudi Barnard up the mountain.

Barnard heaved himself out of the car and crossed to the BMW. He peered inside, saw nothing out of the ordinary. He tried the doors. Locked. Then he lumbered around to the trunk and tried that. Also locked.

He lit a cigarette, checking out the surroundings, taking in the luxurious homes hidden behind high walls and gates. The street was quiet. Not even a pedestrian in sight. Not like the Flats, which teemed with people hanging out on street corners, gangsters doing deals, kids playing soccer in the streets, neighbors hurling abuse at one another. Not here, in this sanctuary of privilege.

Barnard went back to his car and got a crowbar; then he attacked the trunk of the BMW. Under the Michelin man suit of fat was a lot of power, and within seconds he'd sprung the lid. No bodies inside. Nothing but a couple of empty beer bottles and a pile of rags.

He smashed the side window of the car, reached in a meaty arm, and unlocked the door. Wheezing, red in the face, he leaned into the car and checked behind the seats and in the glove box. Aside from a used condom, a couple of nipped joints, and a half-empty bottle of vodka, he found nothing of interest.

As he heaved himself upright and leaned against the car to get his breath back, he glimpsed a half-breed with a dog up on the building site, looking down at him.

When Benny Mongrel saw the fat man looking up at him, instinct told him to duck back out of sight. Even though the man was in an unmarked car and wore civilian clothes, Benny Mongrel knew instantly he was a cop. Just like he had known the other men were gangsters. That radar came standard when you lived the life he had.

"Hey!" He heard the cop shouting down in the street. He ignored him. Bessie growled a low growl. He quietened her with a pat. "Hey, up there, I'm fucken talking to you!"

Benny Mongrel knew it would be better to show himself. He stepped forward. The fat cop was standing with his hands on his hips, looking up.

"Come down here. I want to talk to you."

Benny stared at the cop, saying nothing. The cop was getting impatient. "What, haven't you got fucken ears? I said get your fucken ass down here. Now."

Benny Mongrel let go of Bessie's chain, took the knife from his pocket, and slid it under a cement bag. Better not to have it on him in case the boer searched him. Gut instinct told him not to take the old dog down there with him.

"Stay, Bessie," he told her softly. She whined as he disappeared down the stairs but did as he ordered.

Benny Mongrel stepped out of the unfinished house and approached the fat cop. It was instinctive for him to hunch slightly as he walked, like a tire deflating, and he fixed a submissive look on his face. He deliberately didn't look the cop in the eye.

"Evening, boss."

"This car, when did you first see it?" The cop pointed to the red BMW.

"This morning, my boss."

"Never saw these guys arrive?"

"No, my boss."

"You fucken lying to me?"

"No, my boss."

The fat cop was scanning Benny Mongrel professionally, taking in the scarred face and the tattoos. "When did you get out?"

"Last year."

"Pollsmoor?"

"Yes, my boss."

"You a fucken 28?"

"No more, my boss."

"Don't bullshit me."

"I'm clean, my boss."

"My ass is clean. You see anything last night? This car?"

"No, my boss."

"You fucken lying to me?"

"No, my boss."

The cop hit him with an open hand, right across the face. It was like being struck by a speeding taxi. Benny Mongrel had to put a hand to the wall of the house to stop himself from falling.

The cop raised his hand again. "You better not fucken lie!"

It was then that Bessie, normally the most pathetically docile of creatures, dragged herself from the house. She threw herself at the fat cop, baring her teeth at him, growling.

The cop was wearing heavy boots, and he took his massive leg back and kicked her in the ribs. Benny Mongrel could hear the air explode from her lungs as she spun in the air, her teeth clacking as she hit the ground. Bessie lay there panting. The cop had a pistol in his hand, pointed straight at Bessie, his trigger finger tightening. Bessie lifted her head and showed him her teeth.

Benny Mongrel grabbed her chain, dragging her away from the fat cop. "Please, my boss, no. Please."

The cop was panting like a midnight donkey, still pointing the gun at Bessie. He looked up at Benny Mongrel. "Now tell me the fucken truth. You see the guys who came in that car?"

"No, my boss. I was sleeping."

The cop stared at Benny Mongrel for what felt like forever before he lowered the gun and holstered it. "Fucken useless piece of shit."

Suddenly, he seemed to have grown bored with the interrogation. He threw Benny Mongrel a last contemptuous look and then turned toward the street.

Benny Mongrel knelt down beside Bessie. She was gasping for air, trying to get up, her claws scratching at the cement, her crippled hips sagging under her weight.

He stroked her and crooned softly. "Easy, Bessie. Easy, old thing. Easy now."

Burn took a beer from the fridge. Mrs. Dollie, the middle-aged domestic worker, was chatting in the kitchen with Matt. Mrs. Dollie had come with the house. At first Burn had wanted to get rid of her, not wanting a stranger in their lives. But Susan had felt sorry for the woman, and they decided to keep her on.

She was short and skinny with olive skin and gray hair that escaped in tendrils from beneath her Muslim headscarf. She looked frail but was not. Burn had seen her effortlessly moving furniture as she vacuumed. She spoke rapid-fire English with the local accent that had Jack and Susan continually asking her to repeat herself. Which she did, with a great show of patience, as if, shame, it wasn't these foreigners' fault they were so slow, was it?

Matt loved her and seemed to have no problem understanding her. He watched as she dusted the leaves of the potted plants in the kitchen.

"Now look it here, Matty, when youse is by the house and I'm not here, you must look nicely after the plants, okay?"

Matt nodded, earnestly. "I'll water them."

"Ja. Nicely. No matter what they say about water restrictions. A plant must get its water."

Mrs. Dollie grabbed a bucket and a mop and headed to the tiled dining room, Matt trailing after her. Burn watched as she attacked the tiles energetically, her thin arms pumping as she mopped the area where the bodies had lain. He felt a moment of panic. Had he cleaned the blood properly? Had some of it caked in the grout between the tiles? But Mrs. Dollie noticed nothing. She never stopped chatting to the boy as she mopped, and he heard Matt laugh.

Burn walked away from the conversation, out onto the deck, sipping the beer. His son seemed okay, but how could he be? His world had been upended; he had been dragged across the planet and had witnessed something last night that he wouldn't be allowed to watch on TV.

Burn stood drinking his beer, watching the sun sagging down toward the ocean. Unbelievably, it was less than twenty-four hours ago that those men had come.

The door buzzer sounded, startling Burn. He hesitated, instinctively wanting to ignore it. Then it sounded again. Whoever was down there kept his finger on the buzzer.

Burn walked across to the wall-mounted intercom monitor. On the screen he saw a huge man crowded into the street door recess. Burn picked up the phone.

"Yes, can I help you?"

The man held up an ID to the camera. "Police. Can I talk to you, please?" He had a guttural accent, hard to follow through the intercom.

Burn hesitated. "Okay. I'll be right down."

Burn felt sick in his gut.

He walked across to Mrs. Dollie and Matt. He ruffled his son's hair. "I have to talk to somebody outside. You stay here, with Mrs. Dollie, okay?" Matt nodded.

Burn locked the front door to make sure that Matt couldn't follow him and walked down the pathway.

Was this it? Was this where the whole thing ended?

He opened the street door.

CHAPTER 7

Burn felt as if he were confronting a Table Mountain of fat. The cop was massive, tall and obese, and he stank, a mixture of acrid body odor and something vaguely medicinal.

"Can I help you, officer?"

"I'm Inspector Barnard." The man's body odor became a sweet memory when the force of Barnard's halitosis hit Burn. He took an involuntary step backward.

Burn tried not to breathe. "Is there a problem?"

Barnard was squinting at him. "You American?"

"That's right."

"On holiday?"

"Yeah, I guess. We're renting for a couple of months."

"Nice part of town." The cop smiled, showing yellow teeth beneath a mustache as bushy as a skunk's tail.

"It is, yes. Look, Mr. . . . ?"

"Barnard. Inspector."

"Inspector, is there something I can help you with?"

"Just routine, sir." Barnard had a notebook out. "Can I have your name, please?"

"Hill. John Hill."

"Mr. Hill, there have been a couple of break-ins in the area over the last few weeks. You notice anything out of the ordinary, maybe?"

Burn shook his head. "Nothing. No. This is a very quiet street."

"Last night? You didn't hear anything, or see anything unusual?"

"No. Sorry."

Barnard was pointing at the red BMW. "You maybe see who was driving that car?"

"Sorry. Can't help you."

Barnard nodded, sucked his teeth. Then he fixed Burn with a stare. "You live here alone?"

"No, with my wife and son."

"Okay. Can I maybe talk to your wife? See if she maybe heard something?"

"She's in hospital."

Barnard was looking interested. "Oh? What's wrong?"

"She's pregnant. A complication. We had to get an ambulance for her last night, in fact. I was pretty preoccupied with that, as you can imagine."

"Of course, of course. Well, I hope she is going to be okay."

"Thank you. She's fine."

"Okay, good."

Burn stepped back, ready to shut the door. "Is there anything else?"

The fat cop seemed reluctant to leave. "No. Thanks."

As Burn closed the door, Barnard put out a hand and gripped it. The door was going nowhere. "Mr. Hill, what hospital is she in?"

Burn studied the piggy eyes peering out at him from within the folds of fat.

"She's in Gardens Clinic."

"Maybe I can talk to the ambulance crew. They might have seen something. You have a good night now." Barnard released the door and allowed Burn to close it.

Burn breathed easily for the first time, free of Barnard's stench and the weight of his own terror. The cop had traced the car to the gangsters. Did that mean he had found the bodies?

Burn forced himself to calm down. He went back into the house and walked straight to the bottle of Scotch in the kitchen, poured himself a shot, and knocked it back neat. He felt like flattening the bottle, but he knew he couldn't.

He had planning to do.

They were going to have to run again.

Barnard called in a tow truck to impound the BMW; then he drove away from wealthy Cape Town down to the flatlands he knew so well.

What Rikki Fortune and his friend Faried Adams had been doing up there on the mountain wasn't difficult to imagine. They were predators. Always on the hunt. They had been down in Sea Point looking for a whore; then they had seen something as they cruised like shadows through that white suburb, something they desired. Animals like that, half out of their minds on drugs, never made plans. They acted on impulse. Raped. Murdered. Took what they wanted without thought.

But where were they?

Barnard drove to the Golden Spoon for his usual gatsby full house. It was dark by the time he walked out to his car, but the heat was still intense. He sat for a while, chewing like a hippo on a riverbank, washing the food down with the piss-yellow Double O.

Barnard had touched base with the cops at Sea Point police station. No violent crimes, home invasions, or murders had been reported in the last twenty-four hours. And they knew nothing about this John Hill.

Barnard thought about the American. There was something that worried him about the man, something he couldn't name, something that nagged at him worse than the rash on his thighs.

Hill was hiding something. He was sure of it.

Benny Mongrel searched the black trash can and found a plastic container of potato salad. Next he found a half-eaten bar of Belgian chocolate. The greatest prize of all was a T-bone steak, cooked but uneaten.

Tomorrow was garbage collection day for the road on the mountain, and a bin stood outside each house ready for the dawn truck. Benny Mongrel was always amazed at what these rich people threw away. Uneaten food still wrapped in plastic, brand-new clothes, electrical equipment. Last month he'd found a portable TV that worked perfectly and had swapped it with his landlord for rent.

It was no wonder that squads of homeless people seeped from the doorways, gutters, and open fields, to sift through the trash cans of the privileged. Beatings from the police and rent-a-cops were a small price to pay for these rich pickings.

Benny Mongrel put his spoils in a plastic bag and went back to the building site. He climbed the stairs to where Bessie lay with her gray muzzle between her paws, staring silently into the night. The fat cop's boot had hurt Bessie. When Benny Mongrel had felt her ribs, the old dog had moaned and licked his hand. She was tough. Like him. And like him, she wore the visible signs of abuse and ill treatment. There was a scar across her nose. When he stroked her, he felt bumps and lesions from old wounds. The kick from the cop's boot was just more of the rough treatment she had come to expect from the world. Her ribs would heal. That much Benny Mongrel knew. Even so, it pained him that she had been hurt trying to protect him.

Looking at the scarred old dog, Benny Mongrel saw himself.

Benny Mongrel unfolded a scrap of housepainter's canvas in front of Bessie like a tablecloth. Then, with great care, he set the feast out before her, item by item. She sniffed at the potato salad but was not to be drawn. She granted the Belgian chocolate a cursory lick, then snubbed it. Benny Mongrel placed the T-bone steak in front of her. She feigned disinterest for a moment, but the smell was too much to ignore.

She grabbed the bone between her front paws and started working away at the steak, her jaws moving as she chewed. He squatted beside her and rolled a cigarette, sneaking glances at her as she ate. At last she was done, and she lifted her head and looked him in the eye.

Benny Mongrel could have sworn that she smiled at him.

⟵

Burn slept fitfully. His dreams were full of dead men, and the fat cop made a guest appearance. Matt wet the bed again, and in the early hours Burn carried him, still asleep, to the bathroom, where he cleaned him up and put him in a fresh pair of Disney pajamas.

He took Matt back to bed with him and lay listening to his son sleeping until gray dawn light washed the room.

At five thirty Burn was sitting out on the deck, watching the sunrise. Thinking. Thinking how he had been obsessed with chance, luck, the roll of the dice, the spin of the wheel. How he had convinced himself that he had been born with that extra edge, that extra percentage that would always swing things his way. That he was a winner.

Until that day in the bookie's Cadillac.

The deal Nolan had offered Burn was simple: he was putting together a team to take down a bank in Milwaukee. Recruiting people who had no links with Wisconsin, who would leave no trail for the cops to follow. They were going in at night to blow the vault. Nolan needed a security expert to override the alarms and patch a loop into the surveillance cameras. He'd done his homework on Burn and knew he was the guy.

If Burn signed on, not only would his hundred-grand debt to Pepe Vargas disappear, but he would get a chunk of the six million they expected to lift from the vault. If he didn't, Nolan would pay Susan and Matt a visit. There was a deadness to Nolan's eyes that told Burn this was a threat to take seriously.

Burn had thought of running. But with what? To where?

So he had signed on. He told Susan he was attending a security convention in Dallas, and he went off with Nolan and two other men to Wisconsin.

Everything went perfectly. Burn sat outside the bank, in the back of a minivan, working the keys of a laptop. He disabled the alarm without alerting the bank's security. For Burn, who built and installed these systems, bypassing them was easy. Then he fed a looped image of the empty bank vault into the monitors at the bank's surveillance center. The security guys working the graveyard shift drank their coffee, read paperbacks, and dozed without any idea that the bank was being hit.

Nolan and the two other men went into the bank. Burn stayed in the van, in radio contact, sweating despite the freezing weather. Terrified. Every few minutes Nolan's calm voice would give him a terse progress report. The vault door had blown. They were in.

It seemed like hours but took no more than forty-five minutes. The three men returned with the money in kit bags. There was an air of quiet jubilation. Nolan slid into the driver's seat. A big guy who had hardly spoken sat next to Nolan. The third man, a skinny kid in his twenties, joined Burn in the back. He grinned and lit a smoke, offering one to Burn, who shook his head.

Nolan drove through downtown Milwaukee. He kept to the speed limit. He stopped at the lights. Then a prowl car nosed up behind them, and the cop driving whooped the siren.

Nolan pulled over. He looked back over the seat. "Keep cool."

Nolan got out of the van to talk to the cop. The van had a busted taillight. There was another cop in the prowl car who didn't bother to get out. Things seemed under control until the first cop stepped up to the van and shone his flashlight at the big guy in the passenger seat. Something about him must have set off alarm bells. Next thing the cop was asking Nolan to open the rear of the van.

That's when Nolan shot the cop.

And the uniform in the prowl car shot Nolan, who fell down in the snow beside the dead cop. The big guy had a pistol in his hand, and he returned fire. He slid over to take the wheel of the van, and as he pulled away, half of his head disappeared and the van slowed, then stalled.

The cop in the car shot at the van, and one of his bullets pierced the door and caught the young guy in the stomach. He pitched forward groaning, bleeding over the bags of money.

Burn vaulted the seats. He shoved the dead guy out of the van, got in behind the wheel, and took off. The cop was still shooting. Burn floored the van, fishtailing, fighting to get it under control. As he drifted into a corner Burn saw the strobing lights of the cop car in pursuit. A block later it hit ice and spun one-eighty before collecting a lamppost and disappearing from Burn's mirror.

Burn ditched the van in a side street, grabbed one of the money bags from the rear, and took off into the night, leaving the van and the dying kid.

He'd been given fake ID for the job, and he used it to rent a car and drive to Chicago. He called Susan and told her to get herself and Matt on the next plane to Miami and check into a hotel. He would meet her there. It still amazed him that she had listened, even when he refused to tell her what the hell was going on.

In Chicago it was his turn to look up Tommy Ryan, who was connected. Fitting that what began with Tommy ended with him. It cost Burn plenty, but he managed to get nearly two million dollars laundered and the bulk of it transferred to a Swiss bank account. The new identities came next.

He joined Susan in Miami. They both had news. He told her what he had really been doing. She told him that she was pregnant.

She cried, raged at him. She wanted to go home. She wanted their life back.

Then she had stopped crying and agreed to go with him, and the three of them caught a plane to Cape Town.

The kid in the van hadn't died. He'd sung a long and loud plea bargain, and Jack Burn had joined the U.S. Marshals' MOST WANTED list.

—————

The dogs found them first. A pack of strays roaming the Flats were drawn by the smell of the bodies. They ripped open the plastic garbage bags with their teeth and claws, then recoiled at the ripe stench of rotting human. They ran off to root in the trash cans of the nearby houses.

Ronnie September and Cassiem Davids came upon them next, sometime after eight in the morning. They were both eleven years old, in their school uniforms, but they had no intention of going to school.

They headed across the open veld, sucking on illicit cigarettes, putting as much distance between themselves and their homes in Paradise Park as they could. They were going to jump a taxi and head for Bellville to play arcade games.

It was Ronnie who saw the white Nikes sticking out of the grass. He stopped and pointed. "Check that, man."

Cassiem stared. "Those is Nikes."

"I know that. You think I'm stupid?"

The two boys edged closer to the body of a short, skinny man, only partly covered by black garbage bags. Boys their age who grow up on the Cape Flats are no strangers to dead bodies, but the stench was fierce.

"Look, there's another one." Ronnie was pointing to where the body of a tall man spilled from the torn bags. He ran a discerning eye over the lanky corpse's outfit. "His clothes is shit, man."

"God, but it stinks." Cassiem was covering his nose with his hand.

Ronnie sucked on his cigarette and stepped closer to the small corpse. The dead man lay on his back, the jagged slash in his throat gaping at the sky. "Yaaaw. He was cut, hey?"

Cassiem was looking over Ronnie's shoulder. "Those pants is nice. Diesel."

"It's full of blood, man." Ronnie stooped a little lower. "Maybe he got a phone."

"I'm not putting my hands in there."

Ronnie was eyeing the shoes. "That Nikes is brand-new."

"I saw them first!"

Ronnie gave his friend a shove. "So, you gonna take them off him? Do it then!"

Cassiem said nothing, took a step back.

Ronnie shook his head, disgusted. "My little sister got more balls than you, man."

"Ja, okay, then let me see you do it. Come."

Ronnie eyeballed his friend. He'd always kept a safe distance from the bodies he had seen before, watched as cops or paramedics had shoveled them into bags and carted them away. This was different. Shit, this was fucken disgusting.

But he looked down at his torn and scruffy running shoes, inherited from his brother. There was no way he was ever going to afford a pair of Nikes like these.

Ronnie took a deep breath and knelt down and pulled loose the laces of one of the shoes. He almost puked from the stink. He untied the other shoe. Then he tried to get the shoe off. The corpse had bloated and stiffened, and the shoe was tight on the foot. Ronnie was tugging, and that set the dead man's head lolling back, the wound opening even wider, and a fat white worm crawled out.

It was too much for Cassiem, and he spewed his breakfast of egg and leftover mince curry onto his shoes.

Ronnie wasn't giving up. He tugged again and finally managed to get a shoe off, falling onto his butt in the process. Then he attacked the second shoe and separated it from the dead man's foot.

Ronnie stood, triumphant. He held the shoes up in front of Cassiem, dangling them by the laces. "Gottem."

"They fucken stink."

"Yours stink, and you aren't even dead yet."

Ronnie walked away from the bodies, Cassiem tagging after him. Ronnie sat down and pulled off his old shoes and threw them as far as he could into the bush. He slipped on the new Nikes.

"They fit perfect." He stood, lifting his trousers to his ankles, flexing his toes.

Then he grabbed Cassiem by the tie and pulled him close. "You keep your fucken mouth shut about this, okay?"

Cassiem nodded. Ronnie was already walking toward the road. Cassiem shot a look back over his shoulder at the red socks sticking out of the garbage bag; then he followed his friend.

CHAPTER 8

Burn fetched Susan from the clinic shortly before noon. She looked pale but composed as he helped her into the front of the Jeep. He lifted Matt into the back and belted him into the car seat.

Susan didn't look at him as they drove. "Where are we going?"

"Home. To the house."

She shook her head. "I don't want to go back there, Jack."

"Susan . . ."

"I mean it. Not after what happened."

He said nothing, then realized that his knuckles were white on the steering wheel. He forced himself to relax. "Where do you want to go then?"

"I don't care. A hotel. Anywhere but that house."

He pulled over and stopped. An almost absurdly beautiful expanse of sun-washed ocean and mountain spread out below them. Neither of them was looking at the view.

"Susan, it's important that we don't do anything out of the ordinary. Anything that could attract attention."

"You mean like kill a couple of locals in our dining room?" She was furious, two red spots touching her cheekbones. Susan shut her eyes briefly and took a breath, her hands resting on her swollen belly. She looked over her shoulder at Matt, who was staring at his parents anxiously.

Susan reached back and caressed Matt's hair. "It's okay, Matty. Mommy and Daddy aren't fighting."

Burn, watching in the rearview mirror, saw an uncertain smile touch his son's lips. Susan turned to face forward again, staring down at the ocean below.

"Baby, you need to relax. Please." Burn tried to take her hand. When she pulled it away, he noticed that she wasn't wearing her wedding ring. "Where's your ring?"

She looked at him. "Jack, did you hear a word I said yesterday? About going home?"

"Of course. It's all I've been thinking about."

"I meant what I said."

"I know you did. And I understand." He had to get ahold of himself, force himself to keep it together. "All I'm asking for is some time. To organize myself."

"How much time?"

"A couple of days. A week at the most. Until then, we need to keep up our usual routine."

She was looking at him, intuiting something. "What's going on, Jack? What's happened at the house?"

"Nothing. Nothing's happened."

"Don't lie to me. Please."

He nodded. "Okay. Those . . . those men left a car in the street, outside the building site. It must have been reported. A cop was around asking some questions."

"Jesus, Jack."

"It's fine. He went to every house in the street. It was just routine."

She was shaking her head. "So he's watching the house?"

"No, I haven't seen him again. I told you, it was just routine."

Susan turned slightly to face him, her eyes searching his face. "Three days, Jack. Three days, and then I'm contacting the consulate. Are we clear on that?"

"Yes." He started the car and pulled back onto the road.

His wife had become his enemy.

Berenice September carried shopping bags into her small house. She worked as a cashier at Shoprite, and she'd used her staff discount to buy supplies for herself and her three kids. Like many women on the Flats, she was a single parent. Her useless bastard of a husband had left her for a young slut and then got thrown under the wheels of the Elsies River train.

Good riddance.

Her eldest boy, Donovan, was doing fine. He had a job and brought some money into the house, and her daughter, Juanita, was too young to be any trouble. But it was her middle one, Ronnie, who reminded her of her late ex-husband. He had that same *fuck you* attitude. She would have to watch him.

Ronnie came slouching in while she was preparing supper, heading straight to the room he shared with his brother. She yelled after him. "Hey, come here."

He hovered in the kitchen doorway. "Ja?"

"What time is this?"

He could never resist consulting the huge Batman watch on his skinny wrist. It was a Hong Kong rip-off but still his most treasured possession. "It's ten past five."

"I know the bloody time, Ronnie. I mean why you so late?"

"I had sports."

"You got homework?"

"Ja, I'm gonna go do it."

It was then that she saw his shoes. He saw where she was looking and stepped back out of the doorway. Berenice was a big woman, but she could move rapidly when she wanted to. She grabbed her son by the arm and pulled him into the kitchen.

"Where did you get those shoes?"

He tried to pull free of her grip. "I bought them."

"With what? You little liar! Did you steal them?"

He shook his head. She grabbed him by the throat and pulled him to her. "Tell me the truth before I smack it out of you!"

Ronnie knew his mother never made idle threats. "Can I keep them if I tell you?"

"Just tell me, and I decide, okay?"

"I took it off a dead guy."

She let him go, recoiled in horror. Berenice September lived in superstitious dread of those who had passed on.

She shook her head at her son. What kind of a monster had she brought into this world? Why couldn't he steal off somebody who was alive like any normal bloody person?

Benny Mongrel arrived for his shift intentionally early. Patrol cars zoomed in and out, armed response patrolmen swaggered around with their Kevlar vests and their Ray-Bans and their pistols on their hips. They were the movie stars of the security world.

Benny Mongrel was a bottom feeder. Nobody noticed him.

He knew that Ishmael Isaacs wasn't there. He'd made a big show of telling them that he was taking a course for the day, at the head office in Parow. Hinted that he was up for promotion.

Benny Mongrel paused for a moment, realizing that what he was about to do wouldn't make him popular with Isaacs, but he thought *fuck it*. He no longer wanted to guard the building site. Not after the gangsters. And especially not after that fat cop had kicked Bessie. He wanted to get himself and his dog as far away from there as he could.

So he went up to the young girl behind the reception desk. She sat with her nose buried in a gossip magazine, chewing gum. She ignored him. Benny Mongrel had to find patience from somewhere. In his old world he would have blackened her eyes and bruised that painted mouth before she knew what was coming.

"Missy."

She dragged her eyes from the magazine and stared at him. "What?"

"I want to see the boss."

"Why?"

"Please. I need to talk to him."

He could see she was finding it difficult staring at his scarred face. She looked away and lifted a phone, mumbled a few words. She pointed to a doorway. "You've got five minutes."

Benny Mongrel knocked on the door and walked in. He had never spoken to the white man behind the desk, only seen him driving in and out in his Mercedes-Benz. He wore a dark tie and a shirt so white it hurt your eyes. His office was as cold as a fridge from the air-conditioning.

The man lifted his eyes from a laptop. He didn't stand or invite Benny Mongrel to sit. "What's your name?"

"Uh, Niemand. Benny Niemand."

"Okay. Is there a problem?"

"No, sir. I just was wondering if maybe I could guard a different site, like."

"Why don't you take this up with Isaacs?"

"He's on the course, sir."

The man gave him a long-suffering look. "Where are you posted at the moment?"

"The new house. Above Sea Point."

"Okay. What's wrong with working that site?"

"Nothing. No, I thought maybe I could have something more, I dunno . . . something with more responsibility, like."

The white man laughed at him. "So you're ambitious, hey? Okay, that's fine. Look, you've been with us, what? Two months?" Benny Mongrel nodded. "Why don't we give it another month or so? The house will be completed then anyway, and we'll move you on. Okay?"

Benny Mongrel nodded again. The white man was already going back to his laptop. Then he saw Benny Mongrel wasn't moving. The man looked up, irritated.

"Was there something else?"

"My dog."

"Now what? Do you want a new dog too?"

"No, no, no, sir. She's a very good dog. I was just wondering if, you know, one day I can maybe, like, buy her?"

The man looked at him in surprise. "Jesus, Niemand, what's your problem? We don't sell these dogs; this isn't a bloody pet shop. Now come on, get going. I'm busy here."

The white man was already typing on his computer.

≫

Constable Gershwynne Galant was sure his blood was cooking, honest to God. There was no way he could sit inside the windowless metal container that housed the satellite police station. He took a stool and placed it in the tiny patch of shade outside. His boots were still in the blazing sun, but at least his face and chest were in the shade.

This satellite police station was the result of some visible policing initiative dreamed up by a politician who spent his life inside air-conditioned offices. Since the nearest police station was in distant Bell-wood South, the residents of Paradise Park had shoved the usual rape and murder statistics in the face of local politicians. Finally, a trailer had been towed to a piece of open veld, and the satellite station opened its door.

The plan was to have a police officer on duty from 7:00 a.m. to 7:00 p.m. Which was totally useless as most of the crime happened at night, but what can you do? The first night, after the cop on duty went home, local gangsters had hooked the trailer to a truck and towed it away. Red-faced, the politicians had replaced the trailer with a heavy container, like the ones used on cargo ships.

Manning the satellite station was a punishment detail. Gersh-wynne Galant had made the mistake of getting caught with the takings of a drug dealer he had just busted. So he was frying like an egg, alone, day in and day out for a fucken week. Jesus.

Galant was paging through a magazine he'd found lying outside the container when the woman and her son walked up. Galant looked at his watch. Six o'clock. He would have to listen to their story.

The boy was holding a pair of Nikes. He was walking barefoot with a kind of skip, his bare feet burning on the hot sand. His mother looked like a bloody battle-ax.

Galant listened to what the boy had to say, about bodies in the veld, and decided not to phone this in to Bellwood South. Instead he di-aled Rudi Barnard's cell phone. Gatsby thrived on this kind of informa-tion, and it never hurt to do the fat man a favor.

Galant killed the call and told the mother and son to wait. Some-body was coming.

The battle-ax scowled at him. "And how long must I wait?"

Galant shrugged, his nose already back in his magazine.

The woman sighed, then spoke to the boy. "I got to finish cooking and help your sister with her homework. You wait here and sort this out. You hear me?"

The boy nodded, and she walked off.

Barnard's Toyota scraped across the uneven veld. His great weight dragged the suspension down, and the exhaust smacked the ground alarmingly every time he hit a bump. The little half-breed was flying around in the seat next to him like a turd in a tumble dryer. Barnard's car threw up a cloud of dust in the evening light, heading toward the spot where the kid said the bodies lay.

Barnard slid the car to a stop and hauled himself out, wheezing, wiping a beefy forearm across his sweating face. Ronnie September climbed out, staring at Barnard in mute terror.

Barnard pointed to the Nikes lying on the floor of the car. "Bring those with you." The kid did as he said. Barnard told him to lead the way.

Barnard followed the kid toward a clump of bushes.

He saw Rikki Fortune first. Barnard squatted down. If the stench bothered him, he gave no sign of it. He took in the gash across the throat. Also the torn garbage bags and the duct tape. Who the fuck wrapped corpses up like Christmas presents before dumping them? No gangster he knew.

Barnard snapped a couple of pictures of Rikki with his cell phone camera.

He lifted himself and went across to the tall half-breed. Looked like he had been stabbed in the chest and shot in the stomach. Barnard took a couple more happy snaps.

Ronnie was hanging back, still clutching the shoes by the laces. Barnard beckoned him over. "Come here."

The boy came over to him. "Tell me again what happened."

Ronnie began nervously. "I was coming on here this morning . . ."

"What time?"

"Past eight."

"You alone?"

Ronnie nodded. "I was coming on when I saw that one." He pointed to Rikki. "Then I saw the other one next."

"You see anybody else here?"

The boy shook his head.

"Ja. Then what you do?"

Ronnie held the shoes up. "I took these."

Barnard fixed him with a stare. "And then what?"

"Then I got a taxi. To Bellville. To play games. Then I went home. And my mommy saw the shoes. And I tole her about them." He pointed to the bodies. "And she took me to the cop."

"You didn't bring anybody here?" Ronnie shook his head. "You lying to me?"

Ronnie shook his head even more vigorously. Barnard stared down at the boy. He thrust a hand toward the Nikes. "Gimme those."

Ronnie held the shoes out to him. Barnard grabbed them, flinging them onto the tall guy's body. He poked a finger into Ronnie's chest. "You wait here."

Barnard walked back to the car and popped the trunk. He took a .38 revolver from under the spare tire and shoved it into his waistband. He'd taken it off a dead drug dealer and kept it for special occasions. Like this. Then he hauled out a jerrican and walked back to the kid.

Ronnie looked as if he was thinking of making a run for it.

Barnard stopped in front of him and set the jerrican down. Then he took the revolver from his waistband, cocked it, and shot the kid between the eyes. The little bastard hadn't even seen it coming, just gave him a stupid look and dropped. Barnard shot him once more in the chest, just to make sure.

Barnard dragged Rikki Fortune's body until it lay next to his bean-pole buddy. Then he grabbed the half-breed kid by a bare ankle and slung him across the two gangsters. He emptied the jerrican onto the bodies, set fire to a scrap of cloth, and tossed it, stepping back. The bodies exploded into flame.

There was no way that Barnard was going to let this crime scene into the system. He knew there was only an outside chance that anybody would give a shit about these useless lives ending, but it was a chance he wasn't prepared to take.

No, he knew that the answer to his prayers lay in a house up on the mountain. This was a gift from God.

In very fucken weird wrapping paper.

CHAPTER 9

Burn found Susan making up the single bed in the spare room. "This for me?"

She nodded, tucking in a sheet. "I think it's best."

He tried to help, taking one side of the sheet. She snapped it out of his hand. "I can do this, Jack."

"You know that Matt's slept with me the last couple of nights?"

"Then he can sleep with me." She shook a pillow into a cover.

"He's wetting the bed again."

"I'm not exactly surprised." She levered herself up to standing. "He needs counseling. I want him to get help, as soon as we're back in the States."

He nodded. "Sure." He turned to leave the room.

"Jack?" Her voice stopped him. She was looking at him, in the direct way she had, as if she could read the fine print on his soul. "Do you believe in retribution?"

"Susan, where's this going?"

"Do you ever think of that cop? In Milwaukee?"

"Every day."

"Do you even know his name?" Burn didn't answer her. Susan pressed on. "Do you know he had a wife? And a son?"

Burn said nothing, letting her get done with this.

She walked past him, that splay-footed balancing act. "Just like you, Jack."

≻

When the fat boer showed her the picture on his phone, Carmen Fortune felt a sense of disbelief. Could it really be? Could Rikki really be dead? Did this really mean she would never again feel him shove himself inside her or hit her with his fists?

She stared at the image on the phone. "Is it cut? His throat?"

"No, he's smiling for the camera." Gatsby grabbed the phone out of her hand and slid it into the pocket of his sweat-stained shirt.

"Who did it?"

"Dunno."

"Where is he? His body?"

"Don't worry about that."

Carmen had been out smoking a globe of tik, come back with that crazy rush in her head when she saw the fat boer waiting for her outside her apartment. She had let him in, expecting abuse over the money that Rikki owed him. The cop was bad luck.

But today he had brought her good news. Fuck, it was unbelievable.

The cop was speaking, but she was caught up in the spin cycle in her head. He prodded her with one of his fat fingers, and she nearly fell. "I'm fucken talking to you!"

Carmen had to concentrate hard to keep her head together. "What, man?"

He shook his head at her. "Fucken tik whore." She opened her mouth to protest, but he lifted a hand to shut her up. "Now listen and listen careful."

"Okay."

"People are going to want to know where he is, you get me?"

"Ja."

"But you not gonna tell them he's dead."

"Why not?"

"Because I'm telling you not to, that's why not!" He was looming over her, his stink like a dead thing in the room.

"But what do I do? If people want to know where he gone?"

"You tell them him and his buddy . . ."

"Faried."

"Faried. You tell them you heard them talking about going up the west coast."

"For what?"

"Who gives a fuck for what? For crayfish or abalone. Or Hottentot whores. Just say they went and you haven't seen them since. You understand me?"

Carmen nodded. "Ja. Okay, man."

Gatsby grabbed her by the arm. She could feel her tit lying against his hand. He pulled the hand away. "I hear you saying anything else, and I come and cut *your* fucken throat. You got me?"

She nodded, stepping away from his stench. He looked around the room. "Where's the old alkie?"

"Gone to buy a wine. Don't worry, he won't say nothing."

"And the kid?"

"Social Services took him."

"What, they say you unfit?" She shrugged. "So, no husband. No kid. You can sell your ass again." There was a phlegmy sound from deep in Gatsby's lungs, like a chest wound sucking. He was laughing.

"Fuck you!" Carmen couldn't stop herself.

He moved fast for a huge man, and his fist flew at her. He pulled the punch at the last second, and she felt his clammy knuckles brush the skin of her cheek. They stood like that, eyes locked until he lowered his fist.

"Next time, I'll put you in hospital."

Then he turned and lumbered out, leaving the door open. Carmen shut it.

She sat down on the stained sofa. Rikki was dead. She still couldn't believe it. She had dreaded telling him they had lost Sheldon's grant. Rikki would have blamed her, and, unlike the fat boer, he wouldn't have pulled his punches. Fuck, knowing Rikki, he would have put the boot in.

She felt relief and even some odd sensation that wasn't familiar to her. It was happiness, she finally realized. She was happy. For the first time since she was seven years old, when her father had started visiting her with his whispered, sweaty demands, she belonged to no man.

—————

Burn stood in the kitchen looking through at Susan and Matt on the sofa in front of the TV. Susan held her son's hand. Two days ago this would have made Burn happy. He would have taken this as a sign that Susan was growing close to Matt again, that she was moving out of the closed circle of her and her baby.

But he knew now that Susan was getting ready to turn herself in. She was afraid she'd be separated from her son and was taking what time she could to be with him. Burn couldn't stand watching them any longer, in the knowledge that in a couple of days they would be out of his life.

Probably forever.

He found himself on the deck in the dark, staring out over the lights of the city below. He felt a moment of vertigo as if everything was sliding away from him. He sat down on a wooden chair and deliberately slowed his breathing. Forced himself to calm down. Forced himself to remember who he was.

He had always been a fighter. As a kid, he'd protected his older brother from bullies. He'd worn the bruises and the broken teeth, but he'd never backed down. Ever. There were still men in his hometown who would prop up the bar and talk about the night he won them the high school state championship with his arm broken. His throwing arm. He'd landed his passes on a dime and scored the winning touchdown.

In the marines, no matter what brand of shit hit the fan, he had found a quiet place, some stillness within, that allowed him the time to act.

The night the men had come in off the deck, he had known he was going to take them down. It wasn't a thought; it was a reflex. He was a fighter.

Now he was losing his family, and he wasn't doing a fucking thing. He was letting Susan slip farther and farther away.

He stood and paced the deck, asking himself the tough questions: Did he want her to go? Did he want to be alone, with nothing to lose? Did he want to get rid of everything that made him vulnerable, go deep into a cold place within himself and live out the rest of his days a refugee from both the law and any of the emotions that made him human?

No. He did not.

Burn went inside. Matt was still hypnotized by the TV. Susan was in the kitchen, chopping vegetables.

Burn leaned on the counter and watched her chop. She had beautiful hands, long delicate fingers. She'd been a sculptor when he had first met her. She'd lost interest in sculpting in the last few years, her passion to be an artist diluted by the duties of a wife and mother. It was a pity. She was talented.

Susan ignored him. She scraped the vegetables into a wok and walked it across to the stove.

Burn didn't take his eyes off her. "Ernie Simpkins."

She looked up at him, brushing hair from her face. "What?"

"The dead cop's name was Ernie Simpkins." She shrugged, stirred the wok with a wooden spoon. "I wish to hell I could change what happened, Susan, but I can't. I don't want to lose you. Or Matt. Or the baby."

"It's too late, Jack. You already have."

"I screwed up, big time. I admit that."

She looked up from the wok. "No, Jack, forgetting an anniversary is screwing up. Murdering a cop is in an altogether different category. And let's not even talk about what you did the other night."

Burn watched her as she cooked, determined not to let her anger scare him and drive him into silence. "Baby, do you really want to split up our family? If you do that, you know that we'll never be able to see each other again. The kids will grow up not knowing who their father is."

"You say that like it's a bad thing."

"That isn't you talking, Susan."

"It is, Jack. Get used to it. I'm not your cute little trophy wife anymore."

"You were never that." He came up behind her, tried to hold her, but she spun away from him and crossed to the fridge for soy sauce.

He pressed on. "Let's go to New Zealand."

She laughed in disbelief. "New Zealand?"

He nodded. He had to sell this. He had one chance. "I made a mistake bringing us here. This place is like, hell, I dunno, a candy castle built on a septic tank. New Zealand is beautiful, wild, just about zero crime."

"Now there's an irony. You looking for a place that's crime free." She added soy to the vegetables, stirring rapidly.

"Susan, look at me." Reluctantly, she looked up. "I want another chance. Jesus, I deserve a chance to make things right. For all of us. Stop shutting me out. Because I made some bad choices doesn't mean you have to."

She was looking at him, at least. Holding his gaze. "So, you're saying we go to New Zealand? With me like this?" She pointed at her belly.

"After you have the baby, yes. I'll get us an apartment here until then. In a security block. Tomorrow. We'll pack up and get the hell out of this house. And we'll leave as soon as it's safe for you to fly." He saw that he was reaching her, sensed an opening in her armor. "Susan, I love you. And Matt. I want a chance to make it right."

She shook her head, turned away from him, fighting tears.

He walked over to her and wrapped his arms around her from behind. She tried to free herself, but he held her tight and at last he felt her begin to relax and give in.

Susan almost surrendered, almost let his words convince her. Then she saw him with the knife, crouched over the skinny man, and she broke his hold on her and stepped away from him.

She saw his face, the desperation in his eyes. "Leave me alone, Jack."

"Susan . . ." He was reaching for her again.

"Just leave me the fuck alone!" She shouted before she could stop herself. Burn nodded and walked back out onto the deck. She held on to the kitchen counter, battling to calm herself.

She looked up to see Matt staring at her from the sofa. He was crying.

She composed herself and went across to him, sat down beside him, and put her arm around his shoulders. "It's okay, Matty."

She knew she'd pushed her son away, and she'd been trying, since she got back from the clinic, to reconnect with him. To love him again. But every time she looked at him she saw his father.

The child sobbed as she held him and stroked his hair and whispered reassuring words. She felt his pain and confusion. And she felt her own guilt. God, how could she have done that? To her baby boy?

Matt was calming down; the sobs were not as desperate. Susan blew his nose on a tissue. She pointed to something on the screen, the antics of a cartoon character, and Matt smiled. Then he laughed. Susan sat next to him, held him, until she saw that he was caught up in the swirl of color on the screen. Then she went out on the deck, where her husband stood with his back to her, staring out at the night.

He didn't see her, and she watched him for a few moments. He had always been her rock, the one thing in her life she could trust completely. Not anymore.

"Jack." He turned to her, his face catching the light from the house. The beaten look on his face aged him.

"Okay," she said.

"Okay what?"

"Let's do it. Let's go to New Zealand. Or wherever."

He was staring at her. "You're serious?"

"Yes. But I'm doing it for Matt and for her." She put a hand to her belly.

He came toward Susan and took her in his arms, her belly pressing up against him. She stared over his shoulder, out at the swollen yellow moon hanging like a bruised fruit over the ocean.

"I'm sorry, baby," he said. "I'm going to make it right. I promise."

More than anything, she wanted to believe him.

CHAPTER 10

Why hadn't he smacked the brown bitch in her filthy mouth?

As Rudi Barnard left the Flats behind, drove the Toyota across the railway bridge to Goodwood, he puzzled over that half-breed slut, Carmen, and why he hadn't he hit her. Normally he didn't think twice about something like that. Disrespect or cross him, and you paid the price. He was confused by this aberration in his behavior.

Did he really want to fuck her? No, he decided. It wasn't that. He realized, relieved, that she was someone who would be of use to him sometime. And his intuition was that she had been beaten senseless so often by so many men that it meant nothing to her. In fact, he reckoned he would have more power over her if he didn't hit her.

Barnard smiled to himself in appreciation of his psychological in-
sights. He knew women. Hell, he'd been married to one once, hadn't he?

Fucken bitch.

On impulse Barnard stopped in at a cop bar on Voortrekker Road,
a few blocks from his dingy apartment. The Station Bar had opened back
in the days when men were left alone to do their drinking, women banished to the cocktail bar where a real man wouldn't set foot.

Although by law no woman could now be prevented from entering
the Station Bar, few did. The bar was ugly, it stank, and it was filled with
crude and violent men. It took a certain kind of woman to be drawn to
this sort of company, and most of them were out on the street plying
their trade.

Barnard grabbed a stool. The barman, a bald and wrinkled man
with skin the color of nicotine, shoved a bottle of pine nut Double O
across to him. Barnard grunted his thanks and took a gulp.

He didn't come to the Station for alcohol or company. He was a
teetotaler and a loner. Rather he came here to plug into the cop network;
when mouths were loosened by booze, he often gleaned information that
was to his advantage.

He needed a few questions answered. The grapevine had been
whispering to him, telling him stuff that woke him from his sleep, his
hemorrhoids aching and the itch between his thighs burning like crazy.

He watched a skinny guy with a potbelly and styled hair, dressed
fifteen years too young, in conversation with a half-breed down at the
other end of the bar. The half-breed nodded, laughed at something,
chugged back his beer, and left.

Barnard took his Double O and levered his fat onto the stool beside the snappy dresser. "Lotter."

Lotter looked at him with disinterest. "Barnard."

Waving at the barman who slumped like a dirty rag across the
counter, Barnard pointed at Lotter's empty glass. "Give him a drink."

"Whatever you want from me, the answer is no," Lotter said.

"Who says I want something?" Barnard leaned in close and tried a smile.

Captain Danny Lotter wasn't a squeamish man; in fact he had been known to eat hot dogs during postmortems, but the full blast of Barnard's halitosis forced him back on his stool. He quickly fired up a Camel, not offering one to Barnard.

Lotter's brandy and coke arrived, and Barnard lifted his Double O in a toast. "Good luck."

Lotter grunted, but he didn't turn the drink down.

"Lotter, I've been hearing some funny things."

"Get your ears tested."

Barnard had to restrain himself from grabbing the skinny cunt by his blow-dried hair and pulping his face on the bar. He wheezed, taking it calm. "Things about some task force, anticorruption what-what being set up."

Lotter looked at Barnard. "Ja, so?"

"So, I know you're screwing that girlie in the superintendent's office."

"Marie?"

"Ja. The ugly one?"

"She's not ugly, exactly . . ."

"Lotter, just because you fucking her doesn't mean she's not a dog." Barnard laughed one of his sucking laughs.

Lotter drained his glass and set it on the counter. He stood. "Thanks for the drink."

Barnard put a heavy paw on Lotter's shoulder, easing him back onto his stool. "I'm trying to be nice here. Let's keep it that way."

Lotter looked for a moment like he was going to resist; then he realized it would be foolish and he nodded. "Okay, but take your hands off my jacket. It's just been dry-cleaned."

Barnard took his hand back, and Lotter adjusted his collar. "Look, it's all very hush-hush, and I've only heard bits and pieces, but there is some investigation."

"Ja?"

"Ja. And you one of the people they going to be looking at."

"That so?"

Lotter nodded. "So I hear."

Barnard shrugged. "Fuck them, anyway. How many of these task forces haven't there been?"

"This one's different." Lotter sucked on his cigarette.

"How?"

"Darkies from Jo'burg, sent down from Safety and Security. To clean up the Cape."

"Darkies, hey?"

"In BMWs and suits."

"That so? They got bugger all on me."

Lotter shrugged. "Then you got nothing to worry about." He stubbed out his cigarette, stood, and walked away.

This wasn't entirely unexpected. A man like Barnard made enemies. Often powerful enemies. He had seen what had happened to other cops who had fallen foul of their superiors. The lucky ones were booted out with no pension. The unlucky ones were thrown into Pollsmoor Prison with the half-breed scum they had spent their lives fighting.

This was not a fate that Rudi Barnard was prepared to entertain.

If Lotter was right, and Lotter was too unimaginative to invent any of this, then Barnard had a battle coming. He knew well enough that the way to win a political battle in South Africa—and if there were darkies involved, this was political—was to throw money at the right people. A shitload of money, dumped in the right places, could make anything disappear.

Throw money at people. Or kill them.

Benny Mongrel and Bessie were on the top floor of the house. Bessie slept. She had moved more easily up the stairs that night, and when he'd touched her ribs, where the fat cop had kicked her, she hadn't moaned.

Ever since his conversation with his white boss, Benny Mongrel had been scheming, planning. Lying at home in his shack, unable to sleep, listening to the wind howl like the dying.

Thinking.

He felt at peace now that he had made up his mind. He knew what he had to do. Just two more days, and he picked up his month's pay. A pittance, but it was all he had. Then he and Bessie would start a new life together.

He had sworn to go straight when he walked out of the gates of Pollsmoor, wanted to find a life outside the all-too-familiar structures of prison. Now he was going to commit another crime.

True, stealing a dog, a mangy old bitch with tired hips, was bugger all compared to what he had done in his life. But she belonged to Sniper Security. That alone gave her more value than most of the brown men he'd wished goodnight over the years. Even though she was destined for the vet's needle and then a sack on a dump somewhere.

He had to do this. For them both.

He would build another place for them in the sprawling maze that adjoined Lavender Hill, a shack settlement called Cuba Heights. Nobody would find them there.

Benny Mongrel had a plan for him and his dog. They would find work, guarding the shops and the small factories that were built on the peripheries of the Cape Flats, vulnerable to attack and theft. Most owners couldn't afford Sniper Security, but they would be able to afford Benny Mongrel and Bessie.

"Not long now, Bessie," he whispered. "Not long."

He stroked her as she slept.

Barnard drove up Voortrekker, past the car dealerships and the junk-food joints and the hookers who smiled tik smiles into his headlights. He wouldn't be able to sleep. Not after what he'd found out from Lotter. So there was no point in going home to his cramped apartment in Goodwood.

He was going to need money. Not the small change he got from the likes of Rikki Fortune. Real money. Serious bucks.

He thought about the dead Americans, Rikki and his beanpole buddy, lying wrapped up out on the Flats. Something had spoken to him the moment he saw those bodies. Call it intuition. Call it a hunch. Call it what you wanted, but Rudi Barnard knew that the other American, the one from the US of fucken A, was involved.

John Hill was the key. He was sure of that.

Barnard wanted to drive across to that fancy house with his gun in his hand and kick his way in. Feed his gun down the throat of that fucken American. Slap his pregnant wife. Threaten his kid. Do what he would do out his side of town. Do what he needed to do to get to the truth.

But up on the mountain the rules were different. Money bought lawyers. And the media spotlight. Barnard would have to learn new tactics if he was going to find out what really happened. He was playing for much higher stakes. He would have to take it nice and slow. Be smart. The time would come when he would do what he did best.

Kill somebody.

Barnard had no idea how many people he had killed. Some men he knew kept an obsessive count, but he had never felt the need. Just got on with it. But he remembered his first time. You always do.

At the age of thirteen Rudi Barnard had killed his mother's lover. Seconds later he had killed his mother.

Barnard was born in a forgotten rural village five hours northeast of Cape Town. The town was split in two by a stream that trickled like piss through the semidesert. The half-breeds' hovels were on the one side. On the other the whites' houses huddled around the spire of the Dutch Reformed Church, which pointed like an accusing finger at heaven. Barnard had spent an eternity of airless Sundays in that church, in fear of the hell and brimstone pouring from the pulpit, waiting in vain for God to speak to him.

At thirteen Rudi Barnard was already fat and unpopular. And he stank. One day a bitch of a teacher sent him home early with a note telling his mother to purge his bowels before sending him to school again. Humiliated, Rudi trudged home through the heat, the sun like a fist pounding down on his pink neck.

When Rudi walked up to the house, he saw the ramshackle truck belonging to Truman Goliath, a half-breed handyman, parked in the driveway. His father was paying Goliath to replace some rusted corrugated iron roofing.

Rudi walked into the house, the fly screen door slapping closed behind him. He heard his mother screaming. Barnard ran to his parents' bedroom and flung the door open. It took him a few seconds to understand that Truman Goliath wasn't murdering his mother. In fact she was urging the athletic half-breed on with slaps to his naked haunches and yells of encouragement, unaware that her son stood in the doorway.

It was then that God spoke to Rudi Barnard for the first time.

The young Rudi went to his father's gun room, removed a .22 rifle, and carefully loaded it. Then he walked back to the bedroom and blew the back of Truman Goliath's head onto the wall. The naked Mrs. Barnard, covered in blood, bone shards, and brain matter, stared at her son and opened her mouth to scream, her mouth a perfect operatic oval.

Rudi Barnard shot his mother in the face.

Then he phoned his father at his slaughterhouse. The two fat Rudis, father and son, put their heads together and worked out the story the town wanted to hear. The rape and murder of Elsie Barnard.

Truman Goliath had waited until father and son were out of the house and had forced himself on Elsie. Like a good Boer wife of old, she had managed to get to her husband's rifle and shoot the bastard. Unfortunately, with his last strength, he had wrestled the rifle from Elsie and sent her to the arms of Jesus.

If the half-breeds in the shacks across the railway line had wondered how Truman could have done all this with his head blown away, they had known to keep their thoughts to themselves.

After that first time, killing came easily to Rudi Barnard. He had a talent for it.

Barnard sat at a light on Voortrekker, the sweat flowing from his body. A tik whore hobbled toward him on her high heels. She lifted her skirt to reveal her scrawny thighs, as seductive as a cadaver. Normally, Barnard would have been out the car, ready to make her regret her mistake. But he felt a sudden urgency to get home.

He was going to print out those pictures on his cell phone, the pictures of Rikki and his buddy. He had somebody he wanted to show them to.

⌐══

Burn lay in his sleeping wife's arms. His son slept beside him. He couldn't remember when last he'd felt this good. Tomorrow he would go down to the real estate agents and rent an apartment. Whatever it cost, they would be out of this house by tomorrow night.

Then he would spend time on the Internet, researching New Zealand. He vaguely recalled there were two islands, North and South. The South was meant to be wilder, more remote, less people. High mountains and unspoiled beaches.

It was with these images in mind that Burn fell asleep.

When he awoke, sun streamed into the room. He was alone. He heard water bubbling in the plunge pool beneath the bedroom window. The African shouts and jibes of the builders next door drifted across to him.

He yawned, rubbing a hand across his stubble.

He heard Susan's voice, from inside the house. She sounded like she was in the kitchen. Probably talking to Matt while she fixed breakfast. The idea pleased him.

Then he heard another voice. A man's voice. A voice he couldn't quite place.

Reflex moved Burn from the bed. He pulled on shorts and a T-shirt. Before he knew it, he'd opened the closet and the Colt was in his hand.

Moving silently in his bare feet, he went toward the kitchen. Susan was saying something he couldn't catch. It sounded like a question. The man responded. Now Burn recognized the voice.

The fat cop was in the kitchen with Susan.

CHAPTER 11

Burn stepped into the kitchen.

Susan and the fat cop watched him. Susan looked scared. "Jack, I was about to call you."

The cop leaned his massive gut against the kitchen counter. Susan was on the other side of the counter, keeping her distance.

"How can we help you, Inspector?"

Burn tried to stay cool, relaxed. He didn't want to give anything away. Just a law-abiding guy surprised to see a cop in his kitchen first thing in the morning.

"I just want you and your wife to look at a couple of photographs." Barnard held a large yellow envelope at his side. He lay it down on the counter and slid out two glossy prints.

He handed them to Susan. She took them, one in each hand, and stared at them. Then she closed her eyes for a moment. When she opened them, she stared at Burn. Her face was bled of color.

Barnard had not taken his gaze off her. "Do you recognize either of these men?"

She shook her head and put the photographs down on the counter as if they were toxic.

Burn stepped closer and saw the faces of the men he had killed. Jesus, they had been found. So soon. They looked bloated, mottled. Decomposition already doing its work. He forced himself to stay calm, not allowing his face to tell anything.

He didn't touch the photographs.

Barnard was looking at Burn. "How about you, sir?"

"Never seen them before."

Then Burn was in behind Susan. She was trembling. He eased her onto a stool.

"Look, what's this all about? My wife isn't in any condition to be upset like this."

Barnard slid the photographs back into the envelope. "You know that car that was outside? The red BMW?" Burn nodded. "I think these two men drove it here. To your street."

"I've told you already. We know nothing about the car. Or these two men."

Barnard was heaving his gut off the counter. "Well, I'm glad about that. They weren't nice people." He leered at Susan, yellow teeth like bone fragments in an open wound. "I'm sorry if I upset you, Mrs. Hill."

Susan said nothing, stared at him blankly.

Burn's hands tried to soothe his wife. Her shoulders were tight with tension. She shrugged him off. The cop noticed. Matt came into the kitchen. He looked at the fat cop, then gave him a wide berth and went to the fridge.

"This your boy?" The cop watched Matt help himself to juice.

Instinctively, Burn put himself between his son and the cop. "Is there anything else, Inspector?"

Barnard shook his massive head. "I'll be in touch if there is."

He was hauling himself to the front door. Burn went after him to buzz him out and make sure he left.

Out of the corner of his eye he saw Susan exit the kitchen. He heard the bedroom door slam.

Berenice September was at the satellite police station at seven in the morning. There was no sign of the cop. The sun beat down on the commuters on their way to work. A group of kids in school uniform walked past, shouting out at one another.

Her son Ronnie hadn't come home. Every parent on the Cape Flats lived in fear of this moment. Scores of children went missing every year. Most of them turned up in the veld, raped, sodomized, murdered.

By seven fifteen Berenice was fretting. She was already late for work. She wouldn't be able to pay her bills at the end of the month if they docked her pay. Then she saw the cop, strolling up from the taxi rank like he was with his girlfriend at the Waterfront. Berenice waved at him. This did nothing to speed his pace.

She walked toward him, pushing through a bunch of commuters shoehorning themselves into a taxi. "You remember me? From yesterday?"

It took a moment before the cop nodded. He carried on walking, and Berenice fell in beside him. "I haven't seen my son since I left him by you."

The cop shrugged. They had reached the container, and he fished in his pocket for a set of keys. "I haven't seen him."

"What happened last night, after I left?"

He unlocked the door to the container and pulled it open. The hinges screamed for oil. "Nothing happened."

The cop stepped inside and Berenice followed him. It was like walking into a wall of heat. She was already perspiring, from the sun and from the tension. She felt faint and stepped back out, getting her breath. The cop looked at her with blank disinterest.

She tried again. "Last night, you said somebody was coming. I left my boy, Ronnie, here so he could speak to them."

"Ja. But he fucked off. The kid. Before they got here. He waited for you to go; then he ran."

She was staring at him. "Ran where?"

"How must I know? He's your bloody son." The cop set out the occurrence book and a pen.

Berenice shook her head. She turned and walked back home. She was going to phone in sick. They could dock her pay. She had to find her son.

"That cop knows something, Jack." Susan paced the bedroom, anger flaming her cheeks.

"How could he?" Burn stayed still, deliberately, to counterbalance her motion.

"Then what was he doing here?" she asked, demanding that he make sense of this mess.

"He probably went to every house in the street. It's just routine." In fact, Burn had seen the fat cop get in his car and drive away, but he didn't tell her this.

"Where did you put them? Those men?"

"In an open field. Behind the airport. Miles from anywhere."

"Apparently not. Jesus, Jack." She stopped, put a hand to her stomach, caught her breath.

He moved toward her. "Look, calm down. Sit down on the bed."

"Just get the fuck away from me!" The words stopped Burn as if he'd been struck. Susan never spoke like this.

"Susan . . ."

"Okay, Jack, here's the thing. I, we, Matt and . . . and her"—she pointed at her belly—"had to carry the can for the cop you killed. But we are not, not, going down for what you did the other night. Do you understand me?"

"I understand you. But nobody is going down."

She shook her head. "You're wrong, Jack. You're going down. You're going straight to fucking hell, and you're not taking us with you!"

❦

Beautiful. The fingerprint formed on the monitor of Barnard's computer. The American woman had left a bloody near-perfect right index finger print on the photograph of Rikki Fortune.

Before Barnard had gone to the American's house, he had carefully wiped the photographs clean, then slid them into an envelope. He had hoped to get Hill to touch them, but the man had made a point of leaving them lying on the counter. Which made Barnard all the more suspicious. The woman's prints would have to be enough.

Barnard had left the Americans and headed straight to the police lab. A technician owed him a favor, and he lifted the prints and e-mailed them to Barnard within two hours.

Barnard sat at the laptop at a desk in his apartment. Most people who knew him would have automatically assumed that those sausage fingers wouldn't know their way around a computer, but his hands moved with surprising delicacy across the mouse and the keyboard. He'd skilled up on the latest technology with none of the reluctance of most cops his age; he was smart enough to know that if you were out of the tech loop, you were dead and buried.

People would have been surprised by his one-room apartment, too. It was spartan, and scrupulously clean, almost monastic in its simplicity.

The bed was made, a Bible squared up on the bedside table. The dishes were washed and put away. There was no ring of grime around the bathtub.

If Barnard had no control over the rank and noxious odors his body produced, or remained oblivious to them, he imposed order and discipline on his living environment.

Barnard checked his watch. It would be early morning in Arlington, Virginia, but Dexter Torrance would have finished his prayers. He reached for the phone.

It wasn't often that Rudi Barnard met somebody he felt an affinity with. Mostly he felt scorn and loathing for the rest of humanity, as if their mere presence stood between him and his eternal reward.

Dexter Torrance was different. Outwardly, Barnard and the deputy U.S. marshal couldn't be less alike. Where Barnard was massively fat, Torrance was small and looked to be perpetually hungry. Not for food, but for the succor of the version of Jesus Christ he believed in with a quiet fervor.

Torrance, a member of the Marshals International Fugitives Task Force, had come to Cape Town a few years before to take back to West Virginia a man wanted for the rape and murder of a Charleston Sunday school teacher. The man had jumped bail and, through a series of increasingly idiotic actions, had got himself arrested in Cape Town. The South African authorities had no reservations about extraditing him to West Virginia, a state that, like South Africa, had abolished the death penalty.

It had fallen to Rudi Barnard to hand over the prisoner to Dexter Torrance simply because his senior officers were attending some political shindig hosted by the commissioner of police.

Torrance and Barnard had spent little time together, but very quickly they realized that their worldviews were uncannily similar. Torrance didn't have to say much, merely express his disillusionment that the state in which the crime had occurred had seen fit to abolish the death penalty, for Barnard to recognize a kindred spirit. Barnard felt the same about his own country's liberal constitution, trying his best to remedy the situation by executing as many deviants as he could.

Torrance shook his head while they eyeballed the prisoner in the holding cell. The deputy U.S. marshal was of the opinion that when this sack of crap got back to the States, he would be jailed for ten years and then walk out and do it all again.

Torrance and Barnard found their collaboration to be as easy and pleasurable as a doubles team who had played together for years, each knowing precisely when the other would move to the net. Barnard held the prisoner down while Torrance strangled the man with his own belt, bought for his trip home.

Barnard then held the prisoner up off the ground while Torrance looped the belt through the bars of the cell and around the dead man's neck. They left him dangling there and went and drank tea and spoke as if on first-name terms with the interventionist God they both loved so much.

A constable doing his rounds found the man hanging.

The drunken district surgeon, irritated to be dragged from the youthful juices of his latest catamite, wasted no time in calling the death a suicide and signing the death certificate.

Torrance had flown back to the United States accompanying a coffin. It had pleased him greatly to hand the body over to the dead man's family for burial.

A job well done.

He reserved a special place in his esteem for Rudi Barnard, his brother soldier in the army of Christ, and when Rudi called him that morning and asked him to run a fingerprint through the FBI's database, he said it would be an honor.

Burn drove the Jeep down to Sea Point, a grid of apartment blocks and office buildings that looked out over the Atlantic Ocean.

When Burn had seen Susan handling the photographs, he'd had to resist the impulse to grab them from her and wipe them free of her prints. Hell, her paranoia was getting to him. The cop looked like a moron. He'd been ordered to knock on a few doors, go through the motions. This was Cape Town, a dozen more people would die today; how much time was the cop going to waste on a couple of gangsters?

But what if he had lifted a print? Burn knew that Susan had been busted as a freshman at UCLA, smoking dope at a party. She'd told Burn the story soon after they met, laughing about being driven to Santa Monica in the back of a sheriff's patrol car. Being booked. Kidding a cute-looking deputy about getting her good side when they took her mug shots. Flirting with him when he pressed her fingers down for the prints.

Burn remembered an irrational feeling of jealousy—about something that had happened three years before he met Susan. Now he couldn't get the image of her hands black with fingerprint ink out of his mind . . .

A horn blared behind him. He was daydreaming at a green light. Burn pulled away, trying to calm himself. Even if Susan had been printed, where were those prints now? And how could some Cape Town cop get access to them?

Burn was on his way to a real estate office. The most important thing right now was to get out of that house. Being there reminded Susan of the dead men. It also made them a target for the fat cop.

He would relocate his family; then he would convince Susan about New Zealand. Once the baby had come.

Carmen Fortune almost gagged on the man's dick. She tried to pull her head away, but it banged against the steering wheel. His calloused hands grabbed her by the hair and shoved the thing in deeper, like she was that sword swallower on the TV.

The day had started shit and got worse. The feeling of lightness and freedom that had come with the news of Rikki's death evaporated when she couldn't score a globe. There just wasn't any money, now that Sheldon's grant had disappeared.

She had done some casual hooking as a teenager, before she met Rikki. Most of her friends did it. It was an easy way to buy those designer jeans. But that was years ago.

So, when she caught the taxi to Voortrekker Road, she hadn't known what to expect. She found a corner and stood there, eyeballing the passing motorists. It was payday, and she wasn't ugly. Someone would stop. She knew it was a risk, hooking in daylight. She might have to blow a cop or two. But she couldn't wait until dark. She needed to score. Bad. To get rid of that fucken scratchy feeling, like her nerves were on the outside of her skin.

A car pulled up. Nice new BMW. She stepped forward, ready with what she thought was a professional smile as she bent down at the driver's window.

Her smile faded when she saw the Nigerian at the wheel. Before she could step back, the Nigerian grabbed her by the T-shirt and pulled her half into the car

"This is my territory, you understand? For me and my girls. I see you here again, I kill you." To underscore his point, he swept aside his linen jacket and showed her the massive bloody gun in a shoulder holster.

She nodded, and he pushed her away, taking off fast, almost driving over her feet. Fucken Nigerians.

She went and hung around in the mall for a while. But she was going crazy, starting to scratch herself until she bled. So she went back to the road, a few blocks away from where the Nigerian confronted her, looking around nervously for his BMW.

She only had to wait a few minutes before a dented pickup truck pulled up next to her. The driver was colored, but dark. On the Flats, where the calibrations of color are precise, where the birth of a pale child is cause for celebration and women apply all manner of potions to their skin to lighten it, a dark skin is not a badge worn with pride.

Still, she went to the driver's window. He wore a dirty jumpsuit and smelled of sweat.

"How much for a blow?" he asked. Some of his teeth were missing.

"Hundred." She doubled what she was intending to ask.

"Twenny-five."

"Fifty."

He grinned. "Fuck, you better suck like a vacuum for that." But he reached across and opened the side door.

They drove down a side street, and he parked beside an open lot. He unzipped his jumpsuit and produced his pride and joy. It was massive, and it didn't smell like roses.

Carmen took a condom out of her jeans and tore the wrapping open with her teeth. The man shook his head. "For fifty, no fucken rubber."

"Listen, you think I'm going to put that filthy thing in my mouth without a plastic, you fucken crazy. Take it or leave it."

He shrugged, and she tugged on the condom. Next thing she knew, he had her by the hair and was making her swallow the bloody thing.

Carmen was gagging, but she could hear that he was getting all excited. Now was the time. She knocked away his hands and came up for air.

"Why you stopping?"

"Just relax, speedy. Take your time."

She pulled his jumpsuit down so that it bunched around his knees, then took the kitchen knife out of her jeans. She grabbed his dick with one hand and held the knife against the base with the other.

"Jesus, what you doing?" He stared at her. The thing in her hand was already starting to wilt, like a rubber snake.

"Get your wallet out and put it on my lap."

"Fuck you!"

She gripped the softening dick and jammed the tip of the blade into his skin. He screamed.

"S'trues fuck, I'll cut this thing off!" She jammed the knife in deep enough to draw blood.

"Okay. Okay." He reached down into his pocket and came out with the wallet.

"Put it on my lap."

He did as she ordered.

She kept the blade against his skin, freed her other hand, and opened the car door behind her. Then she grabbed the wallet and slid out backward. He tried to lunge at her but was held back by the jumpsuit around his knees.

"You fucken bitch, I'll kill you!"

Carmen was running, out of the side street, back onto Voortrekker just in time to grab a minibus taxi as it was about to pull out.

The taxi wasn't full, and she sat at the back, alone, catching her breath. She opened the wallet. Saw a picture of a smiling woman and a toddler. Bastard. She pulled out the money and tossed the wallet out the window. Three hundred.

That wasn't going to last long.

⤏

Berenice September fought panic as she followed Ronnie's friend Cassiem across the veld. The afternoon sun blasted down on her, and sweat ran freely from her hair, down her face, pooling between her breasts.

The boy looked at her over his shoulder and stopped, seeing her red face and the blood on her legs where the thorns had torn her skin.

"Is Auntie all right?"

She wouldn't allow herself to stop walking, because she knew if she did she would lose courage and turn back.

"Go, Cassiem. Take me there."

Cassiem trudged on through the veld, the woman panting behind him.

Berenice had spent the day looking for Ronnie. She had gone to his school. He wasn't there. She caught a taxi to the amusement arcade in Bellville, hoping for the first time ever that she would catch him cutting school. No sign of Ronnie.

After school she went to Cassiem's house, two streets away from hers. Cassiem said he hadn't seen Ronnie since yesterday. At first the boy denied all knowledge of the dead bodies. Only after Berenice had threatened to make trouble with his parents did he relent and tell her the truth. He had been with Ronnie when his friend had helped himself to the Nikes.

"I want you to take me there," she told Cassiem.

"Why, Auntie? It's horrible."

"Because maybe Ronnie went back there."

"But why, Auntie?"

She couldn't answer the question. Just knew that she had to be taken to the bodies.

Cassiem walked through thick bush into a small clearing. He pointed toward a clump of thorns on the other side.

"It's there."

"Go on," she ordered him.

The boy was reluctant. Berenice gave him a shove and he walked slowly forward.

Berenice caught the unmistakable smell of burned flesh. Then she saw a mound of something black, burned, unrecognizable.

Ronnie stopped. Berenice found the last of her courage and stepped forward. *Please, God,* she beseeched under her breath.

Berenice approached the bodies. It took her a few moments to make sense of what she was seeing. Two men, she assumed they were men, lying side by side, charred black. Then she made out a smaller form, somehow sprawled across them.

No features were recognizable. Blackened flesh burned off a skull. Scraps of cloth burned into the skin. Then she saw something that made her gasp.

Berenice fought back a wail and sank to her knees in the dirt, to get closer to the bodies, to see—*please, God*—that it wasn't what she already knew it was. On the arm of the smallest body was a watch. A ridiculously large watch, way too big for the skinny wrist. The glass was shattered and the face was blackened and warped, but enough of it remained for her to see the Caped Crusader.

Berenice lifted her face toward the blazing sun and let the wail break loose from her breast, screaming for God's mercy.

CHAPTER 12

Special Investigator Disaster Zondi sat in the interview room at Bellwood South Police HQ, waiting for Rudi Barnard, who was twenty minutes late. Zondi showed no sign of impatience or irritation. He spent the time rereading the file on Barnard. The file was as fat as the cop whose photograph stared up at him.

Disaster Zondi, despite the ridicule his name attracted, flat-out refused to change it. He wore the name, given to him by his illiterate Zulu parents, as a badge of pride. Every time he was mocked, it had made him stronger. Reminded him that he had dragged himself by his fingernails from a life of rural poverty and deprivation. He had won a bursary, earned a degree in criminology, and now answered only to the minister of safety and security. Few people laughed to his face now that power, like an invisible cloak, had settled upon him.

Rudi Barnard and Disaster Zondi were perfect opposites, bookends in the struggle of good versus evil. Barnard was obese. Zondi was trim and athletic. Barnard believed in the power of God. Zondi believed in the power of Justice. Barnard was a glutton, a junk-food junkie. Zondi ate sparingly and was fastidious about what he consumed. Barnard had little interest in sex. Zondi was the owner of roiling passions that continually threatened to upset his equilibrium, but he suppressed and controlled them through sheer force of will.

The nearest Zondi got to a religious notion was the image he had of himself as an inquisitor, riding out through the battlefields of corruption in contemporary South Africa. There was one absolute about Zondi: he could not be bought. He had dealt with men in a much grander league than Rudi Barnard. Politicians and tycoons. He had been offered millions, which he had rejected without pause. He had been offered power and position. These held no appeal.

He had been offered women: wives, daughters, mistresses, the bodies of female miscreants themselves. These offers had been more difficult to resist. He had been forced to dig deep into his resolve. But he had stood firm. He had resisted.

Disaster Zondi believed that the police were the bulwark, the thin blue line that stood between society and anarchy. His mission in life was to weed out the bad cops merrily enriching themselves off the back of South Africa's miracle of transformation.

Zondi was well aware that Rudi Barnard was a dinosaur who'd somehow managed to escape the ice age of apartheid's end. He had carved out a fiefdom for himself here in Cape Town, murdering and extorting out on the lawless Cape Flats. It was extraordinary that he had got away with it as long as he had. Well, his time had come. Special Investigator Zondi was here to bring an end to the reign of Rudi Barnard.

The door opened, and the massively fat cop wheezed his way in. Zondi saw the little eyes, like cigarette burns in a pigskin sofa, scanning his dark features, white shirt, and Roberto Cavalli suit.

He saw that Barnard didn't recognize him. Why would he? The last time Zondi had seen Barnard, through a veil of pain and blood, had been nearly twenty years ago. He had been just another faceless black kid.

Zondi rose and extended a perfectly manicured hand.

"Disaster Zondi," he said.

They climbed onto the minibus taxi in Mowbray, two teenage girls crippled by skin-tight jeans, bumping past Benny Mongrel, taking the seat behind his. Their eyes widened at the sight of his nightmare of a face. As the taxi rattled away, they were whispering about him, sure that he couldn't hear them over the racket.

But he could.

"You see his face?"

"Ja. It's horrible!"

"Imagine waking up with that in the bed."

"I would scream. Honest."

"Think he got a wife?"

"If he do, she must be blind!"

They were giggling into their hands with false nails like claws.

Benny Mongrel wanted to turn and tell them that he didn't need no mean-mouthed bitch of a wife. Scare the living shit out of them. But he did nothing, tuned them out.

Anyways, he'd had his fill of wives. In Pollsmoor Prison an officer in the 28s could take his pick. Benny Mongrel had walked among the newcomers, and when he saw a young body untouched by gang tattoos, he had pointed a finger.

The man would always follow.

Benny Mongrel would install the man in the bed beside him. He would give him protection and in return demand that his food was cooked, his clothes were washed and ironed, and his toenails clipped. And at night, in the crowded cell, Benny would lie face to face with the boy and bugger him.

The duties of a wife.

If you suggested that Benny Mongrel was homosexual, he would kill you. There were gay men in prison, outrageous queens who wore short T-shirts as dresses, grew their hair and rolled it in curlers, had lipstick and rouge smuggled in. These men—the prisoners called them *moffies*—were tolerated. They were amusing; they were part of the prison culture. But Benny Mongrel never went near them.

Benny Mongrel never kept a wife longer than a few weeks. There was never any question of intimacy. It was cold, brutal, and functional.

In the last few years he was in jail, Benny Mongrel had stopped taking wives. He had lost interest. He had no desire to touch or to be touched. He had lain alone in his bunk and tuned out the animal sounds of rape and lust.

It had meant nothing to him.

Now that he was out, the last thing on his mind was taking a woman. By force or otherwise. He saw the way they looked at him, like the little sluts sitting behind him in the taxi. Like he was a monster. He could take them at knifepoint, drag them into the bush by their hair, and have them. He had done it before. But he had no appetite for this any longer.

He had resigned himself to being a man alone.

Until he met Bessie.

To his surprise, he had found his still-point, a place of peace, with the old dog. Bessie was a constant. She was pleased to see him in the evening. She slept beside him, ate the food he gave her, and asked for nothing more. It was strange, but when he was with her he felt a different sense of himself. For the first time in his life, he could simply be.

Just two more days, and he could start the new life he had wanted since he got out of prison.

The taxi lurched to a halt in Salt River, and Benny Mongrel climbed out. It was a short walk to Sniper Security and the start of his shift.

The hot wind roared with a ferocity that got the nerves screaming like tight banjo strings. And the fires had started. A carelessly flicked cigarette, a spark, a shard of broken glass concentrating the sun onto the dry scrub—any of these was enough to get the mountain blazing.

Burn stood next to the plunge pool, watching as a helicopter hovered over the ocean, scooping water into the basket suspended beneath its fuselage. The chopper lifted, battling the weight of the water and the force of the wind, and passed almost directly over him. He watched as it banked over the fire that ate its way down Lion's Head and released its load of water. Then, lighter, it flew down toward the ocean again.

Dark orange smoke blotted the setting sun, obscuring the top floor of the buildings in Sea Point.

Burn felt trapped.

The house on the mountain was like a magnet for Rudi Barnard. He couldn't explain rationally why he was parked up the street from the American's house, but he didn't question the impulse. His hunches were usually right.

Barnard sat in his car watching the helicopter clatter over, so low that drops from the basket splattered his windshield. He finished the last drag of a cigarette and flicked the still smoking butt out into the street. Fuck it, he couldn't give a shit if the whole bloody place burned to the ground.

His hemorrhoids were killing him, but his mind was on that monkey in a suit. Disaster Zondi. What a fucken name.

The face-to-face with Zondi had gone as Barnard's intuition had warned. The darky had sat there and looked at Barnard like he was shit under his expensive shoe, tapping his fingers on the thick file that lay in front of him. The file that had Barnard's name on it.

Zondi hadn't confronted Barnard with anything, just said that he was under investigation. Called this a preliminary meeting. Said they would have some more face time. Used those words, *face time*. His voice, a kind of semi-American drawl, had grated on Barnard's nerves like a hangnail on a blackboard.

He knew men like Zondi. Hell, he had spent a whole chunk of his life hunting, torturing, and killing them. Some had screamed like women, begged for their lives, but others had stared him down until death glassed their eyes over.

Zondi had that look. Like he wanted to take Rudi Barnard down and nothing would stop him. Least of all Barnard's so-called superior officer.

Superintendent Peterson was everything that Rudi Barnard hated. A half-breed who had benefited from affirmative action to pole-vault over the careers of more qualified white cops. A minor politician who wore a policeman's uniform but wasn't fit to direct traffic. A PR man whose tongue had grown permanently attached to the asses of his masters.

After the confrontation with Zondi, Barnard had gone straight to Peterson's office. Barnard knew that his commanding officer was terrified of him. Barnard was a law unto himself, who kept his badge through cunning and manipulation. Those who could be bribed he bribed. Those who refused his bribes he intimidated. Over the years Barnard had built up a massive database of information about his fellow cops and his superiors. He knew who was crooked; he knew who had falsified arrests; he knew who was never booked for driving drunk; he knew who took favors from hookers; he knew who screwed brother officers' wives.

As Barnard sat facing Peterson in the superintendent's office at Bellwood South HQ, he was aware of the half-breed's fear. The man had splashed himself with tons of aftershave, but he stank. Barnard, unaware or uncaring when it came to his own stench, was acutely attuned to others'.

Peterson, a happily married, churchgoing paragon of New South African virtue, had become involved with a much younger woman a few years back. Her husband was a scrap merchant who dabbled in stolen cars. Barnard knew for a fact that Peterson had planted stolen parts at the scrap yard and had used his influence to make sure that the man was sent away for a couple of years. The unfortunate bastard had died in prison, the victim of gang discipline.

Peterson knew that Barnard knew. Simple as that.

So Barnard wrote his own ticket, seldom bothering to come into headquarters. But today he was here for a purpose. He leaned in close to Peterson.

"I want this darky off my back."

Peterson shook his head. "I have no jurisdiction here, Inspector."

"You're not hearing me, Peterson. Make the fucker go away."

Peterson fidgeted with an expensive pen on his desk. "You have to believe that all of us are being kept out of this loop. It is being run by the ministry directly."

"So, you're saying it's okay if he hangs me by my balls?"

Peterson shrugged. "I'm sorry. My hands are tied."

Barnard nodded. He even tried a smile, which was terrifying to behold. "How's your girlfriend?"

The smell of fear washed across the desk. "Rudi, please. I've put all that behind me. I am not your enemy in this, please understand. There is nothing I can do to change the situation with this man from Jo'burg. I'm powerless."

Barnard had stood and loomed over Peterson like a wall of stinking fat. "Just remember. I go down, I take people with me."

Sitting in his car, Barnard lit another smoke, eyes fixed on the American's house. Lights were on in the gathering gloom.

Barnard needed to throw money at this Zondi thing. A lot of it. And if he couldn't buy his way out of the situation, he'd have to do what he did best. Zondi wasn't some crack whore on the Flats; he was a darky with a fancy badge, but that didn't make him bulletproof.

He would die like all the others.

Barnard found himself smiling at the thought. His smile evaporated when he became aware of headlights in his rearview mirror. A car was creeping down the road toward him. An armed response vehicle.

Barnard loathed rent-a-cops, who fed off the paranoia of the wealthy. They looked down on the real cops, smug as they cruised around these privileged areas. Normally, he would have relished a face-to-face with the cowboy driving the car, just for the pleasure of it, knowing his badge always trumped a rent-a-cop's ID.

But not tonight.

He didn't want to be placed near this house. Barnard started his car and drove away before the rent-a-cop could reach him.

———

Burn went into the house and saw that Susan lay on the sofa, asleep or pretending to be. Matt was in front of the TV. Usually, Burn would get the boy away from the screen, fighting the kid's desire to lose himself in the numbing banality of the tube.

But right now it was almost a relief to see Matt occupied, distracted from the rupture in his parents' relationship.

Burn had come home and found Susan reading a fashion magazine, sitting with her feet in the plunge pool, taking the edge off the heat. Matt was splashing in the pool, wearing flippers. Mrs. Dollie was inside, wielding the vacuum cleaner like a weapon, the high-pitched whine making her deaf to anything Burn was saying.

Burn told Susan he had found an apartment. It was right on the ocean, overlooking Clifton Beach, and, most important, it was unoccupied. The agents asked him for a day to send a crew in to clean it, and then his family could move in.

Susan had stared at him, shrugged, and went back to her magazine.

The chopper clattered overhead once again, and Susan opened her eyes to find him staring down at her. She closed her eyes.

"Susan?" He had to pitch his voice above the noise of the helicopter.

"Yes?" Her eyes stayed closed. A cartoon man was squashed flat by a rock, and Matt laughed.

"I'm going out."

Her eyes flicked open. "Sure."

"Come if you want. I just need to get out of here for a while."

She shook her head. "No. We'll stay."

"Are you going to be okay?"

"We'll be fine, Jack." She wasn't even trying to mask her irritation.

"If you want me to stay, I will."

"No. Go. It's better if you do." She closed her eyes again, dismissing him.

"Keep the doors locked. Okay?"

She didn't reply.

He grabbed the car keys and headed for the garage.

As he reversed the Jeep out, he saw the blaze was leaping lower on the mountain. Now two choppers were fighting it.

Disaster Zondi sat in a coffee shop on the ocean, not far from the Waterfront, drinking a poor excuse for a cappuccino. Too much foam, not enough kick.

He spooned some excess foam into his saucer, but when he lifted the cup to his lips some of the froth came dangerously close to dripping onto his silk shirt. He replaced the cup in its saucer and pushed it away.

It was dark now, and he was the only customer left in the coffee shop. The staff were circling like vultures, eager to get rid of him.

After the interview with Barnard, Zondi had suppressed the urge to rush back to his hotel and take a shower. The man's stink had nearly taken his breath away. No mere body odor, it was something far more toxic, fetid. Sulfurous. From nowhere a memory came to him, from his Anglican mission school upbringing, that the Devil had a foul stench, like sulfur. Of course Zondi no longer believed in the Devil. Or God.

But still.

He hadn't expected to be as disturbed by the encounter as he was. He had kept it deliberately short, just fired a shot across the fat man's bows. Let him know that Zondi was on to him. The proximity to Barnard had come close to thawing Zondi's cool, the layer of permafrost he kept between himself and the world. He told himself he was letting this get personal. He needed to slow down. Detach himself. Keep his focus.

He had escaped Bellwood South HQ and driven his rental BMW back toward the city as the sun set over the ocean, the last rays painting Table Mountain gold. Cape Town putting on its show. Even the pall of smoke from the blaze on Lion's Head couldn't mute the splendor.

Cape Town offended Zondi. Its languid slowness and devotion to sun worship, wine tasting, and the deification of its natural beauty struck him as decadent and fatuous. Like a woman obsessed with nothing but her appearance. This place didn't even look like Africa. It was like a bit of Europe transplanted onto a mountainous peninsula that stuck out toward the South Pole like it was giving it the finger. Even the climate was Mediterranean.

And it was the only sub-Saharan city where a black man was in the minority.

Zondi had no wish to go to his hotel, so on impulse he had stopped for the coffee. The undrinkable cappuccino.

The colored waitress whipped the cup away from him. On her way back to the kitchen she paused to chat with another brown-skinned woman, who was mopping a table and setting salt and pepper shakers straight.

They spoke softly, in the local patois, but Zondi could hear them. And understand.

"Can't he see we want to go?"

"Typical darky behavior. I'm sorry, but it is."

"They behave as if they own the place."

"But they do. Now."

"I know. It makes me sick."

"I mean, did you hear on the radio this morning, they even saying that God is black."

"No!"

"I'm telling you."

"I'm sorry. I can deal with God being white. But not black. I can still work for a white boss!"

They laughed and walked to the back of the shop.

Zondi allowed himself a tight smile. His cell phone chirped. Bellwood South HQ.

⌇

Carmen Fortune put her lips to the globe and sucked hungrily. The glass burned her lips, but she didn't feel the pain, too anxious to get the smoke into her lungs, desperate for the rush that followed like a train hurtling from a tunnel.

Sweet Jesus, her head felt like it was going to fragment into a million shards of bone and brain matter. She saw the tattooed hand, nails black with dirt, take the globe from her before she collapsed back onto the stinking mattress and closed her eyes. The rush passed, and she was left with the glow, the euphoria, the feeling of owning the whole fucken world.

She opened her eyes and smiled. Conway Paulsen squatted, watching her, a mushroom cloud of tik smoke exploding from his mouth. He returned the smile, exposing teeth blackened by years of abuse.

Carmen sat up, light-headed. She was in Conway's zozo, a wooden hut built in the yard of his parents' house. Conway, still in his teens, was a connection of Rikki's, an American wannabe who was used as an errand boy but was never allowed the full initiation he dreamed of. He was simpleminded, the butt of endless mean-spirited jokes.

"So, you gonna tune Rikki. About me? That I wanna sell for him?"

"Ja. Soon as he get back from the west coast."

"What he doing up there anyways? I hear some abalone deal with the Chinks?"

"Fuck, I dunno. Maybe."

"Or, is it tik? Is he, like, supplying towns right up to Namibia?"

She shrugged. "You know Rikki."

Conway laughed. "Ja, he's big time."

"Ja. He's fucken big time, okay."

Using the wall for support, Carmen pulled herself to her feet. She thanked Conway and went out into the night.

Carmen walked down Tulip Street, passing the rows of identical houses, stepping around potholes, heading toward her ghetto block. The heat was oppressive, and she felt as if she were being suffocated under a blanket of stale air. Snatches of Cape Flat's life wafted out to her as she walked: shouts, curses, the low keening of a crying woman, a drunken man laughing.

A chopped-down Honda Civic, tuned loud, bumped down the road toward her, forcing her to give way. She saw the four boys inside, slumped low in the car, their eyes sliding across her as they passed, gangsta rap thudding in their wake.

Little fuckers.

Carmen walked faster. She passed three housewives gossiping on a corner, under a streetlight. Two of them had their hair in curlers; all three sucked on cigarettes like they were life support systems. Their eyes locked onto her.

Carmen pretended to ignore them, their whispers echoing after her like sticks dragged along a wooden fence. She heard *tik whore* and *slut* before she was out of range.

When she heard her name being called, she ignored it. More insults. Then she felt a tugging at her sleeve and found her hands in fists, ready to lash out. She turned and saw the wife of her useless brother.

"What you want?"

Carol was a runt of a girl who caught a fright at her own shadow. She let go of Carmen's sleeve and stepped back. "It's your father, Carmie."

"I don't got no father."

"He's very sick."

Carmen stared at the girl. "Good. I hope that rotten thing dies."

Carmen walked on. That was enough good news for one night.

Burn couldn't lose.

No matter what he did, he kept on beating the dealer. He sat drinking Scotch at the blackjack table out at Grand West Casino, Cape Town's answer to Vegas.

The dealer, who was sitting with a queen, dealt Burn a ten and a six.

Burn tapped his cards. "Hit me."

There were mutters of disapproval from the others at the table. Fuck them. The dealer was looking at Burn inquiringly. "You heard what I said. Hit me."

The dealer dealt him a five, then pulled a six for himself and then a ten. Too many.

The dealer shoved a stack of chips Burn's way. Burn flicked a couple of chips back toward the dealer, who tapped them, then dropped them into a slot in the table.

Burn finished his drink and held up the empty glass to a passing waitress. What the hell, he could have one more.

He knew it was crazy to be here. Stupid. Reckless. Gambling had caused all the pain in his life. Got him running from a cop dead in the snow. His pregnant wife and his kid were about to be lost to him forever, and he was gambling again. Blotting out reality.

But he felt some of that old excitement, the thrill that gambling had always given him, like a shot of adrenaline straight into the heart. He loved it.

Even now.

The dealer dealt him a ten and a seven and pulled a king for himself.

The man next to Burn, a dark man with gold teeth, made his feelings clear. "Just, stick, okay?"

Burn ignored him, tapped his cards. "Hit me."

The dealer gave him a bland look and dealt him a four. Twenty-one. Then the dealer went bust by pulling two picture cards.

Burn laughed out loud and reached for the Scotch that had appeared at his elbow.

He couldn't lose.

CHAPTER 13

Disaster Zondi stared down at the charred bodies. The howling wind rattled the portable klieg lamps that beamed down a merciless glare, threatening to topple them even though they were weighted with sandbags. The yellow crime scene tape sang and flapped in the wind, and the technicians battled the dust as they worked.

The wind flung snatches of conversation Zondi's way. The crime techs were wondering why the hell they had been called out for just another Cape Flats mess. Glances were shot in his direction, as if this had to be his doing.

Zondi tuned all this out, impassive, communing with the dead.

The small figure was definitely a child, and the mother swore blind that it was her son. In the morning they would run dental records, but

Zondi didn't doubt she was right. Mothers weren't wrong about things like that.

Zondi was aware that he had stepped outside his brief by being here. Call it research, the man from Johannesburg steeping himself in the crime that gripped the Flats by the throat. This hardly seemed typical, though. The bodies of two men would have indicated a gang killing. The body of the child alone would have been just another victim of the homicidal pedophiles the Flats produced with terrifying regularity.

But the three bodies together? This hinted at an altogether different beast at work.

Superintendent Peterson, station commander of Bellwood South, was on the scene. Zondi had no doubt this was for his benefit. Peterson had the well-fed look of a man who left the dirty work up to others.

A uniformed sergeant came up to Peterson. "Superintendent, we have Constable Galant." He pointed at a patrol car.

Peterson followed the uniform. Zondi caught up with him.

"Okay if I tag along, Superintendent?"

If Peterson objected, he wasn't about to say so. "Of course."

Constable Gershwynne Galant, the reluctant minder of the satellite police station, sat in the back of the patrol car. He was wearing jeans and a T-shirt and smelled as if he had been brought in from a tavern somewhere. He looked sullen and nervous.

"Get the mother, Sergeant." The superintendent nodded to where Berenice September sat in the passenger seat of Peterson's car.

Berenice came across, walking slowly. She stumbled, and the sergeant had to steady her. Her face caught enough of the spill from the kliegs to show the hell she was living through.

Peterson pointed at Galant. "Mrs. September, is this the constable you took your son to?"

Berenice looked at Galant. He returned her stare, then looked away. "Yes. That's him."

Peterson told the sergeant to take the woman back to his car; then he slid in beside Galant. Zondi leaned in through the passenger window, listening.

"What happened after that woman left her son with you, Constable?"

"He ran away. Like I tole her."

Peterson shook his head. "Now we both know that isn't what happened." He paused. "The woman says you phoned somebody. On your cell phone. Now either you tell us who you phoned or we get your phone logs. Believe me, if you cooperate, I'll be more inclined to go easy on you. Do you understand?"

Galant nodded.

"Okay. So I'm asking you again. Who did you phone?"

Galant wiped the back of his hand against his nose, sniffing. "It was Inspector Barnard."

Zondi looked across at Peterson. Was that fear he saw on the man's face?

"And what happened next?" Peterson seemed almost reluctant to ask the question.

"The inspector came and took the boy away. In his car."

Peterson slid out of the car and turned to the sergeant. "Lock him away. Single cell, okay?"

The cop nodded and got behind the wheel of the car, started the engine, and drove away. Zondi and Peterson stood in the howling wind, trying to shield their eyes from grit.

"I'm going to issue a warrant for Barnard," Peterson said, blinking.

"I think that's a good idea. I want to be along every step of the way, Superintendent."

"Of course. Absolutely."

Berenice September walked back toward them. She had caught the tail end of the conversation. "Is it Gatsby what did this?"

Zondi looked at Peterson quizzically.

Peterson shrugged. "Gatsby. A street name for Barnard." He turned to Berenice. "It's too soon to say."

Zondi took the woman's arm and walked her to the car. Peterson looked as if he was about to follow; then he hung back.

"Do you know this man, Barnard?" Zondi helped her into the car.

"Ja. We all do. He makes his own law."

"I think those days may be over."

Berenice said nothing, busy with the nightmare in her head.

Zondi walked off toward his BMW, the wind snatching at his suit, his eyes tearing up from the dust. In the distance Table Mountain blazed, tongues of flame leaping against the night sky.

———

Rudi Barnard hated the wind. In all the years he had spent in Cape Town, he had never got used to it. It made him feel lonely. Barnard took pride in his self-sufficiency; he trusted only himself and his God. He had little use for human interaction, but tonight he needed to speak to somebody. He needed reassurance.

Barnard drove through the back streets of Goodwood until he hit the railway line. He sat in the car, looking up at a crumbling building, two apartments over an African traditional healer. The healer's rooms were closed, but streetlight fell across the crudely painted windows offering cures for everything from impotence to AIDS. COME INSIDE NOW BEFORE IT IS TOO LATE, urged a sign.

The last time Barnard was here, the place had been a pet shop. Things change.

A light burned in one of the apartments. Barnard hesitated; it had been months since he had visited, and he almost lost his nerve. But he left the car, cursing as he took a gust of grit full in the face.

Fucken wind.

He hurried to the doorway of the building, stepping over a man and a woman asleep under cardboard boxes and plastic, anesthetized by cheap booze. Barnard trudged up one floor, panting as if he had run a marathon, and banged on an apartment door. There was rustling and thudding inside, then shuffling steps as somebody stood on the other side of the door, listening.

"It's me, Pastor. Rudi Barnard."

Many keys were turned, bolts drawn back, and the door cracked a sliver. A yellow eye regarded Barnard suspiciously. Then the door opened to reveal a tall, skeletal man with greasy gray hair framing a wrinkled face the color of urine. His mouth twitched a smile, and ill-fitting dentures clicked wetly.

"Come in, Brother Rudi."

Barnard was the least sensitive of men, but he battled to hide his shock at the pastor's decline since he had seen him last.

Johan Lombard, once master of the Army of God Church, had fallen on reduced circumstances. Five years in Pollsmoor Prison for sexually abusing street children had left him fearful and even more paranoid than when he went in. Lombard swore he was innocent, that he had only been doing his duty by introducing the children to Jesus. Why he had also introduced them to his penis he could never fully explain. Rudi Barnard believed implicitly in the innocence of Lombard, believed he had been the victim of the lies of godless half-breeds and had paid the price.

Lombard wore a pair of soiled gray flannels, carpet slippers, and a frayed shirt that had once been white.

"I haven't woken Pastor, have I?" Barnard was at his most deferential, still convinced that Lombard's bloodless lips were close to the ear of God.

"Who can sleep, Brother Rudi? In times like these?"

Lombard shuffled ahead into a small living room, crammed with a molting sofa, two ball-and-claw chairs, and piles of books on theology.

He pointed to one of the chairs. "Please, sit."

Lombard's shirtsleeves rode up to his bony elbows, and Barnard saw the needle tracks from the self-administered morphine shots. Lombard perched on the sofa, his hands on his knees. As Barnard lowered himself into one of the chairs, his stomach growled like a cement mixer. He patted it.

Lombard attempted a smile. "You are looking well, Rudi."

Barnard nodded. "I'm okay. And you?"

The pastor shrugged. "It won't be long before I get my eternal reward. Praise the Lord." Cancer had eaten through most of Lombard's liver and was nibbling at other organs in the vicinity. "And your work? Are you still fighting the good fight?"

"I'm trying, Pastor."

"You are a brave man, Rudi. You must stay strong."

"I do my best, Pastor."

"Do you still ask God for his guidance?"

Barnard earnestly nodded his massive head. "Every morning and night, Pastor."

"Good. And he listens. I see his strength in you."

"Thank you, Pastor."

Lombard's clawlike hands gripped the sofa as a tremor of agony racked his body. Sweat sprang from his forehead, and his eyes pulled shut like dusty drapes.

Barnard felt uncomfortable. Expressions of sympathy did not come naturally to him. "I shouldn't be bothering Pastor."

Lombard fought his way through the pain, then sighed and sat back. He opened his eyes and held up a shaking hand. "No. Please." He sucked air. "Is there something worrying you, Rudi? You look preoccupied."

Barnard shrugged. "I don't want to burden the Pastor."

"Speak to me, Rudi. If I can help in some small way . . ." Some color had crept back into his sunken cheeks.

"I'm facing a battle. Maybe the biggest that I have fought."

"Can you put a face to your enemy?"

"Yes."

"Then God will give you strength, Rudi. See this as an opportunity, a chance to walk through the fire. A gift from him."

"I am trying."

A manic glint had come into the eye of Lombard. "Your enemies are sinners, Brother Rudi. Just as that mountain is burning tonight, so will their souls be lost in a lake of fire. Those fires of hell will melt their very bones and their lungs. A terrible stench will arise from them. And this fire is a fire that will burn for all eternity." He gasped for breath but would not surrender the imaginary pulpit. "But you, Rudi, will walk through the fire, and you will receive the Holy Spirit! I know; I have walked that path!"

Lombard stood. "Come, my son, kneel."

Barnard wrestled his bulk from the chair; then he folded down on bended knee before the quivering man. He closed his eyes.

Lombard lifted his face to where he believed heaven to be, some-where beyond the stained ceiling, and squeezed his eyes shut. He placed a trembling hand on Rudi Barnard's forehead, and a torrent of glottal, unintelligible words flowed from his lips, growing ever more powerful and louder.

Barnard kneeled like a small boy as the gift of tongues rained down upon him.

Berenice September was in her living room, the TV mumbling in the background, some politician lying about crime statistics in South Africa. Juanita sat next to her on the sofa, crying softly. Berenice put her arms around her daughter, trying to find enough strength in herself to comfort her.

The front door opened and Donovan came in from working late

shift at the Goodwood McDonald's. He still had a McD's shirt on and carried a bag of Big Macs and fries.

He stood looking at his mother and sister. "Mommy?"

Berenice looked up at him. "I found him."

Donovan put the bag down on top of the TV. "Tell me."

Berenice stood and kissed Juanita on the forehead. "Stay here. I need to talk to your brother."

Juanita reached for her, clawing at her blouse, grabbing the fabric in her fingers. Berenice gently broke the girl's grip. "You wait here, my baby. We won't be long."

Donovan followed her into the kitchen, and she told him as much as she could bear to repeat. He was eighteen, a man. He deserved to know the truth. Donovan stood, his face gray. All at once he was puking; half-digested Big Macs spewed into the kitchen sink. She came up behind him and wet a dish towel, wiped his mouth off while he got his breath back.

When he could speak, he looked her in the eye. "You're sure it's Ronnie?"

She nodded. "I'm sure."

"And it was Gatsby? What did it?"

"That's what they are saying, ja."

Donovan nodded. Saying nothing. He was the quiet one, her oldest son. So quiet, sometimes, that it worried her.

"Donovan."

He stared at nothing, trying to process what she had told him.

"Donovan, look at me." His eyes found hers. "I want you to promise me that you aren't going to do something stupid now. The police will sort this out."

He spat into the sink. "The police. Fuck the police." He never spoke like that. He rinsed his mouth, then turned to her. "I'm sorry, Mommy."

"It's okay. You're a good boy. I just don't want you getting into trouble."

He nodded. She came up to him and put her arms around him. "Promise me, Donovan."

He stared over her shoulder. "I promise, Ma."

Benny Mongrel huddled against a wall with Bessie, trying to escape the southeaster. The builders had left a mound of sand uncovered, and the gale flung it up against the unfinished house. The dog wheezed and moaned, disturbed by the wind. Benny Mongrel stroked her coat. He could feel the grit sticking in the matted fur. Sniper Security treated their watchmen like animals and their dogs like shit. He didn't know when last Bessie's coat had seen water.

That's the first thing he was going to do when he got her to his shack, put that tin tub out in the yard and fill it with water. Then he was going to take Sunlight soap and wash her. And if the knots refused to wash out, he would cut them out with his knife.

The wind drove Benny Mongrel crazy too. He had a cloth wrapped around his ears and mouth, but still the sand got in somehow.

He squatted, watching the flames dance on the mountain above him, acrid smoke and ashes raining down on him and Bessie. The helicopters were still at work, chattering overhead and dumping water into the mouth of the inferno.

It reminded him of being in Pollsmoor, when the mountain burned, and the inmates started pacing, restless, when even the old-timers who could endure anything started trying to bend the bars open with their hands.

A year ago, during the winds, an idiot, another Mongrel who was due for parole, had lost his mind and stolen food from Benny Mongrel's bed. He had caught the man, and the other prisoners in the cell had waited for Benny Mongrel to say goodnight.

But Benny Mongrel ordered that the man be held down, and a

towel was forced into his mouth to keep him quiet. Benny Mongrel then amputated the fingers of both of the man's hands with his prison shank, a job that required time and strength. Benny Mongrel left him his thumbs. Blood spurted, and the man passed out from the pain.

One of the prisoners had a hot plate in the cell. Benny Mongrel had taken the bleeding stumps and cauterized them on the hot plate, and the smell of burning flesh mingled with the smell of smoke from the mountain fire.

In the morning the warders took the man to the prison hospital. He refused to say a word about who amputated his fingers. Within a week he was back in the cell, with bandages on his hands and a new nickname.

Fingers.

The men had asked Benny Mongrel why he left the man's thumbs. So he can hitchhike home, he told them. They had laughed. He had not.

This fucken wind made men go mad.

Benny Mongrel heard the car engine. He knew it was the Jeep from next door and didn't bother to get up. During a lull in the wind he caught the rattle of the American's garage door rolling up; then he heard the car ease forward. Then the sound of metal scraping brick.

Bessie growled. Benny Mongrel stood and went to the edge of the balcony.

The American had driven into the wall and caught his right fender. He reversed and got out to have a look at the damage. He was drunk, and Benny Mongrel could hear him curse. He got back into the car and drove it into the garage, and the door came down.

Benny Mongrel huddled back against the wall, waiting for the wind to blow itself out.

Barnard drove, still excited by the intensity of his visit to Lombard. He had felt a force, a heat channeled through Lombard's hand into his body. He felt renewed, filled with the fervor he needed to handle what lay before him.

His cell phone chirped, and he pulled over, so he could work it free from his pocket. When he saw caller ID, he answered eagerly and heard Dexter Torrance's slow drawl.

"Rudi, hi. I have news."

"I'm listening."

The deputy U.S. marshal told Barnard that he had run the woman's fingerprint and come up with a minor drug case years ago. Then he had cross-referenced a number of other databases and found out that the woman was married now. And the name of her husband. And what he was running from.

Barnard thanked Torrance profusely.

Then he killed the call and thanked his God for sending him Jack Burn.

CHAPTER 14

Barnard drove home, knowing that he had received the clearest possible message. About this American who called himself Hill but was in fact a fugitive who had escaped from the States with millions of dollars.

Barnard intended to make Burn pay.

Dexter Torrance, the deputy U.S. marshal, had no interest in making his findings known to the American authorities. "Burn killed a cop, Rudi, whether he pulled the trigger or not. But he had the dumb good luck to do it in a state that doesn't have the death penalty. I have no interest in seeing him spend time in prison on the taxpayer's dollar. He deserves to pay the ultimate penalty."

Rudi Barnard assured Torrance that he would take care of that. The American would get what he deserved.

But first Barnard needed money. Simple blackmail wasn't going to work. This American was clearly tougher and more resourceful than Barnard had suspected. At the first hint of exposure he would disappear.

No, Barnard had to do something that left Burn no room to maneuver.

Barnard, his mind working through the permutations, approached his apartment block. When he saw an unmarked cop car parked outside, he thought nothing of it. Many cops lived in the area. Then his eyes traveled up to his fourth-floor apartment. The curtains were drawn, but through a gap he saw a light was burning. Had he left it on? Not that he remembered. He pulled over, engine idling. Was he being paranoid? He didn't think so. As Lombard had so graphically put it, this was a battle between the forces of good and the forces of evil. They would stop at nothing.

Barnard drove away.

Disaster Zondi stood in Barnard's apartment, watching the detectives search the place. It was small and, given the man's repulsive physical appearance, surprisingly neat. Just one room with a bed, a sturdy chair in front of a desk, and an open-plan kitchen. No TV. No sound system. No photographs. No memorabilia. Zondi caught the unmistakable stink of Barnard, as if his essence had soaked into the curtains, the worn beige carpet, and the outsize clothes hanging in the closet.

Zondi took in the atmosphere of the room. He found it oppressive, depressing. The functional furnishings, the lack of any noticeable aesthetic. Most of the corrupt cops he investigated were greedy materialists, funding their appetites with their illegal activities. In Soweto last week Zondi had seen a plasma screen so big, it overshot the wall and hung halfway across a passageway, forcing his team to duck around it until he'd ordered them to remove the bloody thing. He was used to searching houses littered with electronic gear and leather sofas, closets bursting with designer wear and bling, garages with doors that couldn't close on fat-assed SUVs.

It was almost reassuring to come across the physical manifestation of man's basest urges. There was no ambiguity. You knew exactly who you were dealing with.

But this was the refuge of a fanatic. A man driven by an inner certainty that not only was he right in doing what he did, but he *had* to do what he did. In the old days of apartheid Zondi had come up against a few men like that. Different from the boozers and the cowboys, the profiteers; they were the believers. The ones with a mission.

He recognized them because, he supposed, he was one himself.

Zondi shook himself free of his thoughts and walked across to the desk. A laptop, lid closed, lay next to an empty notepad and a cheap ballpoint. Zondi slipped the laptop into its bag and slung it over his shoulder. Then he walked across to the bed and opened the Afrikaans Bible that lay on the bedside cabinet. He saw the inscription in cramped writing: TO RUDI. FROM YOUR FATHER ON YOUR TENTH BIRTHDAY.

Even monsters had fathers. And mothers.

Zondi sat on the bed and slid open the cabinet drawer. A *Hustler* magazine, well thumbed, and a tube of Preparation H hemorrhoid ointment. Zondi, a fastidious man, recoiled from the image of the obese Barnard applying the ointment to his fundament. He slid the drawer closed.

He opened the door to the cabinet and saw a small pile of right-wing Christian tracts. Illiterate bile. Predictable. A photograph, the first he had found in the apartment, lay beneath the pamphlets.

Zondi lifted a faded color shot of four men cooking meat over an open fire out in the bush. They were all white, beefy, holding beers in their hands, and mugging for the camera. He recognized one man immediately, a former Security Police captain who had later publicly apologized for the atrocities he committed during the apartheid years in order to avoid prosecution. The man on the captain's right was the young Rudi Barnard. No mustache, still heavy, but much slimmer than the mountain of flesh who had wheezed into the interview room the other day.

Zondi stared at the photograph. The quiet conversation of the detectives faded from his ears.

He slipped the photograph into his pocket.

Barnard was parked across from the Station Bar. He saw Captain Lotter step out of the bar and walk toward a new Nissan. Barnard crossed the road and dropped into the passenger seat of the Nissan before Lotter pulled away.

Lotter took one look at Barnard and started shaking his blow-dried head. "I had nothing to do with this. Nothing."

Barnard laughed one of his sucking laughs. "Relax. If I was going to plug you, I would've done it already."

"So what do you want?"

"Just tell me what's going on."

"All I've heard is that there's a warrant out for you."

"What for?"

"Killing a kid. And two unidentified males."

This was unexpected. He'd anticipated some trumped-up charge, but they had connected him to the little half-breed. "I didn't kill those two bastards."

Lotter was looking at him. "And the kid?" Barnard said nothing. Lotter shook his head. "Jesus, Barnard."

"Have they got Galant?"

Lotter nodded. "He's locked up at Bellwood South. Hear he's already sung."

"Piece of shit." He sucked on his mustache, staring ahead.

"You better disappear bloody fast, Barnard. I don't fancy your chances in Pollsmoor."

Barnard said nothing as he lifted himself from the car. He watched Lotter drive away, probably already on his cell phone to Peterson.

Barnard went back to his car and got the hell out of there.

The pressure was on him. He had to move—and fast. The only way he was going to survive this was to get enough money together to go deep underground, change his identity. The irony wasn't lost on him.

Just like his American friend.

The helicopter cut through Burn's sleep, low enough for him to hear the blades whipping. The sound of the chopper and the acrid smoke in his nostrils spun him back to February 1991, as an Apache attack helicopter swooped over Burn and his platoon driving through the smoldering wreckage on the Highway of Death.

The four-lane highway through the desert, jammed with vehicles laden with plunder from the Iraqi sack of Kuwait City, had been bombed the night before. Vehicles were riddled with bullet holes, cars blown up, hundreds of Iraqi soldiers and civilians incinerated.

Then Burn woke up. He was in Cape Town. The mountain was burning, and he had the mother of all hangovers. He lay in the spare bedroom, and the windows were closed, the room airless.

He pulled himself to his feet, still fully dressed. His mouth tasted like shit. He put a hand in his pocket and found a wad of notes. Last night's blackjack winnings. He cursed himself for his weakness and stupidity.

He headed off to the kitchen to find an aspirin.

Susan was making breakfast. Bacon and eggs. The smell of the food was enough to make him puke. Matt sat at the counter, swinging his legs, reading Dr. Seuss. A book that Burn used to read to him at night back home. Jesus, how long ago had that been?

Burn ruffled his son's hair. "Morning, Matty." His voice sounded like a work in progress. A poor one.

Matt nodded, absorbed in the book. Susan didn't look around from the stove.

Burn found aspirin in the drawer and washed two of them down with a glass of water. Susan dished food for herself and Matt. She set the boy's plate before him and walked out onto the deck with hers. It wasn't much after seven but the sun was already fierce.

Burn followed her outside, squinting.

The mountain above them was charred, black, smoldering. Choppers were dousing any last sparks. The wind, mercifully, had stopped.

Susan sat down at the table on the deck, her eyes hidden behind black Ray-Bans.

Burn didn't sit. He hovered over her. "I'm sorry."

She said nothing. It was as if he wasn't there.

There was nothing more he could say to his wife. He knew that she would find peace only when he turned his back on her and left.

Disaster Zondi sat at a table in his room at the Arabella Sheraton and ate his breakfast. Fruit salad with extra kiwi, poached eggs, and whole-wheat toast. Freshly squeezed orange juice. No bacon. He never touched pork. He wore his suit trousers and white shirt without a tie. His Italian loafers gleamed.

When you worked for the ministry, you were looked after. You flew business class; you rented BMWs and Mercedes-Benzes. You had an expense account that allowed you to afford the Cavalli suits. Almost. And why the hell not? It was a tough job, trawling the dark pits of corruption, facing the very worst of human nature day after day. A few small luxuries were a balm to the soul.

He carefully picked crumbs off the white tablecloth and placed them on a plate. Then he put the breakfast dishes on a tray and deposited it in the corridor.

Zondi returned to the table and booted up Rudi Barnard's laptop once again. He had spent the previous night, into the early hours of the morning, trawling through the contents of the hard drive. It didn't reveal much, which didn't surprise him. Barnard wouldn't be stupid enough to leave details of his activities on a computer.

Searching his e-mail files had produced mostly innocuous correspondence: police pension fund updates, an objection to a rental increase at his apartment. Then Zondi had found the e-mail to an anonymous Yahoo address with a JPEG of a fingerprint attached. Zondi had pondered it at length the night before, studying the whorls as if they would lead him to some further understanding. None came, and he had forced himself to sleep.

After breakfast he returned to his meditation on the fingerprint. He knew somehow that this was important, that it could lead him to Rudi Barnard. Who had vanished.

Zondi had the photograph of the smiling men at the bush barbecue propped up next to the laptop. As he sipped his cup of Earl Grey, he allowed himself the indulgence of memory.

It was 1988. Zondi was eighteen, at university in Johannesburg, running with a crowd of youth activists. His best friend, Jabu, was a student political leader with a high profile. Zondi was at Jabu's Soweto house one night when the security cops raided. Beefy white men in jeans and T-shirts, with blunt haircuts and shoulders like rugby forwards. One of them was the captain in the photograph. They threw Zondi and Jabu into a car and drove them to John Vorster Square in Johannesburg.

Zondi and Jabu were separated, locked up alone. Over the next few days a succession of men came into Zondi's cell and tortured him, demanding to know the names of Jabu's associates. Zondi didn't know the names.

The younger Barnard had pulled a wet sack over Zondi's head and then pushed his head into a bucket of water, until he was sure he was going to drown. Then the fat man had kicked him and stomped him. Barnard and another man tied Zondi's legs together, kept the wet sack over his head, and carried on kicking him. Broke his ribs.

They pulled the sack off his face, just as he was about to lapse into unconsciousness. He was bleeding from the nose, mouth, and ears.

Barnard again demanded answers that Zondi couldn't give him.

Barnard kicked him into unconsciousness.

Zondi woke up bleeding and wet, in the cell. He was held for another two days, beaten regularly; then without explanation they took him to a car. He was driven to Soweto and dumped in a field. Aside from the broken ribs, his kidneys were bruised and his right arm was fractured. But he was alive.

He never saw Jabu again.

Nine years later Zondi sat with Jabu's mother and sister, in an anonymous Johannesburg office building, listening to the captain in the photograph offer his apologies before the Truth and Reconciliation Commission. To avoid prosecution. On the tribunal facing the captain were an Anglican archbishop, a lawyer, a doctor, and an academic, their faces haunted by the horrors they had absorbed over the past years.

The captain, an ingratiating man with a shit-eating grin, told how Jabu had died during interrogation. His body was taken to an isolated spot and cremated over a log fire for seven hours until all traces had been destroyed. During the cremation a group of security policemen drank and cooked meat at a separate barbecue.

As Jabu's mother folded forward in silent horror, the captain had provided more detail. While the security cops were drinking, cooking, and eating their supper, they would tend the cremation fire, turning the buttocks and upper part of the legs frequently during the night to make sure that everything burned to ashes. And the next morning, after raking through the ashes to make sure that there were no pieces of meat or bone left, they had all gone their own way.

When Zondi had been given the file on Barnard, he had not remembered him immediately. It was only when he read Barnard's Security Police record and saw the ID shots from the eighties that Zondi had realized who he was dealing with.

Knowing who Barnard was changed nothing for Zondi. He was a professional. And he would behave like a professional. But Zondi knew he'd raise a glass of single malt to Jabu when he brought Rudi Barnard down.

CHAPTER 15

Barnard reversed a brown eighties Ford out of the storage container, leaving it empty. He locked up and drove through rows of similar containers to the exit.

He had kept the Ford for just such an emergency, making a ritual of charging the battery every second Sunday. On those Sundays, while the battery charger ticked over, he had sat and cleaned and oiled a Colt Cobra .32 and a Mossberg 500 Special Purpose pump-action shotgun. The weapons, and the small stash of banknotes he had kept in the container, were in the trunk of the Ford.

After dumping his police Toyota in Goodwood the previous night, he had caught a taxi into the city center and booked into a cheap hotel, far from his usual haunts. He had paid cash in advance. He hadn't slept well. Not out of fear; he didn't believe the door was about to give way and Disaster Zondi enter like an avenging angel. No, it was the anticipation of what was to come.

In the morning he had caught another taxi to within a few blocks of the storage depot, waiting for the cab to disappear into the rush-hour traffic before he went to retrieve the Ford and the weapons.

Now, as he drove toward the city, he ran through a checklist of what had to be done. He had his plan.

He knew exactly what was in store for the American.

It was the toughest day of Burn's life. It was the last day he would spend with his son.

Burn and Matt drove down the peninsula in the Jeep. Although the fires were dead, some still smoldered in places, the mountain looking like a lunar landscape. But the sky was blue and the wind had died. The ocean went from turquoise near the shore to a deep aquamarine farther out.

They were listening to the Beach Boys as they drove, singing along to "Good Vibrations" just as they always did.

Burn forced himself to keep it light, to keep Matt laughing. Otherwise he would start to cry, and he didn't think he would be able to stop.

That morning Burn had selected a new identity from the safe. William Morton. He took the passport and a wad of dollars down to the travel agent in Sea Point and booked a flight to Denpasar, Indonesia, by way of Johannesburg and Singapore. His flight left Cape Town airport at 10:00 a.m. the next day. He had chosen Indonesia because it seemed a lot more hospitable than Algeria, Angola, Moldova, Yemen, Zimbabwe, or any of the other countries that didn't have an extradition treaty with the United States.

Now that he wouldn't have a pregnant wife or a small child with him, the sprawl of Indonesia seemed appealing. And there were worse places than Bali to stitch his life back together.

He had made peace with the fact that Susan was going to give herself up. He hoped the U.S. authorities would be sympathetic, and that Susan's punishment would be light.

Sometime in the future they would be together. He had to believe that.

Burn and Matt stopped at a small harbor and walked out onto the pier, watching as men lazily fished from the breakwater. Brightly painted wooden fishing boats chugged in, loaded with their catch.

Burn bought a cod fresh from the ocean. Maybe he could cook it that night, as a kind of undeclared farewell meal. He intended to wait for Matt to go to sleep and then tell Susan of his plans. He would say good-bye to his son before he left in the morning. That was the only way he could imagine doing the unimaginable.

Matt held Burn's hand and stared in fascination as a bronze-skinned woman in gum boots sat on a crate surrounded by fish innards and gutted their cod. She worked the filleting knife without needing to watch her hands, all the while flirting with fishermen in the singsong local patois. She had a raucous laugh, the kind that is marinated in cheap booze and cigarettes.

She winked at Matt. "Pretty boy," she said in heavily accented English. "He got his daddy's eyes." Then she looked up at Burn. "He gonna break some hearts." She laughed again as she scraped the last of the pink fish guts onto the ground.

Burn walked back to the car still holding Matt's hand, carrying the fish in a plastic bag.

Barnard drove the Ford along Main Road, Greenpoint. He stopped at a red light and lit a smoke while he waited. He felt the nicotine infuse his system, slowing things down just a fraction. He knew he was hyped. Primed for action. That was good. But he needed to keep his focus. This was a critical time.

A police van stopped next to Barnard, the uniformed woman cop looking down at him. He returned her look and then stared straight ahead, feeling the sweat flowing down his chest, his jeans chafing his thighs. He had that fucken rash again, inflamed red pustules on his ocean of white flesh. He needed a shower, and to change into some of the clothes he'd brought from the container.

The light changed, and he pulled away slowly, working his way through the gears. The cop van surged ahead, getting lost in the traffic. Barnard passed a couple of teenage hookers in short dresses. One of them blew him a kiss. Any other day he would be out the car, flash his badge, and run them off. Scare the hell out of them. Not today. Today his profile was as low as that of a man built like a tank could be.

He saw a sign advertising rooms and turned off into a parking lot. The hotel was small, cheap, and nasty. Home to hookers and dealers and low-rent adulterers. It would suit him fine.

Barnard popped the trunk of the Ford. He had stashed the weapons, money, and clothes in a kit bag. He locked the car and went into reception, carrying the bag.

An unenthusiastic colored man sat watching cricket on TV. He hardly looked at Barnard, took the cash he offered, and slid him a key. Barnard humped his fat up a flight of stairs and into a cramped room. The air-conditioning was noisy, but it worked.

First thing, he stripped and headed for the shower. There was no separate shower cubicle, just a curtain around the bathtub. It was diffi-cult to maneuver his bulk in the tight space, and the spray from the noz-zle was weak and tepid.

But at least he was clean.

He parted his butt cheeks and slathered on his ointment. The hemorrhoids had been playing up, aching like hell. He lumbered naked into the bedroom and took a plastic container of baby powder from the kit bag and rubbed it under his arms and between his thighs where the skin chafed when he walked. Then he dressed in jeans, T-shirt, and heavy boots. He sat on the bed, the springs compressing under his weight.

He laid out what he needed. First the Mossberg 500 pump-action, barrel chopped to the length of the magazine tube. The stock was cut almost to the pistol grip. Barnard had taken it off a Flats gangster, forced him to eat the barrel, then pulled the trigger. He had liked the way it lifted off the top of the gangster's head and decided to keep the gun.

He cleaned it, checked the action, and pumped two cartridges into the chamber. Then he cleaned, oiled, and loaded the .38 he'd been carrying for the past couple of days. Lastly, he prepared the .32 and strapped it into an ankle holster.

He took a roll of duct tape, a pair of surgical gloves, a piece of cloth, and a couple of black plastic cable ties from the kit bag and stowed them in the small waist bag he'd attached to his belt.

He shrugged on a shoulder holster and slid the .38 into place. He drew it a couple of times, adjusting the hang of the holster until it was comfortable. Then he wrapped the sawed-off in a garish beach towel he found in the bathroom and put it in the kit bag. He zipped the bag, checked around the room to make sure he hadn't left anything, then headed to the door.

He wasn't coming back.

If she didn't go now, she would lose her courage.

Susan Burn walked to the front door, carrying a small overnight suitcase. Mrs. Dollie was washing the picture window in the living room, vigorously working newspaper across the glass until it offered an unblemished view of the world outside.

"Can I help you, Mrs. Hill?"

Susan shook her head. "No thanks, Mrs. Dollie. I'm fine." Susan tried a smile, but she could see from the concern on the older woman's face that it was unconvincing.

Mrs. Dollie hesitated for a moment; then she stepped across the employer-employee divide and gave Susan a hug. Susan almost gave in to her tears, wanted to clutch onto this kindly woman and pour her heart out, sob until she was as dry as that burned mountain looming over them.

But she freed herself from the embrace and managed a more effective smile. "Thank you, Mrs. Dollie. For everything. Tell Matt I'll see him soon."

Mrs. Dollie nodded. "You look nicely after you, okay?"

Susan maneuvered herself carefully down the stairs, unlocked the door at the bottom of the garden, and went to the waiting taxi. When he saw her bulging stomach, the taxi driver, a middle-aged brown man, hurried around the vehicle to open the rear door for her. He helped her with her case.

"Where am I taking madam?"

"Gardens Clinic."

The taxi pulled away, and Susan shut her eyes, the air-conditioning taking the edge off the heat.

She had made the decision that morning before Jack and Matt had left her alone in the house. She was going to the clinic to have her baby induced. Her doctor would support her decision after the episode with the detached placenta. She could no longer stand the waiting. Or seeing the effect her fragmenting marriage was having on her son. God, she owed Matt that at least.

After her daughter was born, she was going to call the U.S. Consulate. By then she hoped that Jack would be gone, to New Zealand or wherever the hell he wanted to run to.

When she had said good-bye to her husband that morning, she had made up her mind that it would be the last time she would see him.

When Benny Mongrel reported for his shift in the late afternoon, he went immediately to the kennel to fetch Bessie. She lay panting on the floor of the cage, a dry water bowl in front of her. These bastards couldn't even see to that. He filled the bowl at a tap and watched her lap all the water down.

Then he hooked her up to her chain and walked her toward the truck. A voice stopped him. Ishmael Isaacs, the shift foreman, calling for him to wait. Isaacs came striding across the yard, his paramilitary uniform sharp with knife-edged creases. He carried a clipboard.

Isaacs gave him the once-over. "Boss tells me you were in there hassling him the other day."

"I just wanted to ask him something."

"Why didn't you speak to me first?"

"You wasn't here."

"You don't go over my head, ever. You understand me?" Benny Mongrel nodded. "Anyways, I'm pulling you off that building site, as of tomorrow."

"Why?"

"You experienced enough now to go to one of the factories. One of the new boys can take your place." Benny Mongrel nodded. Suited him. He turned to go. "By the way, you being assigned a new dog."

Benny Mongrel stopped and faced the foreman. "Why?"

"Look at her." Isaacs nudged Bessie's back leg with the toe of a shiny boot. She whined. "Her hips is fucked, man. We had the vet in here today, and he say she no longer fit to work. Tonight is her last night."

"Can I buy her then?"

"What for?"

"I want to keep her."

Isaacs shook his head. "No. These dogs are trained attack dogs. They can't be released into the civilian population."

"So what will happen to her?"

Isaacs sneered at him. "What, you gone soft or something? Why do you give a fuck? Her days are numbered; she'll be put down."

He walked away, with the clipboard under his arm.

Benny Mongrel looked down at Bessie. So, that was it. It was decided. Tonight was the night they would escape. Only two days to payday, but that couldn't be helped.

Benny Mongrel walked Bessie toward the truck.

The sun was low in the sky by the time Burn and Matt arrived at the house. When they walked inside, Mrs. Dollie was sitting in the kitchen.

Matt went up to her, carrying the fish. "Look what we got."

She smiled at him. "That's a very big fish."

Burn was puzzled. "Where's Susan?"

Mrs. Dollie looked uncomfortable. "She ask me if I would stay the night with Matt. She say she had to go somewhere."

Burn's mind was racing. Was she in touch with the consulate? Would the cops be here any moment? He calmed himself. "Where did she go, Mrs. Dollie?"

The woman looked at him, saying nothing, incapable of lying.

Burn spoke as reassuringly as he could. "Mrs. Dollie, I know Susan told you where she was going. I need to know. Please."

She nodded. "She took a taxi. To the clinic."

"Is she okay? Was she bleeding?"

"She seemed fine. It didn't look like there was any problems."

Burn headed for the phone and punched in the number of the clinic. He spoke to a woman in admissions, who refused to give out any information over the phone.

Burn grabbed his car keys. "Mrs. Dollie, I need to go to the clinic. Will you give Matt something to eat?"

Mrs. Dollie was looking at the fish. Burn shook his head. "No, just make him a hot dog or something. The fish can wait."

He took the plastic bag and put it in the freezer. Then he headed down to the car.

Barnard sat in the Ford, a few doors up from Burn's house. It was almost dark, and the streetlights were on. He had been there for two hours, tuning out the heat, the boredom, and the rash that was itching like a bastard beneath his balls.

An hour ago he had seen a taxi pull up. The blonde woman had come out alone. She had climbed into the back of the taxi, and it drove away. A few minutes later a half-breed in a domestic worker's smock had come out and swept the deck. No sign of the man or the boy.

Then, ten minutes ago, the Jeep had passed him and turned into the garage. Burn driving, the kid strapped into the seat in the back.

Now the garage door rolled up, and the Jeep reversed out. The American on his own.

Barnard watched the Jeep slow at the stop sign, brake lights glowing red in the dusk. Then the Jeep turned down to Sea Point and disappeared.

The half-breed woman and the child were alone.

Barnard would wait a few minutes, until it was completely dark. Then he was going in.

CHAPTER 16

Burn walked up to the desk at the clinic. The young receptionist, a bottle blonde with dark roots, flashed a professional smile.

"I'm here to see my wife. Susan Hill. Where do I find her?"

The woman's fingers flew over her keyboard. She hummed to herself. "Excuse me just a moment."

She left him and went across to a telephone that was far enough away to be out of earshot. Her conversation was brief, punctuated by a number of nods and head shakes.

She came back without her smile. "I'm sorry, sir, but Mrs. Hill has requested that she have no visitors."

"I'm her husband."

The woman shook her head. "I'm sorry. Those are my instructions."

Burn headed toward the stairs, ignoring the woman calling after him.

He took the stairs two at a time, until he found himself on the floor of private wards. He went to Susan's previous ward, shoved open the door, and stuck his head in. A man sat next to a pale woman propped up on pillows. The woman was weeping and the man held her hand. Burn mumbled an apology and closed the door.

As he approached the next ward, a nursing sister and a uniformed security guard fell in beside him. The sister was a bruiser who looked like she could go ten rounds with Mike Tyson in his prime. She did the talking. "I'm sorry, sir, but you'll have to leave."

"I want to see my wife." Burn tried to push past them. The security guard, a big man, laid a warning hand on Burn's shoulder. Another guard hurried toward them, speaking into a walkie-talkie.

The sister was trying to calm Burn. "Your wife instructed us that she doesn't want to see you right now."

The second security man joined them. Burn held up his hands in supplication. "Okay. Fine. At least tell me how she is."

"She's fine. Everything is normal."

"Then why is she here?"

"The procedure will be perfectly routine."

"What procedure?"

"Your wife, given her condition, has requested that we induce labor. The child will be born a few weeks premature, by cesarean section if necessary, but there is no danger."

"And when will this happen?"

"Tomorrow morning." The sister tried a smile. It looked like she was spitting out a mouth guard. "I really think it's best if you leave. I'm sure once the child is born, and your wife is less . . . less emotional, she'll want to see you."

Burn nodded. He turned for the stairs, the two security men flank-
ing him.

⌒

Fires had sprung up again on the mountain, tongues of flame lick-
ing the night sky, and the smell of burning reached Benny Mongrel's
nostrils. He was tense, now that the time had come. If they left now,
they would have nine hours to make their escape.

Benny Mongrel was about to attach the chain to Bessie's lead and
start the walk into their new life when he saw the fat cop hauling himself
down the road. Benny Mongrel stayed still. Waiting. He saw the cop ring
the buzzer at the American's house, heard him saying something into the
intercom.

⌒

Barnard filled the recess in the wall as he pressed the buzzer, his
finger bulging like a dick in a condom through the surgical gloves. After
a moment he heard a woman's voice. The half-breed domestic, nervous.
Asking who was there.

Barnard held his police ID up to the camera, tilting it so that it
caught the light above the door. "Police. Let me in, please."

The woman's voice was tentative, full of Cape Flats' wariness of
the cops. "Mr. and Mrs. Hill aren't home."

"I know. That's fine. I need to talk to you."

"What about?"

"Listen, lady, what is your name?"

Hesitation, then a nervous reply. "Mrs. Dollie."

"Mrs. Dollie, if you don't want trouble from me and your boss, you
better open this door now. You hear me?"

The threat in his voice worked, and the door clicked open. Barnard stepped inside and shut it after him.

⌁

Time to move.

Benny Mongrel hooked Bessie to the chain and clicked his tongue softly. "Come, Bessie. Let's go." The old dog heaved herself to her feet, taking a while to get movement into her back legs.

They had a long walk ahead of them. Benny Mongrel knew that he didn't have a hope of a taxi driver letting him and the dog on board. They would have to do it on foot, stopping frequently so the old dog could rest. Benny Mongrel and Bessie walked down the uncompleted stairway, between the piles of sand and rubble, toward the gate and freedom.

Then a red Sniper armed response car pulled up. Right under the streetlight. Benny Mongrel saw Ishmael Isaacs at the wheel, looking straight at him.

⌁

Burn sat in his car outside the clinic. He didn't know what to do. His mind had been made up; he was ready to shove the pain of leaving his family into some deep vault and get on the plane in the morning.

Now things had changed. Susan was in the clinic. Their daughter would be born the next day. Burn couldn't leave Matt. He trusted Mrs. Dollie, but there was no way he could just leave the boy with her and fly away. Not until Susan was back at home, in some condition to look after herself and Matt. It came almost as a relief, the feeling that the decision had been made for him. He was staying.

He started the car.

━◇━

Isaacs lit a Camel and took a long pull before blowing the smoke in Benny Mongrel's face. He sat behind the wheel, the Sniper car idling, staring up at Benny Mongrel.

"Where you going?"

"Just patrolling."

"Patrolling?" The sneer in Isaacs's voice grated on Benny Mongrel. Another time, another place, this bastard would be on his way to Allah. "Where you patrolling?"

Benny Mongrel kept himself cool. Not long now. "We walk the front here every hour."

Isaacs nodded. "Okay." He puffed, exhaled. "With the fires we got extra units out. These people here are nervous their bloody houses will burn down."

Benny Mongrel said nothing, keeping his mind blank the way he had learned in prison.

Isaacs put the car in gear. "I might make a turn here later, so don't patrol too far, okay?" Isaacs laughed to himself and took off with an unnecessary burn of rubber.

Asshole.

Now they would have to wait.

━◇━

The half-breed maid stood behind the security gate, watching Barnard as he wheezed up to the front door of the house. He saw she was middle-aged, and Muslim, judging from her head scarf. He had no time for them, bloody heathens.

"Good evening, Mrs. Dollie."

"Good evening."

"I'm Inspector Barnard." He kept his hands, in the surgical gloves, out of sight.

"Yes?"

"Can I come inside, please?"

She was unsure. "I can't let anyone in. My boss has told me that."

"I'm not anyone. I'm the police."

Barnard tried to look reassuring. It spooked her more. She shook her head, stepping back from the security gate, reaching into her pocket for her cell phone. "I'm going to phone Mr. Hill. You can talk to him."

Before she could move out of reach, Barnard stuck a meaty arm between the bars—it just squeezed through—and grabbed her by the throat, lifting her onto the tips of her sensible shoes, her feet kicking. Her eyes bulged with terror as she gasped for air. He grabbed her phone and pocketed it.

The key was in the security gate, on her side. Still holding her, Barnard reached in with his free hand and turned the key. He pushed the gate open and let the woman drop.

She hit the floor hard, fighting for breath as she started to crawl on her hands and knees toward the living room. She was trying to shout something, but no sound came from her throat.

Barnard closed the door. Then he dropped onto her with his full weight, his knee ramming into her back, pinning her to the floor. He grabbed her head between his hands, and with one twist he broke her neck like she was a backyard chicken. Moving quickly to avoid the stream of urine that flowed from her, he got to his feet and found himself looking down at the boy.

The kid, in a pair of pajamas covered in Disney cartoon characters, stood staring up at Barnard. Then his mouth opened, and he was winding up to let rip with one hell of a scream.

Barnard was across to him in an instant, the palm of his hand squashing the scream back into the boy's lungs. Barnard held on to the boy's face with one hand and unzipped the waist bag with the other. He took out the cloth and the duct tape. He removed his hand from the boy's face, allowed him to grab a breath, then shoved the cloth into the kid's mouth. He taped his mouth closed.

The kid was hyperventilating, sucking air through his nose, his blue eyes wide with terror. Barnard spun him onto his stomach, pulled his hands roughly together behind his back, and slipped one of the cable ties around his wrists, pulling it tight enough to cut into the skin. He did the same with the kid's bare ankles.

Barnard grabbed the boy, holding him under one of his massive arms like he was a bag of oranges, and stepped over the dead woman on his way to the door.

CHAPTER 17

One thing that Benny Mongrel knew how to do was wait. Spend more than half your life in prison, and you develop a Zen-like ability to live in the moment. Those who don't, kill themselves or go crazy. Or get themselves killed.

He dug Rizla papers and a bag of tobacco from his pocket and set about rolling a smoke. He would give Isaacs an hour. If the bastard wasn't back, he and Bessie would start their journey.

Isaacs was all show. There was no way he was going to spend his night driving around the slopes of the mountain. No, some woman in a head scarf, fat thighs whispering beneath a Punjabi pantsuit, was waiting at home with a pot of curry on the stove, ready to serve him.

Benny Mongrel paused in his cigarette making and stroked Bessie's matted coat. The old dog looked up at him, and her tail slapped the cement as she wagged it. Then she groaned from deep in her throat and rolled onto her side, sighing contentedly. She was still hooked up to her chain. Benny Mongrel unclipped it.

Let the old girl relax; she had a long walk ahead of her.

Benny Mongrel finished rolling the cigarette, ran his tongue along one side of the paper, and glued it together with his fingers. He spat out a shred of tobacco, shielded the cigarette from the wind that was starting to gust again, and fired up.

He took a long drag, feeling the movement of the smoke deep into his lungs, and then allowed it to trickle out of his mouth and nose. Smoking was another prison ritual. Sucking on a cigarette and allowing time to pass by. That was life in prison. Minutes, hours, days, years, flowing away like a muddy river.

Benny Mongrel stood and walked to the edge of the balcony, smoking, staring up at the flames that were being fanned by the wind, zigzagging along Lion's Head.

Then the wind died. Suddenly. Like a TV being switched off. He could hear the murmur of traffic down in Sea Point, a car alarm wailing somewhere far below, and the distant clatter of the choppers circling the mountain like dragonflies.

And he heard the click and buzz of the door of the neighboring house. This got him moving back into the shadows. Fuck. He had forgotten about the fat cop. There the bastard was, sticking his big head out, looking up and down the street, before he stepped out and slammed the door. He had something under his arm.

The fat cop took off up the road, his legs chafing together and his ass shaking like a belly dancer's. The thing under his arm was moving, writhing. Benny Mongrel watched the fat cop stop and change his grip, right under a streetlight. That's when Benny Mongrel saw what the cop was carrying. A boy with blond hair.

The American's kid.

Fucken little bastard. He was small, but he was fighting like a cat in a sack. Barnard held him in both arms, squeezing the boy's face against his chest, smothering him. That seemed to calm him down a bit. For good measure he brought the side of his hand down into the kid's guts, hard. He felt the boy jerk, knees digging into Barnard's fat; then he was still.

Barnard arrived at the Ford, went back to holding the kid in a one-armed grip while he fished in his pocket for his keys. While he was battling to work the keys past the rolls of fat that hung from his hips, the kid kicked his bare feet against Barnard's paunch and propelled himself out of the cop's grasp. The little shit fell to the pavement and hit his head, hard. Barnard saw blood, dark against the kid's blond hair.

Wheezing, Barnard popped the trunk. Then he bent, his legs spread wide like a sumo wrestler getting into first position, as he grabbed the boy and threw him into the trunk. He heard the kid gasping and saw the tears and snot streaking his face.

Fuck him.

Barnard slammed the trunk closed and leaned on the lid, fighting to get his breath. Sweat rolled freely from his forehead, into his eyes. His shirt clung to his back, and the itch between his thighs stung like a thousand mosquitoes had nailed him.

When his breathing was easier, he stood up and looked straight at the building site. Was that half-breed bastard with the dog up there, watching? Barnard couldn't take the chance, couldn't risk being tied to this kidnapping.

He was sure the American would keep his trap shut. But if the cops got wind of a foreign kid being abducted, there would be hell to pay. Very bad for the tourist industry. This wasn't the Flats, where a child's life was cheap. There would be a manhunt, pictures on TV and in the papers. Rewards offered. All of which would severely fuck up Barnard's plans.

He got into the car, didn't start the engine, just freewheeled down until he was level with the entrance to the building site and pulled up the brake. He wiped his sweating hands on his jeans, moved his wet shirt out of the way, and slid the .38 from the holster.

He stood up out of the car.

The knife was in his hand. Benny Mongrel waited at the top of the stairs, behind the half-built wall, listening. He heard the crunch of heavy feet as the fat cop walked across the builder's sand and gravel.

Benny Mongrel was in a place within himself that he had been in many times since he had killed that American gangster when he was a boy. It was a place of perfect focus, all his senses honed, every muscle and sinew waiting for the command that would send the blade deep into flesh.

The cop had entered the building site. He was making no attempt to move quietly. From where he stood, two flights up, Benny Mongrel could hear the wheeze of the fat cop's lungs as air sucked through phlegm like a clogged pool filter. The cop coughed and spat.

The fat man walked the two planks that spanned a plumber's ditch and led to the ground floor of the house; the planks creaked and bounced under his weight.

Benny Mongrel heard the cop's voice. "Hey, watchman. You there?"

Bessie growled behind Benny Mongrel. The growl was low and deep. She had rolled up and was trying to stand, the nails of her back paws scrabbling at the cement floor as she fought to lift her hips. Benny Mongrel stared at her, willing her to be quiet. He held out a warning hand. She seemed to understand, and the growl died in her throat. She raised her long snout and sniffed the air. But she stayed where she was.

"Watchman? I got something for you, man. Some cash. Want you to gimme a hand with something." The fat cop was heading up the first flight of stairs, his boots heavy on the cement.

Benny Mongrel stood dead still. Let the bastard come to him. The moment he stepped onto the landing on the top floor, Benny Mongrel would strike.

He heard the cop reach the landing on the floor below. He was wheezing like he'd climbed Table Mountain, his breath coming in short gasps. "Watchman? Don't make me fucken come and look for you . . ."

The sound of the cop's boot on the first step leading up to the top floor. Not long now. Benny Mongrel was ready for him.

And then, before he could stop her, the old dog was flying past him, digging deep into muscle memory and finding some last echo of the speed and strength she had once known. Benny Mongrel made a leap for Bessie, tried to grab her by her thick coat, but his fingers found air and he hit the cement hard, his knife spinning away from him.

***

Barnard was on the second step, panting toward the top floor of the house, when he saw the dark shape flying down toward him. The fucken dog. He raised the .38 and got off a shot, knew he had missed.

The dog's paws hit him in the chest. A smaller man would have been sent flying backward, but Barnard did nothing more than lean, before righting himself. The dog bounced off him and hit the stairs with her back. He heard the crack as her left hip shattered. The dog moaned, but she was still fighting to get up at him, snarling, yellow fangs visible in the spill of the streetlight.

Barnard shot her at point-blank range, in the chest.

The shot almost deafened him, bouncing off the hard cement walls, reverberating through the unfinished rooms and escaping out into the night. Unbelievably, the dog was still coming, a sound somewhere between a growl and a scream coming from her bloody muzzle. He shot her again.

She was still.

Dogs in the houses next door started to bark, a chorus that kept collecting new voices as it rolled across the suburb.

When he heard the first shot, Benny Mongrel was racing across to retrieve the knife that had spun from his grasp and come to rest against a cement bag. He grabbed the knife, felt the reassuring shape of the hilt as he curled his fingers around it.

Then the second shot.

Benny Mongrel took off for the stairs.

From where he stood Barnard could see out through the unfinished rooms and across the streets and houses below.

An armed response patrol car, hazards flashing, barreled down the street three blocks away. The shots had been heard.

Barnard needed to go upstairs and finish this.

He looked back toward the patrol car, saw it brake, skid, and fishtail as it avoided an SUV that had reversed out of a driveway into its path.

The moment he needed.

Benny Mongrel was at the top of the stairs. He knew he would be silhouetted against the light from outside. He knew the cop would have a perfect target. He didn't care.

He launched himself at the stairs, and the bullet smashed into his shoulder. It was his knife arm, and he heard the knife clatter as it fell from his grip. He had been shot before, but it wasn't a feeling you got used to, the smack of the bullet into your flesh. The deadness. No pain at first. But you knew it was coming.

He managed to twist and throw himself backward and sideways, so that he landed away from the stairs, shielded by the low wall. Benny Mongrel lay on his side, waiting for the fat cop to come up the stairs. His right arm was useless. He could feel the blood flowing from the shoulder, down his arm, pooling onto his fingers.

He reached out his left hand and found a half-brick. At least that was something.

He heard a car in the distance, driving fast, racing through the gears. He heard the cop, coming up one step. Then another.

Barnard climbed the stairs. He looked down at the street. The patrol car burned rubber as it started toward him again. Two blocks away. Barnard made up his mind. He turned and ran, moving as fast as his huge frame would allow.

He burst from the building site, hurtled across the planks, and took off for the road, legs pumping, heart threatening to explode from within its housing of fat and cholesterol.

The Ford was ahead of him. Not far.

He looked over his shoulder. The patrol car wasn't there yet, hidden from sight, around the corner. He could hear it, though, screaming through the gears.

He was at his car. Unlocked it, dropped inside, feeling it sag under his weight.

Key in the ignition. Smashed gears into reverse and took off, away from the house, away from the patrol car, clutch burning.

Then he was over the rise and reversing down out of sight.

When he heard the planks bounce as the fat cop ran away, Benny Mongrel dragged himself to his feet, the brick still in his left hand. He went down the stairs.

Bessie lay on the landing below. She wasn't moving. Benny Mongrel stood over the dog, dropped the brick, and slowly knelt down. He knew she was dead before he touched her. The streetlight shafted onto the landing, and he could see her mouth drawn away from her bloody teeth in a rictus of death. Blood matted her coat and spread like a dark stain away from her body.

Benny Mongrel knelt down in the blood, and with his good arm he cradled the dead dog. Then he did something that he hadn't done since he was thrown on the garbage dump all those years ago.

Benny Mongrel cried.

CHAPTER 18

When Burn saw the flashing lights of the police car, he felt a moment of blind panic. His first urge was to drive straight past his house and get the hell out of there.

Then he saw the cops were at the building site next door. An ambulance was parked in front of the cop car and an armed response vehicle up on the sidewalk. He saw the night watchman, the man with the disfigured face, being led to the ambulance. The watchman's shirt was open, and Burn could see his arm was in a sling and his shoulder bandaged. The cops eyed Burn incuriously as he stopped outside his garage door and pressed the remote.

He nosed the car inside the garage, and the door rolled down. He sat for a moment and enjoyed the sense of relief. He was safe. For now. And he wasn't going to leave tomorrow. Maybe, just maybe, once their daughter was born, Susan, awash in the sensation of motherhood, would change her mind. Give him—give them—another chance.

Burn remembered the birth of Matt, Susan digging her nails into his palm hard enough to make him bleed. He hadn't felt a thing, so caught up was he in the drama of this new life.

Now it seemed impossible to him that he had thought of saying good-bye to his son.

He climbed the stairs up from the garage and came into the house through the kitchen. The familiar mayhem of the Cartoon Network blared from the living room, and two plates were laid out on the counter in the kitchen.

"Matt?" Burn dropped his keys on the counter and walked through toward the TV. That's when he saw Mrs. Dollie lying sprawled on the tiles near the front door, her head at an impossible angle, eyes staring at nothing. The living room was empty.

Burn was running. "Matt!"

He ran through every room in the house, checked under the beds, in the closets. Knowing that his son was gone.

At last he returned to Mrs. Dollie, went through the futile exercise of feeling for her pulse. He let her lifeless hand drop to the floor. Burn checked his watch. He had been gone less than an hour. Whoever had taken his son would already have lost themselves in the sprawl of the city by now.

They were in the wind.

There were cops outside. He could walk out and ask for their help. Step back and let them handle it. He knew it would probably mean that he would be exposed. He didn't care. All he cared about was his son.

But he knew that going to the cops could get his son killed.

Someone had taken Matt because they wanted something. This was no home invasion. Nothing had been stolen. Mrs. Dollie had been killed so she wouldn't be able to identify his son's kidnapper. Burn believed that somebody would contact him with a demand. He would wait for that.

It was the best chance Matt had.

Maybe the only chance.

They took Benny Mongrel down to Somerset Hospital. No fancy clinic for him, just the public hospital. It was underfunded, understaffed, and overcrowded.

The paramedics left him sitting in the emergency room amid accident victims, men bloody from brawling, homeless people in distress, and, most memorably, a man who walked in with an ax embedded in his skull. Even the jaded ER staff took notice of that one.

A duty sister cast a disinterested eye over Benny Mongrel's wound, saw that it wasn't life threatening, and told him to wait.

Benny Mongrel waited. He had nothing better to do.

When he'd heard Ishmael Isaacs come pounding up the stairs like Clint Eastwood, his pistol in his hand, he had stopped crying, laid Bessie's head down gently, and stood up. He had wiped the tears from his good eye. Isaacs was on the landing, pistol out in front of him, raking the area like he was auditioning for one of those fucken action movies they showed them in prison.

"They gone," said Benny Mongrel.

Isaacs lowered the pistol, like he was disappointed he couldn't shoot somebody. "What the fuck happened here?" As if whatever shit had gone down had to be Benny Mongrel's fault.

"Two guys came in." Benny Mongrel was pressing his fingers to the wound in his shoulder. It didn't feel too bad. He tried to keep his eyes away from Bessie. He didn't want Isaacs to see him crying.

"Who were they?"

Benny shrugged his good shoulder. "Pair of rubbishes. *Lighties*, little shits. Wanting to steal tools and go score tik, probably."

"You okay?" Isaacs asked grudgingly.

Bennie nodded. "My dog went for them. They plugged her."

Isaacs grunted and gave Bessie a disinterested kick with the toe of his boot. "Saves the vet the work."

That's when Benny Mongrel hit him, a looping left to the nose. Benny wasn't a big man, but there wasn't much you were going to teach him about fighting. He felt the foreman's nose break under his knuckles.

Isaacs's hands flew up to his face, blood dripping between his fingers. "You fucken bastard." This came out muffled. Benny Mongrel kicked him in the balls.

That was when the two cops came in, with their guns out. There was confusion when they came upon the pair of bleeding security men and the dead dog.

It took a bit of explaining. One of them even took notes.

Then the ambulance was there, and they bandaged Benny Mongrel. The paramedic working on Benny Mongrel said he was lucky; the bullet had passed straight through.

The other medic was having a look at Isaacs, told him his nose was broken.

"I fucken know that," said Isaacs, seriously pissed off. Then he looked at Benny Mongrel. "You come pick up your pay next week, Niemand."

"Shove it up your ass," said Benny Mongrel as they walked him out to the ambulance. He had looked back over his shoulder at the dog.

Bye, Bessie.

He didn't want Sniper Security's money or its fucken job. He wanted that fat cop. He was going to cut him open like a pig from his balls to his throat and let his guts fall out, let the fat bastard try to hold himself together while Benny Mongrel watched him die.

They finally got to stitch him. Benny Mongrel was stripped to the waist, his prison tattoos making quite a statement under the harsh hospital fluorescents. The bullet had taken a chunk out of his right shoulder, removed part of his tattooed rank.

The doctor was a young woman, probably just out of medical school. Benny Mongrel made her nervous. Her hands shook, and her stitching wasn't going to win any prizes. She saw him looking down at her handiwork. "It'll look better when it's healed."

He said nothing.

They told Benny Mongrel that they didn't have a bed for him. He could sleep the night on a bench in the emergency room. Maybe they could find him a blanket.

But he was already walking away, out into the early hours of another Cape Town day.

Carmen Fortune stood in the doorway of her apartment and stared at Gatsby, then at the little blond kid lying limp in his arms, tied up like a Christmas turkey. "What in fuck is that?"

"It's a kid. What does it look like?"

Gatsby shouldered her aside and went into the apartment. He threw the boy onto the sofa next to where Uncle Fatty was passed out in his briefs.

"Is it dead?"

"If it was dead, I'd throw it in a fucken ditch. Not bring it here." Gatsby was panting and stinking up the room even more than he usually did.

Carmen closed and locked the front door and went over to the child. A white kid with light hair. Blood clotted on the side of the head. The boy's hands were tied behind his back and his feet were bound. Carmen could see that the circulation was cut off.

The kid was unconscious.

Carmen looked up at Gatsby. "Why you bring him here?"

"You going to look after him for me."

"Like fucken hell!"

"For a day or two."

He pulled out a wad of notes from his waist bag and threw them at her. Carmen caught them with surprising deftness.

She looked at the money hungrily, running a thumb over the notes wrapped in an elastic band. There must have been five hundred there. "I don't want no trouble."

He laughed one of his sucking laughs. "All you people know is fucken trouble. It's in your blood."

He sat down on the arm of the sofa, his arms dangling limply between his legs like he was a big ape. Carmen shoved the money into her bra, circled the sofa warily. "Whose kid is it?"

"You don't need to know. You keep him here, keep him out of sight till tomorrow, maybe day after, I give you another grand."

She stared at him. "Don't talk shit to me."

He wiped a huge hand across his face, moving his pudding-bowl fringe aside. "I'm serious."

"I just got to look after him?"

"That's all. Give him something to eat. Keep him quiet."

"And then?"

"And then I come and get him again. And you can go buy you some tik and have a fucken party."

"Your mother. I don't tik."

Gatsby raised his bulk from the sofa, lifted his shirt, and pulled his jeans down. For a horrible moment she thought he was going to expose himself to her, but he was letting her have a look at the pistol at his waist, surrounded by a mass of mottled pink flesh.

"You be a good little girlie, and you get your grand. You let anybody know this kid is here, and I'll kill you. You get me?" Those dead pig eyes were latched on to her. It made her want to have a bath.

"Ja. I get you."

He dropped the shirt and trudged to the door.

"Hey," she called out to him as he reached for the door handle.

He turned. "What?"

"What's his name?"

"How the fuck must I know?"

"Can I cut him loose? His feet is going blue."

"Do what the fuck you like. Just keep him hidden." And the fat boer was gone, slamming the door after him.

Carmen walked back to the sofa and stood looking at the kid. She reached out a hand, tentatively, and touched his throat. She could feel a pulse, fluttering like a bird. His eyelids flickered but stayed shut.

She pulled the tape from his mouth, then worked the cloth free. He sucked air through his mouth but still didn't regain consciousness. He was a pretty boy, she could see, in his Disney pj's. A soft little whitey whose nice life just went all to shit. Not her fucken problem. To her he was a godsend. A bonus.

She went across to the kitchen and got a knife so she could cut him loose.

Burn sat in front of the TV. Local news. Images of a child's body found in a drain out on the Cape Flats. The child had been raped and murdered.

Burn reached for the remote and changed the channel. MTV. Some writhing Latina singing about love gone bad. Jesus, he wished he was back in the States, where he understood the codes. This fucking country was all about angles that he didn't get. He had the dead gangbanger's pistol next to him. For some reason it made him feel better. Maybe because he knew that if things got too bad he could use it on himself.

He had to believe that his son was still alive. Matt had been taken for a reason. This was about money. About greed. It had to be.

His cell phone rang, and when he saw Mrs. Dollie's name come up on caller ID, he allowed himself to believe, for one split second, that she was calling him from her home, not lying dead near the front door.

He answered the phone.

"Mr. Burn?" The man knew his real name. The voice on the other end, heavy with a guttural local accent, was distorted. As if the caller was talking on speakerphone and had muffled his voice to disguise it.

"Who is this?"

"Never mind. I've got your kid."

"Where is he?"

"The boy is okay. And he will stay that way if you do exactly what I say. Understand?"

"Yes. What you want?"

"I want a million. Cash. By the end of tomorrow."

"I don't have that kind of cash lying around."

"Listen, Burn, fuck with me, and I start cutting off his fingers and stuffing them in your postbox. You get me?"

"I understand. Please, I'll do as you say. Don't hurt my son. I need to transfer money, from offshore. I'm going to need more time."

"How much time?"

"Until the day after tomorrow."

All Burn heard was the wheezing of breath. Then the man spoke. "Okay, but no longer than that. Understood?"

"Yes."

"Now, I know who you are. I know the U.S. Marshals want your ass. So you're not going to do something fucken stupid now, are you? Like go to the cops?"

"No. I won't do that."

"Okay. Because if you do, I'll kill your brat."

"I give you my word."

"Ja, sure." The man laughed. "Now, you get to work on the cash, and you wait for me to contact you, okay?"

"Can I at least speak to my son?"

"Not now. Just get the money."

And the man was gone. At least it was about money. Greed Burn could comprehend; it meant there was still a chance that he was going to get his son back alive.

Something about the voice reminded him of the fat cop. Barnard. It made sense, the man prowling around, showing them photographs. Maybe even lifting Susan's fingerprint. Barnard was foul enough. But Burn couldn't be sure. Still, he felt the urge to do something, to take action. Try to track the fat cop down. Find out if he had taken his son.

He calmed himself. Making those kind of moves would be the quickest way to get Matt killed. Tough as it was, he had to wait. Take it step by step.

Burn crossed the living room, trying not to look at Mrs. Dollie where she lay under a blanket. He went into the spare room, booted up his laptop, and accessed his anonymous Swiss bank account.

The kidnapper wanted one million in South African currency. That was about one hundred and fifty thousand U.S. dollars. Not a lot of money, but double what he had lying in the safe in the bedroom. He completed the transactions, transferring money into two different Cape Town banks. He would attract less attention that way. He logged off and stood up. He needed to do something about Mrs. Dollie.

For the second time that week, Burn had to get rid of the dead.

CHAPTER 19

Disaster Zondi battled his frustration. He prowled the cramped office at Bellwood South HQ, the strip lights buzzing like angry insects. The building was deserted, way after midnight.

The fat man, the very reason for him being in this bloody painted tart of a city, had disappeared. Rudi Barnard, previously so visible, so present with his fat and his stench, so much part of the corner of the Cape Flats he'd made his own, was nowhere to be seen. He never went back to his apartment. He made no contact with those of his informers who could be relied upon to cooperate with the police. Even the woman who supplied him with his junk food had noted with relief that she hadn't seen him.

Gone.

Zondi, via Peterson whom he used like a glove puppet, had mobilized as much manpower as possible to scour the Flats for the rogue cop.
They had come up empty.

Meanwhile Zondi'd had to distract himself by interviewing the
other two bent cops on his list. They were nothing, small-time nobodies
who had their hands in a few pockets. Run-of the-mill. Boring.

His prey was Barnard. And his prey had slipped off the radar.

He knew he had to be patient. Barnard was too used to writing his
own rules; he would screw up, and then they would have him.

Zondi stood at the window staring out at the lights of distant Cape
Town. He fought an urge to go out into the night and prowl for sex; the
more alienated the encounter, the better. Zondi had never married and
had no companion. He had become skillful at fending off the sexual ad-
vances of the female hunter-gatherers of affluent black Johannesburg.
So skillful, in fact, that many thought he was gay.

He wasn't, but he did nothing to contradict the rumor.

Zondi had no use for the comedy of manners that a relationship, or
even an affair, would demand. The mating dance, the shared intimacies,
the endless conversations about careers and status and, God forbid,
where the relationship was going. The idea of waking up with a woman
in his bed, her body slack from sleep and sex, her expensive perfume
mixing with other more pungent smells, frankly revolted him.

Zondi was a hit-and-run man. When he couldn't suppress the urge
any longer, when it became too insistent, he went on the hunt. A pickup
in a bar, or even a street corner—he had no qualms about paying, liked it
in fact—a quick and brutal coupling in the back of his car or an anonymous hotel room and then out of there. Back to his place for a shower, a
thimbleful of Glenmorangie, and, with the smoky tang of the barley and
the peat fire still on his palate, a peaceful sleep alone in his bed, his appetites satiated. For the moment.

But he had made a pact within himself before he left Johannes-burg. No sex, no distractions, until his work in Cape Town was done.

He had to be disciplined.

His cell phone rang. It was the computer technician at the police lab. The man, an Afrikaner barely out of school, surprised Zondi with his efficiency. "Uh, Mr. Zondi, I've traced that IP address, via an ISP in the States."

"In English, please."

"Okay. I tracked back the Yahoo address to a person in the USA."

"Yes. And?"

"He is a deputy U.S. marshal in . . ." The technician paused; Zondi could hear fingers tapping a keyboard. "In Arlington, Virginia."

Now Zondi was interested. "How do you know that?"

"The IP address is registered to the U.S. Marshals' headquarters."

Zondi reached for his notepad. "You have the name of this marshal?"

"Torrance. Dexter Torrance." The technician spelled it for Zondi.

Zondi thanked the technician and killed the call. All thoughts of his howling libido were gone as he sat down in front of Barnard's laptop. It was in sleep mode, and he drew a fingertip across the touchpad, wip-ing his finger on his silk handkerchief in unconscious fear of contami-nation.

The image of the fingerprint faded up onto the screen. Why had Barnard sent it to a deputy U.S. marshal in the States? And who the hell did it belong to? The first question might take some time to answer. The answer to the second question was within his grasp.

His own slimline laptop chimed the arrival of an e-mail. It was from his commanding officer, Archibald Mathebula. His boss had called in a favor and acquired an encrypted password for Zondi, a password that allowed him to access the FBI fingerprint database.

Burn slowed the Jeep and eased it into a parking spot between streetlights. He switched off the interior light of the car before he opened the door. He stood a moment in the quiet street of houses much like the one he rented, watching and listening. It was after 2:00 a.m., and the world was asleep. Aside from a dog barking in the distance and a car whining up an incline blocks away, all was quiet.

Burn walked around the Jeep and came to a steep flight of steps that connected the road he was on to the one below. They were a feature of this suburb built on the precipitous slope. The steps were used by joggers and dog walkers and domestic workers taking a short cut down to High Level Road and the minibus taxis. They were also used by homeless people as a place to sleep. Burn walked halfway down the steps. He saw no dispossessed bundle of humanity.

He went back to the car, looked around once more to make sure he was alone and unobserved before he opened the rear door of the Jeep. Mrs. Dollie lay in the same spot he had stowed the last two corpses. She was wrapped in a blanket. He bent down and lifted her. She was small and thin, easy to carry.

Burn hurried down the stairs. He lowered her gently to the concrete steps and unwrapped her from the blanket. Enough streetlight reached him to see the look of terror on her face. For a moment he felt he couldn't do this, leave this decent woman who had treated his son so tenderly lying like refuse dumped on the steps. Then Burn took the blanket and went back to his car. He checked once more that he hadn't been observed and drove away.

He knew that when the body was found on the stairs in the morning, it would be called a mugging. When the police came, he would add substance to that fiction, tell them that she had left his house at around seven, refusing his offer of a ride, saying that she enjoyed the walk down to the taxi. That it did her good, the bit of exercise. It would be easy enough to reproduce the dialogue that had passed between them many times before.

As he pulled the car into his garage, Burn felt sick. Because of him Mrs. Dollie had unwittingly been drawn into something that had taken her life. He had met her husband, a timid and self-effacing man who could not be persuaded to call him anything other than *Mr. Jack*. He'd also met her daughter, Leila, a young woman in her twenties who was pursuing a career in business, the product of her parents' years of self-less dedication.

Burn knew he couldn't afford the luxury of guilt. He had to keep one thing, and one thing alone, on his mind.

Matt.

Carmen Fortune woke in the morning with the tik craving chewing at her nerve ends. Fuck, she had to score. Then she remembered the white kid, her little present from God. She sat up, the greasy sheet falling from her naked breasts. Where was he?

The night before, she had put him in the bed next to her and locked the bedroom door from the inside. He hadn't woken when she had released his hands and feet. He probably had a concussion. She had made a token effort of cleaning the blood from his blond hair. The hair was so fine and soft under her fingers, not like her Sheldon's, which had grown out hard and wiry, like steel wool.

She saw the boy sitting on the dirty linoleum in his pj's, staring vacantly into space, sucking on his thumb. He didn't look at her when she got out of bed and crossed to the closet, pulling a T-shirt over her nakedness.

She crouched in front of him. "Hey," she said.

He didn't react. She saw that he was sitting in a pool of piss. Jesus, was it her curse to be surrounded by men who couldn't control their fucken waterworks?

She shook him by the shoulder. "Hey, little guy."

Slowly, his eyes tracked up to her face. Carmen, even in her state of low-grade tik withdrawal, could see they were beautiful eyes. Blue, with something almost like purple in them. Like her week-old bruises from Rikki.

"How's your head?" She reached out and parted his hair to see if the cut was healing. The boy flinched and pulled away.

He took the thumb from his mouth and spoke for the first time. "I want my mommy."

The accent was American, like one of those smart-ass kids on the sitcoms. It made Carmen want to laugh. Was this for real? "You'll see your mommy later, okay?"

The kid was starting to cry, the mouth quivering and those beautiful eyes tearing up. Jesus, she wouldn't be able to deal with a bawling brat right now.

She stood and held out her hand. "Come, let's go get you some food." The kid just looked at her. "You wanna watch the TV?" No reaction.

She grabbed hold of his hand and hauled him to his feet. He wobbled a little, then found his balance, pulling his hand away. "What's you name anyways?"

"Matt."

"Okay, Matt. You can call me . . ." She stopped. She couldn't very well tell the kid her real name, could she? "Call me Jenny." Like J. Lo's "Jenny from the Block." Still one of Carmen's favorite songs.

"Are you Leila's friend?" He was looking up at her, desperate to make some sense of what was happening to him.

Who the fuck was Leila? Some Muslim chickie who looked after him, maybe. "Ja, sure. Me and Leila is tight. She tole me to look after you, okay?"

He nodded. When she held out her hand, he took it this time, and she unlocked the door and walked him through to the kitchen.

Uncle Fatty sat on the sofa, just woken up. His hands shook as he tried in vain to squeeze a drop of wine out of an empty foil bag. Then he saw the white kid, and his face looked like he was sure he was having hallucinations.

"You just shut up about this, okay?" she said, pointing at the boy. "I'm gonna go now and get you a wine."

Uncle Fatty nodded, licked his dry and scummy lips. Carmen knew how he felt. She was going to take some of Gatsby's money and go and score a globe. Then Uncle Fatty could get pissed, and she could get high, while the American kid watched cartoons.

Life on the Flats.

⌐

Burn found himself sitting in Matt's bedroom, on the bunk bed with the brightly colored duvet. A Dr. Seuss book lay on the carpet. *The Cat in the Hat*. Burn picked it up, leafed through it, each page imprinted on his memory from the endless nights he had read it to his son. He put the book down.

Was his son still alive?

Burn pushed these thoughts from his mind, went to the landline in the living room, and called the clinic. He finally managed to talk to the nursing sister from the night before—was it only the night before?—who told him Susan's procedure had been postponed by a day. It would happen tomorrow; her doctor was delayed at a conference in Johannesburg. This suited Burn. The longer Susan stayed away from the house, the better.

His cell phone rang. He snatched at it. "Yes?"

A young woman spoke, vaguely familiar. "Mr. Hill?" Definitely not the kidnapper.

"Yes. Can I help you?"

"This is Leila. Leila Dollie."

Oh, Jesus, Mrs. Dollie's daughter. Burn shifted gear, suppressing the feeling of guilt that almost paralyzed him, ready to lie. "Yes, hi, Leila. What can I do for you?"

"Is my mom maybe there?"

"No, she left here last night. At around seven, seven thirty."

There was a pause. A worried one. "I see. I thought she was staying the night at your house."

"No, I think that had been the plan, because Susan had to go off to the clinic. But then I was back early, and your mother preferred to get on home."

"Really? Now I'm very worried. How was she getting home?"

Burn spun his story about the ride he offered being rejected, Mrs. Dollie's determination to get a bit of exercise.

The young woman was battling to control her anxiety. "Ja, that sounds like my mom. Okay, I better go. I think I'm going to check with the police, the hospitals."

"Is there anything I can do, Leila?" Like maybe tell you that I dumped your mother's body on the stairs above High Level Road?

"No, no, thank you Mr. Hill."

"If you need anything at all, please let me know, okay?"

"Thank you. Okay."

Leila was gone. About to face her worst nightmare.

It started as a whisper on the streets. Gatsby was a wanted man. There was a warrant out for him. There was even a price on his head. He had killed a kid, Ronnie September from Tulip Street in Paradise Park. Shot him and burned him with two other men. And now the cops were after Gatsby, hunting one of their own on the streets of the Flats.

The wiser heads shook when they heard this. No way. This had to be a lie. Gatsby had ruled his patch with an iron fist for what? Fifteen years? Seventeen years? He had more blood on his hands than a halal butcher, and no voice of protest had ever come from the law.

The foolish who had attempted to accuse him in the past were found in ditches with the backs of their heads blown away. Executed. A message from the fat man. Fuck with me and this is what you get. So why should now be any different?

There were whispers about some darky, a tall man in a black suit, come all the way from Jo'burg to take Gatsby down. That the big guys up-country couldn't trust the cops in the Cape to deal with him. Some people swore they saw this darky sitting in the back of a cop car as it made the rounds of the Flats, trying to get mouths to talk.

At first, few had.

Then one or two, brave, foolhardy, or greedy, had spoken a little of what they knew. The local cops, brown men, had asked the questions. The darky had just stood and listened, eyes hidden behind his shades, absorbing what was said like he was made of black blotting paper.

So, slowly, the unbelievable became the believable.

Gatsby was a marked man.

〜

After they put her son in the ground, Berenice September's neighbors gathered at her house. The women and the girls were inside, serving cake and tea.

Donovan September stood in the cramped backyard with the men and the boys. The group spoke in low tones, each man and boy swearing to Donovan that they would get their hands on the human filth that did this to his little brother. And they would send the fat boer to hell.

Berenice stood at the kitchen window, filling the kettle at the sink, looking out at her son standing with the men. Donovan caught her eye, and then he looked away from her.

Oh, God, please let this thing end.

CHAPTER 20

Another hotel room.

This one was in Retreat, the ass end of Cape Town. A run-down area Rudi Barnard was unfamiliar with, far away from his turf. The irony of the name wasn't lost on him. He hated going into hiding. Not his way of doing things. Not at all. He lay on the bed, sweat running off his naked chest. There was no aircon in the room, just a desk fan that stirred the thick air, shifted it around, but didn't make it any fucken cooler.

He reached for his cell phone and thumbed a number. Time to check up on the half-breed bitch and the boy. When he got the automated female voice telling him the number wasn't available on the network, he nearly threw the phone at the flipping wall. The bitch hadn't bought herself airtime, probably spent the money he gave her on tik.

Fuck.

He had to restrain himself from going down to the Ford and driving across to the bitch's hovel, giving her a few smacks. No, that was just the kind of mistake that would screw up everything. They were out there, Zondi and his trained monkey Peterson, waiting for him to do something stupid. Tough as it was, he had to stay patient. At least until it got dark.

The promise of more money would keep the little whore from doing anything clever. Keep her in line until it was time to kill her.

And the kid.

He found a Gideon's Bible next to the bed and opened it. Maybe if he read some Old Testament, he'd feel soothed. He was disgusted to see that most of the pages had been ripped out, probably used by some fucken heathens to roll joints.

He shoved the Bible back in the drawer, heaved himself from the bed, and walked to the window. The room overlooked a courtyard full of garbage cans and junk. A scrawny homeless woman in a torn dress and unlaced running shoes, a baby strapped to her back, was going through the garbage. A ragged man stood behind her, swaying on his feet as he watched her digging in the bins.

The man said something that Barnard couldn't catch. The woman swung on him, hands still in the can. Her voice was shrill, hard from years of living on the street. "Your mother's cunt!"

The man mumbled something. The woman found a couple of empties and turned to walk away. The man grabbed at the bottles. The woman evaded his flailing hands and swung one of the bottles, hard, smashing it against his head. The man slumped, blood flowing down his face.

The woman threw the broken neck of the bottle at him. "Now look what you make me do, you fucken rubbish!"

She walked away clutching the remaining bottle, still hurling abuse at him over her shoulder. She had the disjointed, crablike walk that came from years of frying your brain cells with cheap booze. The man was on his hands and knees, shaking his head, drops of blood landing vividly on the cement.

Barnard turned away and walked his gut directly in the path of the fan. It stirred the pelt of gingery fuzz that covered his belly like a worn carpet but didn't cool him at all.

Ja, relationships. Marriage, whatever. It never fucken worked. Not if you were a homeless half-breed or whoever the fuck you were.

His had lasted a year.

He had met his wife at the Army of God Church, the run-down Pentecostal congregation in Goodwood led by Pastor Lombard. When the pastor was jailed as a pedophile, the congregation fell apart and Rudi Barnard had communed with God alone, in the privacy of his own home.

Well, not quite alone. He had met Sanmarie Botha at church. Amazingly, Sanmarie, though not blessed with a powerful intellect, was extremely good-looking in a blonde, corn-fed way. Even more amazingly, she took it upon herself to fall in love with Rudi Barnard. Barnard didn't question why a pneumatic blonde would fall for an aging, stinking, obese wreck like him. He presumed he reminded her of her father. She cooked the cholesterol-intensive food he loved, she washed his clothes, and her sexual demands weren't beyond his limited capacity.

They were engaged and then married. Barnard would spend his days terrorizing and murdering and then come home to a hot meal, a few hours in front of the TV with his wife, and then the dubious comfort of the marital bed. *Happiness* would be too strong a word to describe this period of his life, but he knew a kind of contentment.

But then Sanmarie joined the Living Joy of God Congregation in Monte Vista. A new church, with a young pastor, all teeth and blow-dried hair. She tried to persuade Barnard to worship with her, but the multiracial congregation and the watered-down brand of Christianity peddled by Pastor Marius left Barnard cold.

As Sanmarie spent more time at church, he spent more time eating gatsbys from the Golden Spoon. Sanmarie's sexual demands had ceased entirely. When she left him for Pastor Marius, Barnard had briefly considered some fitting form of biblical wrath to rain down on their heads, then had decided he couldn't be bothered.

A man alone made the perfect soldier in God's war.

He went back to the bed and got the dead woman's phone out of his waist bag and switched it on. He thumbed through her contact list, then hit a number.

The American answered immediately. Eager, anxious. "Yes?"

"How's it going with the money?" Barnard used the speakerphone, intentionally making his voice even harsher than it normally was. Dropping it a register.

"It will all be in place by lunchtime tomorrow."

"Fine. And you're keeping your trap shut?"

"Yes. As I promised. How is my son?"

"He's fine."

"I want to speak to him."

"No. Not now."

"Then how do I know if he's still alive?" The American was trying to sound tough, in control. But Barnard could hear the panic just beneath the surface.

"Just take my word for it, he's okay. And he'll stay that way if you don't screw up." Barnard killed the call.

He sat on the bed, elbows on his knees, arms dangling, drops of sweat plopping onto the wooden floor. Then he decided he was hungry.

There was a Kentucky Fried across the way. A barrel of wings and a Colonel Burger.

It wasn't a gatsby but it would have to do.

Benny Mongrel lay on the mattress in his shack, his shirt off, his right arm still in the sling. The bandage on his shoulder was spotted with blood. He stared at the tin roof and let the index finger of his left hand trace the crude lettering carved into his chest: I DIG MY GRAVE, I CRY FOR BLOOD.

The promise he had made to himself, the one about going straight, was forgotten. He was going to kill that fat cop. Finished. And he didn't care what they did with him after. They could send him back to Pollsmoor and let him rot.

He didn't give a fuck.

He had lost two things the night before: his dog and his knife. He regretted having to leave the knife behind; it was a good one. But he had another almost as good. Bessie wasn't something he could ever replace. When she died, so did the tiny voice of hope and faith that had unexpectedly spoken from his heart. Now his heart was cold. Now he was a Mongrel again.

He sat up and unslung his arm. As he moved the shoulder, he winced, but only slightly. Pain had been part of Benny Mongrel's life since birth. He knew how to shut it out. He moved the arm some more; then he took the sling off and threw it on the dirt floor.

He'd keep the bandage on, unless it got in his way.

He reached under the mattress and found his other knife and the sandpaper. He opened the knife and began his ritual of honing the blade. With each swipe of the sandpaper, he visualized the innards of the fat cop spilling out like trash from a dumpster.

Barnard. The name carried on the wind when he had buzzed the American's door.

Benny Mongrel didn't know where to find him. But he knew men who would, the men he had deliberately avoided since he had come out of jail. The older men who wore the same tattoos he did, who hung out in taverns and cramped houses in Lotus River. They would tell him what he needed to know.

Then he would go back to Mountain Road, to the house of the American guy. Tell him what he saw the night the fat cop dumped the kid in the trunk of the car. Tell him that he would help to track the fat man down and find the boy. He had no interest in the child. Didn't care if it lived or died. It was a means to an end. Nothing more.

The American would lead him to the fat cop. And if the American outlived his usefulness, Benny Mongrel would kill him too.

He knew how to kill Americans.

＞

Burn eyed the bottle of Scotch. It was only lunchtime, but surely he could allow himself one drink, just to steady his nerves? Then he took the bottle from the counter in the kitchen, put it in a drawer, and shut it away.

He couldn't trust himself to keep it at one drink.

He went and flopped down in front of the TV, cricket on the screen. The game made no sense to him. It seemed to be played over days, men in white endlessly bowling balls that were bumped back at them by helmeted batsmen.

He hated this passivity. Sitting and waiting, leaving the play in the hands of the kidnapper, was driving him crazy. All his training, those years in the marines, prompted him to action. Take the gun. Get out there. Find his son.

He played the man's voice over again in his head. Harsh and guttural. He tried to recall the voice of the fat cop, Barnard. Was it him? It made sense, but Burn was no closer to being sure.

The buzzer dragged him to the screen of the intercom. Two uniformed cops stood at the gate, a man and a woman.

Here we go again.

Burn lifted the intercom phone, and within seconds the cops were standing in his living room. The man was white, the woman brown. They both wore blue uniforms, black boots, and Kevlar vests. Must be hell in this weather. They introduced themselves, local names that slid through Burn's memory like water through a sieve.

A woman's body had been found that morning, on the steps above High Level. The victim's daughter had identified the body as that of her mother, Mrs. Adielah Dollie. The daughter said that her mother had left here the night before, walking to a taxi.

Adielah. Burn hadn't known her by anything other than Mrs. Dollie.

Burn feigned shock, even had to sit down. It wasn't hard, the way he felt. "My God, this is terrible. What happened to her?"

The man did most of the talking. "Her, ah, neck was broken. Either somebody did it, hit her, or she fell trying to get away. It was a mugging, we think. Those stairs are dangerous. There have been a lot of incidents."

Burn nodded. "I feel so guilty. I should have insisted on taking her home."

"Mr. Hill, could we see some ID, please?"

Burn went into the bedroom and returned with his John Hill passport. The cop looked at it, then wrote down the number before handing it back to Burn.

"Is there a problem?" he asked as he pocketed it.

"No, just routine. We'll type up your statement. Maybe you can go down to Sea Point police station in the next day or so to sign it?"

Burn nodded. "Of course."

Then they were gone. It had worked. Very little energy was going to be spent on finding Mrs. Dollie's killer.

Llewellyn Hector caressed the racing pigeon sitting in his cupped hand. Hector gently set the bird on a perch in a wire cage. It was night, and a dangling lightbulb cast shadows across the cramped backyard of the Lotus River house. Hector engaged the latch on the cage and turned. That's when he saw Benny Mongrel. Hector was too hard a man to let emotion reach his face, but Benny Mongrel saw in the moment of hesitation before he spoke that the gangster was surprised.

"Hey, brother. Where you come out of?" He walked across to Benny Mongrel. Hector was a squat man, almost as wide as he was tall. His large head balanced directly on his sloping shoulders, like a boulder on a hill, and his muscled arms, seething with tattoos, were unnaturally short. He extended his hand for the insider's shake.

Benny Mongrel took the hand and shook it. "I been here and there."

"But you haven't come and see us?"

Benny Mongrel shook his head.

"Come inside, brother."

Benny Mongrel followed Hector into the tavern that was home to the Mongrels. Hector was a few years older than Benny Mongrel. They had known each other since they were teenagers, had killed many men together, and had spent decades sharing a prison cell. Hector had been out a few years longer than Benny Mongrel, and he was a general, a middleman in the organization. He mobilized members in times of gang conflicts and ran gang-related business interests. Fencing stolen goods and selling drugs.

The tavern was not a place you ventured into unless you were a Mongrel or under their protection. It occupied the front room of a small house, crammed with tables and game machines. The room was full of youngsters, some still teenagers, the cannon fodder of the gang.

Hector led Benny Mongrel through to a private table, where a man in his late thirties sat. Rufus Jordaan. He was a middle-rank enforcer and bodyguard. Hector pulled up a chair and motioned Benny Mongrel to sit. "Look what the wind blew in."

Benny Mongrel had no sooner sat down than a bottle of whiskey and three glasses were delivered by a teenage girl in tight jeans. Hector poured and lifted his glass. Benny Mongrel joined him. Rufus Jordaan didn't.

Hector led the toast. "No excuses, no explanations, no apologies, not to anyone, not ever."

Rufus muttered his assent. Benny Mongrel said nothing. Rufus pushed the whiskey aside and reached for a beer bottle. He made a show of knocking off the cap of the bottle with the sight of his .38 Special. He left the gun lying on the table.

"So," Rufus said, sucking on the beer, "why you been a stranger, brother? We not good enough?" He was a big man who wore his 28s tattoos with pride.

Benny Mongrel just gave him that flat look that he'd perfected in prison. The look that said: *Here I am. I'm not going anywhere. Do what the fuck you like.* Rufus hid behind a shit-eating grin like Benny Mongrel knew he would.

Rufus raised his bottle. "Anyways, welcome home, brother."

Benny Mongrel spoke to Hector. "I need to know about a fat cop called Barnard."

Rufus leaned forward. "Gatsby?" Benny Mongrel shrugged, fixed his good eye on Rufus. "Big fat boer with a mustache? Stinks like shit?" Benny Mongrel nodded. "What you want with him?"

"We got some business."

Hector swallowed some whiskey, wiped the back of his mouth with his hand. "He mainly works Paradise Park. He's in with the Americans there from back in apartheid days, early nineties."

"Where's he based?"

"Bellwood South. He's a bad bastard. Killed more brown men than the HIV. They say he's a reborn."

Rufus laughed. "He do it for Jesus."

Hector topped up Benny Mongrel's glass. "I hear there's a warrant out on Gatsby. Seems like he went too far this time, killed a kid."

Benny Mongrel sat forward. "White kid?"

Hector shook his head. "No, colored. Over in Paradise. The cops is all over the Flats asking questions. You not the only one who want to find him. He's a popular guy."

This was making sense to Benny Mongrel. Why the fat cop was taking the chances he was taking. He had his back to the wall. Good. Benny Mongrel liked that.

Something changed on Llewellyn Hector's face as he looked over Benny Mongrel's shoulder. Benny Mongrel took a sip of whiskey, felt it burn its way down, and then he turned. And saw Fingers Morkel, the man he had operated on in the jail cell a year before.

Fingers stood in the doorway of the tavern, staring at Benny Mongrel. He looked as if he was reliving the agony of the amputation. Benny Mongrel showed nothing on his face, turned back to Hector and Rufus Jordaan.

Hector rolled the liquor around on his tongue. "You need to watch yourself."

"I can handle Barnard."

Hector shook his head. "Not that fat fuck. Him. Fingers."

Benny Mongrel allowed a smile to touch his mouth. "That piece of shit?"

"He's got power out here. His drugs bring in a lot of bucks."

Benny Mongrel shrugged. "He stole from me. He was punish."

Rufus Jordaan chugged back some of his beer. "Says you didn't go to the Men in the Clouds before you chop him."

The Men in the Clouds, the old-timers, usually lifers, who made the law in prison. They mediated in disputes and decided on punishment.

"I didn't need to waste their time." Benny Mongrel looked back over his shoulder. Fingers was sitting at a table near the door, never taking his eyes off Benny Mongrel. He kept his hands on the table, the stumps of the fingers scarred from the hot plate, the thumbs moving nervously on the wood.

Benny Mongrel felt nothing. "Useless cunt is lucky I didn't kill him."

Rufus Jordaan looked on as if the whole thing amused the hell out of him.

Benny Mongrel stood. So did Hector. "His guys won't touch you in here, but outside is another story. He want your blood."

Hector called a boy over, a pimply kid with a desperate attempt at a mustache. Handed him a set of car keys. "Ashraf, take Benny Mongrel where he want to go."

Benny Mongrel shook his head. "I make my own way."

"Just take the ride, okay? I don't want no mess out on my street. It's been nice and quiet lately."

Benny Mongrel shrugged, and the kid went off to get the car. Hector put out his hand, and they exchanged the shake. "Good luck, brother."

Benny Mongrel headed for the door, the young punks getting out of his way. People still knew who he was. He passed Fingers, didn't even look the way of the useless piece of shit. As he reached the door he felt the nudge of a thumb in his ribs.

He turned to look Fingers in the eye. "You know I can't do anything to you here, you cunt." Benny Mongrel stared him down. "But I'll see you again, soon. And I'll fucken kill you." Fingers nudged him again with his thumb.

Benny Mongrel grabbed the thumb and bent it back, saw the pain in the amputee's eyes. "Bring your mother. Save me the trouble of sending you to her."

CHAPTER 21

It was past 2:00 a.m. and Barnard couldn't sleep. He had tried the half-breed bitch every hour, and he still couldn't reach her. Number not available. It was stressing him big time. What if she had sold him out? What if every second that ticked by brought him closer to a trap?

He sat up, wearing only his briefs. He wheezed into the hotel bathroom, drilled a stream of piss into the toilet bowl, and washed his face at the stained basin. The water was tepid, and when he made the mistake of drinking some out of his cupped hand, he spit it right out.

He went back into the airless bedroom and stood by the window, trying to catch a breeze. Nothing. The hotel made its money out of a hookers' bar on the ground level, and darky music beat up through the floorboards.

To calm himself, Barnard thought of the million that would be his tomorrow and the new life it was going to bring him. He was going to leave Cape Town and its seething, Godless hordes and head up the east coast, with a new name and a new identity. One of his old connections from the Security Police days, the only one he stayed in touch with, ran a sport fishing boat out of St. Lucia, north of Durban. There was an open invitation for Barnard to come up and join him. It was time. Now all he needed to do was get his hands on the money.

He grabbed his phone from next to the bed and thumbed the bitch's number. Not available. Fuck that.

In minutes he was dressed, packing his armaments in the kit bag and getting the hell out of there. He knew it was a risk, crossing the Flats to Paradise Park. But it was late at night, and he had to find out what was going on.

He shoved the .38 into its holster and headed for the door.

Carmen watched as Leroy brought the match to the bottom of the globe. The tik started to cook, and smoke swirled inside the glass, turning the globe opaque.

She put her mouth to the empty neck of the globe and sucked the tik deep into her chest. The rush hit her, that feeling that was better than anything she'd ever known, and she lay back on her bed, head pumping like it was gonna burst. But in a good way. She felt bright and shiny, all the shit in her life blown away by the smoke.

Leroy grabbed the globe from her and took a hit. A slow smile glazed his face as he exhaled a plume up to the ceiling. "Ja. This is the thing, huh?" He was a real Cape Flats' Romeo, with his designer labels, his gelled hair, and his muscular arms covered in 28s tattoos. He thought he was God's gift to massage parlors.

Carmen closed her eyes. She was wearing a halter top and a short skirt. The way she lay left her thighs exposed, and she opened her eyes to see Leroy admiring the view. She brought her legs together and sat up, slapping him on the shoulder. "Hey. I'm a married woman."

Leroy handed her the globe to finish. "Where is he anyway? Rikki."

She exhaled, shrugging. "Up the coast. Who the fuck knows?"

"He catch me here, and I'm dead." Leroy reached across and grabbed her leg above the knee.

She swiped his hand away. "Hey, stop it." She stood up. "Don't worry, he's not coming back in a hurry."

The only reason she could have Leroy here was because she knew that Rikki had been burned crispier than a McNugget. Leroy was a Mongrel, a 28, the sworn enemy of Rikki and the Americans. But, hey, he scored some sweet tik. And he was prepared to play Mr. Delivery. She knew it was only because he wanted to screw her, but so what? Let him dream on.

She went to the window, her head still spinning from the rush. She looked out over night on the Flats. It came to her that she had never been farther from here than into downtown Cape Town once, when she was a small child, to see the Christmas lights. She had lived within a couple of blocks of here her whole life, and she would die here, probably.

She made an effort to shake these thoughts and turned to Leroy. He was heading into the bathroom, and before she could stop him he opened the door. Enough light spilled in from the bedroom for him to see the American kid sleeping on a blanket on the bathroom floor.

The kid had been a pain in the ass the whole day. Weeping and snotty, wanting his mommy. By the time night came, Carmen was sick of it. She'd slipped him half a downer in a glass of warm milk, and he'd gone to sleep almost immediately.

Leroy was staring down at the blond hair. "Who the fuck's kid is this?"

Carmen pushed his hand away from the door and closed it. "I'm babysitting."

"I need to take a piss."

"Then piss in the kitchen sink."

He stared at her. "That's a white kid, hey?"

She shook her head. "No ways. He belongs to my girlfriend."

"Bullshit."

"True. The father was something off a boat."

"Looks white to me."

"Ja and what? Are you suddenly some fucken expert?" She gave him a shove toward the front door. She'd had enough of his nonsense. "Time for you to go."

"I want something first."

He slipped a hand under her skirt and grabbed her between the legs. Cape Flats foreplay. Carmen didn't slap; she punched. She punched hard for a girl, putting her weight behind the blow, so when her fist caught Leroy in the ribs he felt it. And he definitely felt her knee in his balls. He grabbed himself, sucking air. She had taken that shit from Rikki because he was the father of her child, but no other man was going to put his hands on her.

"Come. Move." She pushed him toward the living room.

Leroy wasn't about to make a scene here in the middle of Americans territory. He slunk to the door like a wounded dog, past Uncle Fatty snoring and farting on the sofa. She opened the door and Leroy went out.

"I wouldn't put my dick in that dirty thing of yours anyways."

"Ja, rather go put it in your mother."

With the pleasantries over, she slammed the door. What had happened pissed her off. Not the crude attempt at sex, but the fact that she'd got rid of him before she could buy another globe off him.

Fuck it. She'd be okay till morning.

Leroy sat slumped in his pimped Honda, staring out at the dark ghetto block. Fucken bitch. He had a good mind to go back and teach her a lesson. What the fuck was going on in there, anyways? With that white kid?

While he pondered these confusing elements, his fingers were busy preparing another globe. A car's headlights raked the front of the block, illuminating the words *thug life* daubed in white paint. Leroy ducked down even lower when he saw the Ford come to a halt. He knew Rikki drove that red BMW, but still. He was in enemy territory.

He saw a big guy get out of the car. He was wearing a jacket and had a peaked cap pulled over his face, carried a kit bag. The guy walked across to the stairs Leroy had just come down. One light still burned on the stairs, and Leroy realized he was watching Gatsby walking up to the landing.

Leroy laughed to himself. The moment he saw that white kid, he reckoned something was up. Now he knew. Fucken Gatsby. Leroy had heard there was a warrant out on the fat boer, but there was no way he was going to share his news with the cops.

He also knew that some old-school gangster, Benny Mongrel, had been in Lotus River asking around about Gatsby. And that Fingers Morkel was hot to find Benny Mongrel, wanting revenge. If Gatsby was here, maybe Benny Mongrel would follow.

Leroy was only too happy to score points with the man with no fingers. In the Byzantine world of Cape Flats gangster politics, he was a powerful ally. Leroy reached for his cell phone and dialed. He got voice mail and left a brief, not altogether lucid message, telling Fingers what he had seen.

Then he made the mistake of striking a match and bringing it to the globe.

Barnard was on the landing, catching his breath, when he saw the match flare in the Honda. Instinct took over, and he ducked into the shadows, moved across to the fire escape, and humped his bulk back down to ground level. He stayed in the shadows, coming up behind the car.

He saw the driver slouched behind the wheel, and from the glow he knew he was smoking tik. Barnard couldn't run the risk that the man had seen him. He knew that shooting him would be too noisy. Even on the Flats a gunshot wouldn't go unremarked. Barnard was walking across uneven, broken pavement. He set the kit bag down, bent and grabbed a chunk of cement, and headed for the Honda.

The half-breed heard him, dropped the globe, and looked up with a stupid expression on his face, smoke escaping from his open mouth. Barnard reached in through the open window and smashed the cement down on the half-breed's head, stunning him. Barnard opened the car door and hauled him out onto the street. Then he finished the job, pulping the half-breed's head with the cement, till it looked like roadkill on the blacktop.

Then he pulled the keys from the car's ignition and went to the rear and popped the trunk. He hauled the half-breed around the back of the car and dumped him into the trunk. He threw the car keys in after him, slammed the lid, and made sure it was locked. He looked around. All was quiet.

Time to go and check on the bitch and the American kid.

CHAPTER 22

When the half-breed finally opened the door, Barnard grabbed her by the throat and walked her backward into the room. He kicked the door shut behind him as he pushed her into a kneeling position on the floor. In the same motion he produced the .38 from its holster and shoved it into her mouth, grabbing a fistful of her kinky hair with his left hand. By tilting the gun barrel, he forced her to look up into his eyes.

"Okay. Listen to me and listen careful. When I take this gun out your mouth, I'm gonna ask you a question. And you not gonna lie. Understood?"

She nodded, choking on the gun. He slid the barrel from her mouth and she coughed.

"Who was that fucker who was here now?"

She shook her head. "There was nobody here."

He took his arm back and hit her with the barrel. The sight dug deep into her cheekbone, and blood sprang, a red ribbon against her sallow face. She moaned and brought a hand to her cheek, trying to stem the blood that flowed between her fingers.

"There was one light on in the building when he came out. Yours. I'm only gonna ask you one more time. Who was he?"

"My dealer."

"Did he see the kid?"

She was about to lie. He knew it and took his gun hand back, ready to hit her again. He saw the truth come into her eyes. "Ja. He seen him."

"What did you tell him?"

"That it's my friend's kid."

"A white kid?"

"I tole him that the daddy was a sailor."

"He buy that?"

"Ja. I think so."

"Anybody else see him?"

She shook her head. He believed her. He lowered the gun. "Where's the kid?"

"In the bathroom."

He banged past the old alkie, who snored on the sofa, dead to the world, and opened the bathroom door. The kid lay next to the filthy shit pot, so still he looked dead. Barnard lowered himself down and prodded a sausagelike finger into the kid's neck. He could feel a pulse. The kid didn't stir.

Barnard went back through to the other room and found the half-breed at the kitchen sink, holding a wet cloth against her face. The cloth was already turning pink.

"You give him something to make him sleep?"

She nodded. "Half a Mogadon."

"And what if you'd fucken killed him?"

She stared at him, the blood seeping through the cloth. "You gonna kill him anyways, aren't you?"

"What makes you say that?"

She shrugged. Blood dripped through the cloth.

Then he came at her. She shrunk back against the sink, but he surprised her by putting his thumb against the cloth where the cut was, applying pressure. He held it there for nearly a minute, staring at her, his rotten breath rolling over her like the fumes from a septic tank.

"I'm gonna stay here tonight."

"You can't sleep with me!"

"You'd be so fucken lucky." He laughed and released the grip on her face. The pressure had slowed the flow of blood.

Barnard turned and walked over to a threadbare chair, dragged it so that its back was to the wall and it faced the front door. He sat, his fat overflowing the arms of the chair, and unzipped the kit bag. He unwrapped the towel and rested the Mossberg 500 on his lap.

He looked at the door, not at her, when he spoke. "I won't be sleeping. I'll be sitting here waiting for somebody to come through that fucken door."

$$\longrightarrow$$

The helicopters woke Burn again. This time he knew exactly where he was. And where he was made Desert Storm look easy. There had been rules of a sort in that war, if you were an American, that is. You took orders, you moved forward, and you killed people. At night you pissed into your ration pack to get the heater going and ate a turkey dinner while the smoke from the blazing oil fields wrapped you like a blanket.

But now, in Cape Town, the rule book had been lost. Or maybe never written.

Burn looked at his watch, just gone six a.m. His head was thick from the Scotch that had sent him to sleep. Reaching for his phone, he thumbed Mrs. Dollie's number. He heard her voice, self-conscious, uncomfortable with technology, saying that he should leave a message. He killed the call, fighting his guilt at her death. And the terror that the kidnapper had already killed Matt.

Mrs. Dollie's daughter, Leila, had called him again the night before. Her voice had been thick with grief, but she was composed and polite. She accepted his condolences gracefully, then asked him to come to the funeral. Mrs. Dollie was Muslim, and according to Muslim rites she had to be buried as soon as possible. The police had completed an autopsy and released the body to the family for burial. Burn had heard himself saying that of course he would be there.

That was today, later in the afternoon.

He dragged himself from the bed and into the shower, alternating hot and cold to smash himself into some form of alertness. He shaved and combed his hair, dressed in the casually expensive clothes appropriate to the morning's banking.

He looked at his face in the mirror and remembered that he was going to be a father again that day.

Barnard woke to the sound of somebody at the door. Fuck it, he hadn't meant to sleep. He battled his way out of the chair, leveling the shotgun, then realized that he'd heard voices of men in the corridor, early morning workers on their way to the taxi stand. It was light already. He'd meant to get away in the dark.

He looked across at the old drunk, who lay on his back, his mouth gaping, dentures slipped off his gums. The blanket had fallen from the sofa and showed his emaciated body, naked except for the filthy under-pants. Barnard saw that the old alky had a hard-on, bulging out the front of his briefs like a tent pole. At his fucken age.

Barnard lifted the blanket with his foot and dumped it over the old man's balls; then he walked across to the window. The glass was cracked and taped up. Barnard eased back the greasy lace curtain and peered down into the street. His Ford was there, and so was the Honda. From where he stood he couldn't see the blood of the fucker whose brains he'd pulped, but he knew that sooner or later it would be noticed. He had to get out of there.

He bent over the sink and splashed his face, resting the Mossberg 500 on a pile of dirty plates. He wiped his face with his hand, not trust-ing one of the soiled dish towels. Grabbing the shotgun, he lumbered into the bedroom.

The half-breed bitch was asleep, covered by a gray sheet. He could see her naked shoulders, the swell of a breast, the kinky hair squashed against the pillow. He stood over her, looking down at her face. Her left cheek was swollen, the gash from the gun barrel crusted with blood. A vivid purple bruise was already spreading across the cheek toward her eye. Cape Flats mascara, he'd heard a colored cop call it one night dur-ing a domestic disturbance call.

These fucken people, they made a joke of everything in that lingo they spoke, a complex sublanguage of Afrikaans, prison slang, and street talk. Barnard understood it, after all the years out on the Flats. Though he would never bring himself to admit it, he felt more at home among these brown people he loathed than the white world he was supposedly part of.

The half-breed turned in her sleep, the sheet falling away, and he could see her tits. Aside from the stretch marks, they weren't bad. Ja, you knew it was time to leave Cape Town when you started finding a tik whore attractive. He brought the shotgun up from his side and placed the barrel against the side of her head. She didn't move, soft snores escaping her gummed-up lips. Maybe he should finish her now, one less witness, one less drug-fucked mouth to worry about. Finish the kid too, and the old rubbish on the sofa, and get the ransom and drive away from this long-drop of a city.

His fat finger tightened on the trigger. Then it relaxed. No, maybe it was too soon. He might need her and the kid. He could clean up this mess later.

He left the bedroom and walked into the bathroom. The boy was still asleep, curled up on the blanket, lying in the fetal position, sucking on his thumb. Barnard lowered himself onto the pot, lid down, and sat looking at the kid. He couldn't stand children. Maybe because he knew only too well what they grew up to become. Just another fucker who wanted to take away from you what was yours.

Barnard leaned forward and prodded the little brat with the shotgun barrel. No response. He prodded him again, harder, and the kid opened his eyes and looked at him. And his blue eyes widened in terror.

CHAPTER 23

Burn sat at the kitchen counter, an untouched cup of coffee before him. He couldn't remember when last he had eaten. The thought of food made him want to puke. He was waiting for the minutes to pass so he could drive down to Sea Point and withdraw the ransom money. At least he would be able to fool himself that he was doing something. Not just sitting, passive.

His cell phone rang and vibrated, doing a slow dance on the wooden counter. When he saw Mrs. Dollie's name come up, he grabbed at the phone. "Yes?"

"Just making sure you're not doing anything stupid."

"I'm about to get the money. As soon as the banks open."

"Good. I'll call you later. With details."

Burn tried to manufacture some authority. "I'm not going to hand over the money until I get my son."

"That so?" There was a pause; the phone bumped against something. Then he heard the man's voice at a distance. "Say hullo to your daddy."

Then Matt's voice. "Daddy?"

He heard the terror in his son's voice, and it was all he could do to reply.

"Matty, it's going to be okay. Daddy's coming to get you." Then Matt screamed. A piercing scream, followed by sobs. Burn was shouting into the phone. "Stop it, you bastard! Don't hurt him."

The man was back. "Don't worry, just a little pinch to bring some color to his cheeks. But you don't give the orders; I do. Do you get me?"

"Yes. I understand."

"Now you get the fucken money, and I'll call you."

The line went dead.

Susan Burn woke up believing that she had lost her baby. She was sweating, her breath coming in rasps as she fought herself out of the nightmare. It took her a minute to remember where she was. In the private ward at the clinic, bright sunlight behind the curtains. She put a hand on her belly and felt her daughter kick.

Susan lay back, trying to slow her breathing, inhaling long and deep through her nose, the way she had learned in yoga. Her baby was fine. Then she realized that the dream, the nightmare, had not been about her unborn child. It had been about Matt. And a feeling of nameless dread grabbed Susan by the throat. There was something wrong with her son.

She told herself to calm down. She was feeling guilty because she'd been distant from Matt. She tried to convince herself that she had repaired her relationship with him over the last few days. Allowed him back into her heart. But there was no changing the truth. When she looked at her son, she couldn't stop herself from seeing his father.

As she lay there she remembered when she had met Jack Burn. How he had wooed her, pursued her relentlessly. She was young, used to the clumsiness of men, boys really, her own age, and she was no match for this man of nearly forty.

There had been a moment, just before they married, when she felt a momentary chill, as if a cloud had crossed the sun. She panicked. It was all going too fast. Could she really trust this much older man she barely knew?

Jack had done what he always did: took her in his arms and reassured her. Told her he loved her. So they were married, and Matt was born, and she was as fulfilled and happy as she had ever been in her life.

When she found out about Jack's gambling, she thought her premonition was being realized. But he swore to her he would never gamble again.

She had believed him.

Then came Milwaukee and the series of events that had led her to Cape Town. Now she felt a superstitious dread, an almost karmic presentiment, that her happiness had been a borrowed thing, a thing that had never truly belonged to her, that it had come at a cost to others.

And that a price was yet to be paid.

~~~

Burn was at the front door when the landline rang. He was ready to ignore it. He knew it wouldn't be the kidnapper. But what if it was the clinic? What if there were complications?

He went back and answered. Susan's voice, distressed.

"Susan, is everything okay? With the baby?"

"Everything's fine, Jack. I want to speak to Matt."

Burn had to fight to keep his voice level. "He's not here."

"Where is he?" Anxiety tightened her voice.

He heard himself lie. "He's gone for a walk with Mrs. Dollie. She went down to the store to buy some milk, and he went with her." It had happened often enough before.

"Is he okay, Jack?"

"Of course he's okay. Why?"

She hesitated. "I had a bad dream. I dunno. I just felt scared."

"He's fine. You're just . . . anxious is all. Susan, when are . . . when will you have the baby?"

"Later today. Sometime after lunch."

He could hear the distance creeping back into her voice. She was bringing up the barriers again. "Promise me, Jack, that everything is okay with Matty."

"I promise."

She hung up.

Burn hated himself more than he had ever hated himself before.

Disaster Zondi breakfasted in his room, his back to the sweeping view of blazing Table Mountain, the harbor, and the Waterfront. He had no use for scenic panoramas. While he ate slices of ruby grapefruit off a small silver fork, he considered the fingerprint and its owner, displayed on the screen of his laptop.

In April 1997 Susan Ford, a student at UCLA, had been arrested in possession of ten grams of marijuana. She had pled guilty to a first-degree misdemeanor and paid a thousand-dollar fine.

That was all he'd gleaned from the FBI database.

Zondi wiped his fingers on a linen napkin before executing the series of keyboard commands that allowed him to zoom in on the girl's mug shots. Blonde. Pretty. Not looking too fazed at what was going down in her life. In the front view she seemed to be biting back a smile, like she had just shared a joke with the cop shooting the pictures.

Where had Barnard picked up her fingerprint? Was she holidaying in Cape Town, drawn by the mountains and beaches and wine estates like so many foreign tourists? She'd be in her late twenties now, that youthful glow maybe just starting to dim, but she'd still be attractive, he'd bet. He liked that wholesome blonde look.

He was reminded of a boer girl he'd met when he was ending the career of the corrupt commander of a rural police station. She couldn't get enough of Zondi in her parents' bed while they were off at Sunday devotions. Each time she had climaxed, she yelled *Disaster* at the top of her voice. Her father would have echoed those sentiments if he could have seen what was going on between his sheets.

Zondi pushed that thought away, bit into the grapefruit, and winced slightly at the bitterness. He would e-mail a request to U.S. law enforcement, via Interpol, asking for an update on Susan Ford. From prior experience he knew that would take at least a week. If he was lucky.

Zondi had run a check on Deputy U.S. Marshal Dexter Torrance, the man Barnard had e-mailed Susan Ford's print to. Torrance, a member of the Marshals International Fugitives Task Force, had been in Cape Town a few years ago to escort an American fugitive back home. The fugitive had hanged himself in his cell, and Torrance had ended up accompanying a coffin. The suicide took place at Bellwood South holding cells. Where, no doubt, Barnard and Torrance had met. And become friendly enough for the U.S. marshal to do Barnard a favor. Zondi wondered about the kind of man who would feel an affinity with Rudi Barnard. Probably some redneck who let his sidearm do the talking. No shortage of those, he was sure.

Zondi scrolled his computer to a new page and faced the images of Barnard's Cape Flats human barbecue. The two unknown men. And the boy, Ronaldo September. Ronnie. At least Mrs. September had been able to bury her child. The charred remains of the men burned with him lay in the police morgue awaiting their inevitable disposal in a pauper's graveyard.

Forensics had given him very little beyond confirming that the victims were male and, based on surviving dental work, possibly in their twenties. They had found a .38 slug still lodged in what was left of the abdomen of the tall man. It didn't match the .38 bullet they found in Ronnie September.

Two men in their twenties. Most likely from the Cape Flats. Most likely gangsters, given the world in which Barnard ran. Something occurred to Zondi, and he shifted windows, his fingers moving with deft certainty on the keyboards. There. Two nights before he disappeared, Barnard had put out an APB on a car, a red 1992 BMW 3 series with a CY registration plate. Wealthy Cape Town and the downtown area carried CA license plates; the working-class suburbs and the Cape Flats that sprawled north and east of the city carried CY plates.

So Barnard was looking for an early-nineties Beemer, car of choice for Flats gangbangers. It would seem that he had found it.

With two men inside.

Burn drove the Jeep up the hill toward the house, on his way back from the banks in Sea Point. Lion's Head was above him to his right, etched against the blue sky. The slopes were blackened, and smoke rose like a funeral pyre. The helicopters were gone, but the wind was picking up, ready to carry sparks to the dry brush. The choppers wouldn't rest for long.

Burn had the money crammed into a duffel bag on the seat beside him. It was after ten, and he had heard nothing from the kidnapper. He slowed outside his house, thumbing the garage door opener. Burn eased the Jeep into the garage. He stepped down from the car and reached across for the bag of money.

Out of the corner of his eye Burn glimpsed the silhouette of a man as he ducked under the descending garage door. The door bumped as it hit the cement floor. The man was locked in with him.

Chapter 24

Instinctively, Burn swung the duffel bag. The man was fast. He grabbed the bag with his left hand, deflected it, and pushed Burn back against the car.

It was then, when a shaft of light from the small window above the garage door struck the man's face, that Burn saw the livid scar and the empty eye socket. The watchman from the building site next door. In that moment everything made sense to Burn. The ugly freak had spied on them. He'd broken in and killed Mrs. Dollie and kidnapped Matt.

All the pent-up fear and rage exploded in Burn, and he went for the bastard's throat. His fingertips had just brushed the watchman's neck when he took a massive blow in the abdomen and fell to his knees, useless. He knew now that the watchman would take the money and disappear. And he would never see his son again. Then, as he was gasping for breath, he saw the watchman squat down in front of him, their faces almost level, the dark man looking at him like he was some alien life-form.

"Where is he?" Burn asked, his voice strangled.

"Who?"

"My son. What have you done with my son?"

The watchman shook his head. "I don't got your son."

Burn was sucking air, trying to get to his feet. The watchman was standing, too, helping him. Burn pushed his hands away. "Look, stop playing fucking games. Tell me what you want."

"I don't got your son. But I saw who do."

Burn stared at him. The watchman continued slowly, the heavy accent grating on Burn's ear. "I use to work next door, by the building site."

"I know who you are."

"That night, I seen him. He come and take your boy; then he come and shoot my dog. And me."

Burn remembered arriving home the night Matt was taken. Seeing the watchman bleeding as he was led to the ambulance. "Who was it? Who took my son?"

"The fat cop."

Burn knew then that the watchman was telling the truth. "I'm sorry."

The watchman shook his disfigured head. "It's okay."

"Please, come into the house. Tell me what happened."

Burn took the duffel bag of money and walked to the stairs, his stomach still tender. The watchman wasn't big, but he punched like a heavyweight.

They walked into the open-plan living room, all glass and light and Scandinavian design. The watchman looked around, taking it in. He was out of uniform, wore a pair of jeans meant for a bigger man, cinched in at the waist and rolled at the cuffs that fell onto a very tired pair of sneakers. His check shirt was frayed, short sleeved, showing plenty of prison artwork. He wore a cap, which he took off now that he was inside, standing holding it in his left hand, like it was something he'd been told to do. Burn found it hard not to stare at the dented, ravaged left side of his face.

Burn put the duffel bag down. "What's your name?"

"Benny."

"Just Benny?"

"Jus' Benny is okay."

"I'm Jack."

"Ja, you tole me."

Burn invited him to sit, which he did reluctantly, forward on the chair, his elbows on his knees, hands fidgeting with the cap. He told Burn what he had seen, expressionless, no emotion when he gave the details.

"He locked him in the trunk?"

"Ja."

"But he was still alive?"

"He was, like, kicking. Ja."

Burn battled to process this. His four-year-old son trying to fight off the huge cop. "You didn't tell the police any of this?"

A smile touched the watchman's scarred face. "Me and the cops don't talk." Then he was serious, his good eye fixed on Burn. "The fat cop. He tole you what he wants?"

"Money," Burn said.

"And when you gonna give it to him?"

"When he calls me. Later today."

"I wanna be there."

"Why?"

"He kill my dog. I'm gonna kill him." Like he was saying he took milk in his tea. No emphasis. No emotion. And no doubt that he meant it.

"Look, I understand. But I have to get my son back. Alive."

"You think he gonna give him to you?"

"Yes. If I pay him."

The watchman shook his head. "Man like that, he take your money, but maybe he don't give you your son."

Burn heard the scarred man give voice to his deepest fears. Right now the fat cop held all the cards.

"Ja. I find out about this cop. His, his moves, like. Where he operate and such. He's dangerous."

"Okay, I get that much," Burn said. "You have an idea? A plan?"

"I go with you when you drop the cash. To watch your back, like."

Burn nodded, taking this in. Trying to figure out whether he could trust this man and whether he would be risking or saving Matt's life by getting the watchman involved.

◁━

The wind howled across the Flats, picking up sand and grit and firing it at Zondi like a small-bore shotgun. He felt it in his ears, up his nostrils, and it sneaked in and found his eyes behind the Diesel sunglasses. He kept his mouth shut and his hands in his suit pockets as he followed the uniformed sergeant through the rows of cars at the police pound.

Wrecked vehicles, endless minibus taxis, and a surprising number of luxury cars spread out across the yard. The cop carried a clipboard and seemed to know where he was going. He stopped and pointed. "There's your car."

A red BMW four-door with all the gangsta accessories: chopped suspension, fat tires with chrome mags, louvers, spoilers, and tinted windows. Zondi saw that the side window on the driver's side was smashed and the trunk lid banged in the wind. The lock had been forced.

"Did it come in like this?"

"That's right, sir." Calling this black man *sir* stuck in the throat of the colored cop.

"That window too?"

"Yes."

Zondi opened the trunk and looked inside. A spare tire and a jack. A couple of empty beer bottles and rags. An old newspaper and an empty brake fluid container. He walked around to the driver's side and opened the door, looked inside.

"Who did you say this car was traced to?"

The sergeant consulted his clipboard. "A Mrs. Wessels of Tableview. She reported it stolen two years back. Wouldn't recognize it now."

"No, I bet she wouldn't. Not something she'd use in the carpool."

Zondi sat in the front seat. He popped the glove box: a couple of nipped joints and a half-empty bottle of vodka. He moved the bottle aside and saw a used condom.

"Pass me your pen, please, Sergeant."

The cop obliged, and Zondi lifted the condom out with the nib of the pen and held it to the light. Damned if he was going to use his Mont Blanc. There was a good squirt of semen in the tip of the condom. He took a folded paper evidence bag from his jacket pocket and shook it open. He dropped the condom into the bag and held the pen out to the cop.

"Thanks."

The sergeant hesitated, then shook his head. "You can keep it."

Zondi dropped the pen onto the floor of the car. He had a quick look around the interior, saw nothing more of interest, then slid out, back into the howling wind. "So this car was found up above Sea Point?"

The cop wiped sand from his eyes, then squinted at his clipboard. "Ja, we towed it from Thirty-eight Mountain Road."

"Write that address down for me, won't you?"

"Yes, sir." The sergeant muttered to himself as he bent to retrieve his ballpoint from the car.

Zondi was already walking away, back toward the shelter of the office. How did people live in this bloody place?

⟶

The wind whipped across the graveyard, blowing the imam's Arabic chant back toward the Maitland railway line. Burn stood at the rear of a small knot of mourners—all men—some dressed in traditional Muslim garb, others wearing knitted kufi caps with Western clothes. Burn had been handed a kufi as he joined the group, and he had to hold it down with one hand to stop it blowing away. He stood with the duffel bag containing one million in notes between his feet. His other hand was on his cell phone in his pocket, to feel the vibration if Barnard called.

Mrs. Dollie's body, wrapped in a white cloth, lay next to the open grave as the imam droned the prayers. Mr. Dollie, small and bearded, looked almost lost inside his Muslim clothing. His face was pinched and drawn, and a young man in a suit had to steady his arm, as if the wind might take him.

Burn wasn't sure why he had attended. He could have made an excuse, that Susan was about to have a baby. It was a valid excuse; the cesarean section was to be performed that afternoon. He knew it was ridiculous, but he felt that by attending the burial, facing Mrs. Dollie's husband, that he was at least atoning for some of his actions.

Burn had been brought up a Catholic but had lost touch with religion by the time he was a teenager. He was surprised to find that now, in his midforties, the idea of guilt and retribution should be so present. As he stood and listened to the Arabic prayers directed at a god he was not on first name terms with, he heard a voice making a deal with some invisible force out there: I'll face up to my guilt, I'll take what comes to me, but just save the life of my son. It was his voice. He knew it was superstitious. He knew it was irrational. He didn't care.

It was all he had right now.

That and a disfigured brown man with prison tattoos, sitting in the Jeep in the graveyard parking lot. The watchman had made it clear that he was going to shadow Burn until this thing was over, until he could get to the fat cop.

And kill him.

Burn had no reason to trust the watchman, which was why he stood with the bag of money between his feet, and the .38 Colt belonging to the dead gangster in his waistband. He knew that the watchman was a killer, but for now, at least, they wanted the same man dead: Barnard.

Men stepped forward and carried the wrapped form of Mrs. Dollie toward the grave. They lay the body on its right side, facing Mecca. The prayers moaned along with the wind.

Burn felt his phone vibrating, and he stepped away from the mourners as he looked at caller ID. Mrs. Dollie. He was almost moved to hysterical laughter at the surreal juxtaposition of her body in the grave and her name on his phone.

Then he took the call from his son's kidnapper.

CHAPTER 25

Benny Mongrel sat beside the American, who sped through Salt River, toward Woodstock, on the frayed fringes of the city. Burn was tense, checking his mirrors, nosing the Jeep into gaps. Then he made a visible effort to calm himself, and he slowed down, dropped to the speed limit.

Benny Mongrel had a cell phone in his hand, looking at it as if it might bite him. He'd seen people using them, sure, the guards at Pollsmoor, many people since he was released. But he had never held one in his hand. Never mind used one. Burn had given it to him earlier, saying it was a spare he kept as a backup. It would allow them to keep in contact during the drop-off of the money.

They had stopped at a light. Burn was looking at him. "You understand how to use it?"

"Ja."

"Call my phone. Just to see everything is okay."

"It's okay."

"Do it. Please. We can't afford screw-ups."

Benny Mongrel shrugged and jabbed a finger at the tiny phone. Burn had showed him that he only had to push that one number, the three, and it would dial his phone. Burn's cell, lying on the seat between them, chirped and flashed.

"Okay, hit the red button."

Benny Mongrel's finger searched, found the red button, and jabbed at it. The chirping stopped. They were driving again.

"You clear on how we're going to do this thing?"

Burn overtook a minibus taxi, which suddenly veered into their lane, and he had to swerve, almost colliding with an oncoming truck, horn blaring.

"Jesus!" When they had passed the taxi, Burn shot him a look. "You clear?"

Benny Mongrel nodded. "Ja."

He was clear. Burn would drop him off just before they got to the Waterfront. Benny Mongrel would make his way to the place where he could observe the drop-off point. Burn had drawn him a map. He would watch the fat cop pick up the money and follow him. If the cop didn't leave the boy, Burn wanted to know where the fat man was, to go after him. Benny Mongrel had no doubt the boy wouldn't be left. The fat cop would take the money, and he would go back to his car. Benny Mongrel would follow him and kill him. He had no use for this stupid little phone.

Burn was talking, asking him to run through details of the plan. Benny Mongrel grunted, nodded, but his hand was in his pocket. He gripped the knife, the blade honed to perfect sharpness.

The Waterfront, Cape Town's dockland development, attracted twenty-two million visitors every year, and it looked like most of them were there that day. Part shopping mall, part theme park, the Waterfront sprawled around the working dock. Restaurants, street musicians, boat trips, and spectacular views across the city packed in the crowds.

Burn, duffel bag hanging from his shoulder, pushed his way through throngs of European tourists, skins fried Bockwurst pink by the African sun. They strolled in their shorts and sandals, digital cameras slung around their sunburned necks, wallets bulging with euros. Burn checked his watch; he had five minutes to get to the drop-off point.

Barnard's instructions had been clear: Burn was to leave the bag on the stairs of the Mandela Gateway and cross the pedestrian bridge toward the shopping mall. Once the money was in place, Barnard would call his cell and tell him where in the Waterfront he could find his son. Burn's gut instinct was that Matt was nowhere near the Waterfront. Barnard would be keeping him as an insurance policy.

If he was still alive.

Burn had tried to argue that he wouldn't part with the money until he saw his son. Barnard's counter was simple: if Burn didn't shut up and follow instructions, he would remove one of Matt's fingers. Burn shut up.

Burn skirted a group of black boys stripped to the waist, doing a loud and energetic gum boot dance. They blew whistles and clapped, the boots like gunshots on the cobbles. He approached the Mandela Gateway. The area teemed with tourists, queuing up for the half-hour boat ride across to Robben Island, to see where Nelson Mandela spent twenty-seven years in jail. Shortly after getting to Cape Town, Burn and Matt had taken the trip. Susan had begged off; she was suffering from morning sickness, and there was no way she was getting on a boat. While Burn had stood and looked into Mandela's cramped cell, he had felt uneasy. Too vivid a reminder of where he could end up.

Burn checked his watch. Two twenty-nine. He forced himself not to look up at the first floor of the shopping area—curio shops and African theme restaurants—where he had told the watchman to take his position.

Burn headed for the stairs. He knew that Barnard wouldn't waste time collecting the bag. The Waterfront had been the target of bomb attacks in the late nineties, and the security personnel were ultravigilant. An unattended bag would be spotted immediately.

Two thirty. Burn stood on the stairs, gave the area a sweep, then set the duffel bag down against a pillar. He headed off toward the pedestrian bridge, not looking back.

Barnard sat under an umbrella at a table outside a German restaurant, his eyes not moving from the Mandela Gateway. An untouched mug of pilsner stood in front of him. He thought it made him look like a tourist. He wore his cap and a pair of sunglasses, sweating into a T-shirt. Barnard took the sunglasses off and wiped the sweat from his eyes. He checked the watch that cut into the fat on his massive wrist. Almost two thirty.

Then he saw him. The American. Carrying a bag, heading straight toward the stairs. Barnard would let the American drop the bag and walk away. Then he would collect the money and drive over to Paradise Park. Put the Mossberg to the heads of the half-breed bitch and the American kid. Shut them up for keeps.

He regretted that he wasn't going to be able to kill the American. He'd made a promise to his friend U.S. Marshal Dexter Torrance that

Burn would be made to pay. Well, his dead son would have to be payment enough.

The fat man stayed seated until he saw the American place the bag on the stairs and walk off in the direction of the pedestrian bridge. Barnard stood, hitched up his trousers, shifted the position of the holster under his T-shirt, and went to get his money.

———

Benny Mongrel waited at the railing on the first floor, outside an African restaurant, his cap pulled low. He watched the stairs. He saw Burn drop the bag and walk away. Benny Mongrel kept his eyes locked on the bag. He was aware of somebody coming up next to him, on his right side. Instinctively he felt for his knife; then he saw it was some young white girl with blonde hair, wearing a backpack.

"Excuse me, can you tell me where I find the taxis?" To Benny Mongrel's ear, the German accent was nearly incomprehensible.

He turned to her, favoring her with the carnage of the left side of his face. "Fuck off."

She saw his face, blanched white under her tan, and did as he said.

Benny Mongrel looked back toward the bag. It was gone. He scanned the crowd and glimpsed a fat shape about to disappear up the flight of stairs that led to the street.

Benny Mongrel was running.

———

As Burn approached the pedestrian bridge spanning the waterway, he heard a shrill blast of a whistle and the gates at the front of the bridge closed. A yacht with a towering mast approached the low bridge, en route to its mooring. With agonizing slowness, the bridge swung away from where Burn stood and traveled in an arc until it hugged the opposite bank.

The yacht glided slowly past, a tanned man in shorts at the wheel and a ridiculously good-looking woman sipping a glass of wine on the deck, neither deigning to look at the rabble on the banks.

Burn couldn't resist a glance over his shoulder, up to the first floor. He saw the watchman take off, running, toward the stairs to the street. On the tail of Barnard.

Burn couldn't stop himself. He turned and plunged into the crowd.

The call that Disaster Zondi was dreading came as he piloted his BMW southbound on the N2, cruising toward the city that huddled at the foot of the mountain. His outward appearance of imperturbable calm belied an inner turmoil. He sensed that Barnard was close, so close he could almost smell him. He couldn't shake the feeling that he was dogging the fat man's footsteps. But how far behind he didn't know.

Zondi had decided to leave Superintendent Peterson and the rest of the cops at Bellwood South HQ out of the loop. He couldn't risk a leak now. He knew it would take him more time to do everything himself, but he needed to keep control.

His phone, hooked up to a hands-free, was yapping on the seat next to him. He sneaked a glance at caller ID. His commanding officer. He was tempted to let it go to voice mail, but at the last moment he took the call. "Zondi."

"Afternoon, Zondi."

To Archibald Mathebula, Zondi was always just Zondi. He called his other investigators by their first names, but it was as if giving voice to the name Disaster was an insult to his sensibilities. He would have fought to the death to defend Zondi's right to the name, but it conjured up an African world that was too rural, too primitive for a man of his refinement.

"And how is the Cape?"

"Windy," said Zondi.

Mathebula chuckled. "Yes, it can be. Now I understand that you have completed your task?"

"Well, not entirely."

"But an arrest warrant has been issued for this Barnard?"

"That's right, sir."

"And you've made recommendations regarding the other policemen?"

"I have."

"Then it's time for you to return to home and hearth."

"There are a couple of loose ends, sir, that I'd like to tie up."

Mathebula dropped the avuncular tone. Under the genial exterior that he worked so hard to project, Zondi's boss was a hard man. A killer. Zondi, of course, had compiled a dossier on his superior and knew that during the struggle years, when Mathebula had been a commander in the ANC's armed wing, he had personally executed nine of his men whom he suspected of selling information to the apartheid government. No trial, just a bullet in the head and an unmarked grave in the Zambian veld.

"Zondi, I know of your history with this man, Barnard."

"That is not influencing me."

"We don't do vendettas, Zondi. I have cut you some slack, but now I'm losing patience. My p.a. will liaise with you regarding your flight back to Johannesburg. I want you back in the office in the morning."

"Yes, sir."

Mathebula was gone. Zondi cursed quietly. He was passing the Ratanga Junction Theme Park and saw that one of the rides, the cobra, had stalled in midair, people dangling upside down while men in a cherry picker battled to get to them.

He knew how they felt.

His phone beeped as a text message came through. Zondi drove one-handed and sneaked a look at the message. He was flying out at 8:00 p.m. He had six hours to do what he needed to do.

Mathebula was right. It was a vendetta. He wanted to be there when Barnard was taken down, to bear witness. He didn't yearn for the closure that the daytime TV shrinks peddled like twenty-first-century snake oil, the fuzzy notion that you faced up to things and then went on with your life. He wanted revenge. It was as simple as that.

He wanted blood.

>

Barnard shouldered his way through the crowd, deaf to the angry complaints thrown his way. Pounded his bulk up a flight of stairs and crossed an open plaza, his body as wet as if he'd walked through a car wash. He had avoided pay parking and left the Ford in a narrow road at the bottom of a ramp that led back to the city. He unzipped the duffel bag as he walked, just enough to glance inside. It was stuffed with notes. He felt like laughing. He sent a quick glance heavenward. *Thank you, God.*

He would get down on bended knee and offer a prayer of thanks as soon as he was safe.

>

Burn ran, dodging tourists. He lost sight of the watchman for a few seconds, then saw him heading up the stairs. There was no sign of Barnard. Burn hit the stairs, pumping his legs, racing to the top. He slowed when he hit the plaza above. The tourists were thinner on the ground here; he couldn't risk being spotted.

He saw the watchman, using a minibus loaded with tourists for cover, walking toward the ramp that joined the main road into downtown Cape Town. Burn speed-dialed the phone he had given to the watchman.

Benny Mongrel shadowed the minibus, which crawled as a giant tour bus passed, waiting to swing out into a lane and accelerate. The phone in his pocket started to ring and vibrate. Benny Mongrel threw it into the gutter and walked on. The fat cop looked back, but he couldn't see Benny Mongrel.

Then the cop ducked off the ramp and hauled his fat ass down a narrow flight of stairs that led to the road below. The road flanked a dry dock, and Benny Mongrel could see a group of Chinese sailors scraping and repairing their rusted trawler. One of them saw the cop's man-breasts jiggling as he humped down the steps, and he said something to his friend and they stopped scraping and laughed. The cop didn't notice. He was heading toward a brown Ford that was parked outside the old fish canning building.

Benny Mongrel knew he was going to be exposed on the stairs, but he had no choice. If he didn't make his move now, the cop would be in the car and away. He hit the stairs at a run, two at a time.

The fat cop was at the rear of his car, popping the trunk, his sweating back to Benny Mongrel. He dropped the bag into the trunk, slammed it, and turned. And clocked Benny Mongrel, who was closing in fast. Surprise, astonishment even, crossed the cop's face. He had to get both his fat and the T-shirt out of the way before he could draw the revolver at his hip, and that saved Benny Mongrel's life.

Benny Mongrel closed the gap and kicked the fat cop in the balls while he was still trying to draw the gun. The cop made a sound like air escaping from a blimp and sagged but didn't fall. Benny Mongrel kicked him again, in his ribs. And the cop was on his knees.

The Chinese sailors were chirping excitedly, hanging over the railing of the boat. It was better than a Jackie Chan movie. Benny Mongrel had the knife in his hand, and he flicked the blade open on the pocket of his jeans. The fat cop was looking up at him, gasping for air, stinking. Benny Mongrel held the blade so that it gleamed in the sunlight, grabbed the cop by his thatch of hair, and pulled his head back, exposing his throat.

Time to say goodnight.

Benny Mongrel felt the cold barrel of a gun shoved up against the back of his head. "Drop the knife," said Burn.

CHAPTER 26

Benny Mongrel wondered if he would be quick enough to cut the cop's throat before the American shot him. He held the blade against the jowls that hung like accordion bellows from the fat man's neck, a rivulet of blood already snaking down to the cop's T-shirt. One motion, quick and true, and it would be done. Benny Mongrel didn't care if he died, but there was no way he was going to die without taking the fat cop to hell with him.

He heard the gun cocking, a sound he had heard many times before in his life.

"I mean it," said Burn. "Drop the knife or I'll shoot you."

Benny Mongrel believed the desperation he heard in Burn's voice.

He looked into the cop's eyes, saw the fear, smelled the stench of his body. Then the message from Benny Mongrel's brain moved down his arm and reached his fingers, and he loosened his grip on the knife.

There was a moment of absolute silence, broken only by the clatter of the knife as it hit the road. Then the Chinese sailors were jabbering again, in high excitement.

Benny Mongrel felt the pressure of the gun barrel ease as Burn stepped back. He turned and saw Burn reach down and pocket the knife. The fat cop, still down on one knee, was moving a hand toward his ankle. Burn's gun arced and fixed on the cop.

"Search him," said the American.

Benny Mongrel found the .32 in the ankle holster and set it down on the road. He removed the .38 from the fat man's hip and placed it next to the other weapon.

Burn held the gun steady, unwavering, pointed at the fat cop. "Where is my son?"

The cop sneered. "Fuck you." Burn's finger was tightening on the trigger. "Shoot me, and you can kiss his little ass good-bye."

"Open the trunk of the car," said Burn, the gun moving between Benny Mongrel and the cop. Benny could see that Burn knew how to use it.

Benny Mongrel popped the trunk. Burn leveled the gun at the fat cop.

"Get in." When the cop tried to protest, Burn pointed the weapon at the cop's leg. "I'll shoot you. I mean it."

The cop shook his head again. "Fuck you."

And Burn shot him. The bullet took the cop above his left knee, in the meat of his thigh, passing through his flesh without doing serious damage. The cop bit back the pain and grabbed at his leg. The Chinese sailors were chattering like monkeys.

Burn waved the gun again. "Now get in the trunk."

Blood was flowing down the cop's leg, and he cursed as he hauled himself to his feet, keeping his weight on his right leg. With a series of actions that under any other circumstances would have been comical, he contrived to load his bulk into the trunk.

"Close it," Burn said to Benny Mongrel.

When Benny brought the trunk lid down, it hit the cop's massive belly and refused to close. He leaned his weight on it. He heard the cop grunt and curse. He had to lift himself off the ground, lie on the lid, before he heard it catch.

"Kick the guns over to me."

Benny Mongrel did as he was told. He watched as Burn pocketed the weapons.

"Now you drive." Burn gestured with the gun toward the car.

Benny Mongrel shook his head. "I don't drive."

Burn stared at him. "You're kidding me?"

"I never learn."

"Fuck." Burn shook his head. "Okay, get into the passenger seat. Slowly."

He got into the Ford, and Burn slid behind the wheel and started the car.

"Where we going?" asked Benny Mongrel.

"To my house. To get him to talk." Burn was doing a juggling act, the wheel, the ignition key, the revolver.

"It's okay."

"What is?"

"I won't try nothing." Burn was looking at him. "You want your boy? You need to know where to get him?" Burn nodded. "I help you if you do one thing for me."

"What?"

"You let me work on him." He jerked his head back toward the trunk. "To make him talk. I wanna do that."

Burn nodded. "Deal." He started the car and sped off, the revolver shoved between his seat and the door.

Benny Mongrel thought that maybe things had turned out okay. Maybe the American had done him a favor. Cutting the fat cop's throat was too easy, too quick. Now he had the chance to take his time, put to good use the torture practices he had mastered in prison.

He was looking forward to that.

Burn drove toward his house, battling with the gears on the right-hand-drive stick shift. He had driven only the automatic Jeep since coming to Cape Town. Then he started to get it, felt the mind-muscle coordination kick in.

As he threaded the anonymous brown Ford through the traffic on Greenpoint Main Road, he checked out his passenger. The watchman sat absolutely still, staring straight ahead. Maybe that is what prison taught you, to live in the moment. To conserve your energy for when it was needed, and to go into sleep mode when you faced that endless succession of days. Burn knew that he might well be learning those lessons himself soon.

Somehow he no longer cared. He felt detached from himself, from his own ego and desires, for the first time in his life. He understood how shallow, how immature and superficial most of his urges had been. Now all he cared about, all his very being was focused on, was saving his son. If he could achieve that, he would step quietly into whatever uncertain future awaited him.

Burn changed back to second gear as he turned up Glengariff. The car struggled, and he felt the exhaust scrape under the weight of the massive man in the trunk. Burn had to pump the clutch and shift back to first to get the car moving up the hill.

The watchman was laughing, with no sound escaping his lips. Maybe that was another trick you learned in prison.

—◁—

Barnard battled for breath. The exhaust of the Ford leaked, and noxious fumes found their way into the trunk, making him feel as if he was being gassed. His leg throbbed, and he could feel the blood pooling under him. He'd underestimated the American, hadn't thought he'd have the balls to pull the trigger.

Barnard cursed himself for his stupidity. He had been too sure of himself. He was accustomed to dealing with people out on the Cape Flats, who were shit scared to act against him. But he swore to himself that he would tell the American and the half-breed nothing. They had formed an unholy alliance, but they would not break him.

The car hit a bump, and his forehead and nose smashed up against the lid of the trunk. He felt blood flow from his nose, back into his throat. He couldn't move his head, wedged in like a meat loaf in a mold. The blood, combined with the fumes, convinced him that this was it. He was about to die. The irony was that he was trapped in the trunk with the duffel bag of money, his passport to a new life, squeezed painfully up against his ribs.

He tried to slow his breathing, offered a prayer to God. For some reason God felt very far away.

—◁—

The Ford was parked in Burn's garage. The fat cop was still in the trunk. The steel door was down, and the room was very quiet, cut off from the world outside. Not even the shouts of the men tossing bricks on the building site penetrated the garage.

Benny Mongrel was very precise in his requests. He needed a kitchen chair strong enough to hold the fat cop's weight, a length of nylon rope, a few rags, some newspaper, garbage bags, and duct tape.

And he needed his knife back.

Burn hesitated a moment, considering the request. Then he reached into his pocket and brought out the folded knife. He handed it to Benny Mongrel. The two men went upstairs and gathered the items Benny Mongrel had asked for. Then they went back down to the garage.

Burn watched as Benny Mongrel spread the newspaper. The garage was large enough to hold two cars, so there was plenty of space next to the Ford. Benny Mongrel was methodical, making sure that the edges of the newspaper overlapped. Then he ripped the black garbage bags apart and placed them over the newspaper. Only then did he set the chair in place.

He looked at Burn and nodded. Burn pointed the .38 at the trunk. Benny Mongrel popped the lid. The fat cop was gasping, his face bright red, blood crusted around his nose and in his mustache. He hauled himself upright.

"Fuck youse," he said and vomited down the front of his T-shirt. He wiped the back of his hand across his mouth.

"Get out."

Burn waved the gun toward the chair. It took a couple of tries for the fat man to lever his weight out of the trunk. At last he managed it, like a side of beef coming out of a freezer truck, and stood wheezing, blood from the leg wound flowing into his shoe.

"Sit down," said Burn.

Barnard shook his head. Benny Mongrel kicked him in the right kidney, hard enough to make the cop piss blood for a week. The fat cop made a sound like a pig fucking and stumbled, fighting not to fall to his knees. He staggered across to the chair and lowered himself with a series of whining grunts. The wooden chair protested but held his weight.

While Burn held the gun on the cop, Benny Mongrel tied the fat man to the chair, quickly and efficiently immobilizing his arms and legs. Then he shoved a rag into Barnard's mouth and taped it in place. He opened his knife and cut away the cop's jeans above his left knee. He pressed a cloth against the wound and taped it up. He didn't want the fat boer to die of blood loss before he had a chance to work on him.

Benny Mongrel laid the knife on the trunk of the Ford. He took a length of white mutton cloth and tore it with his teeth until he had the length he needed. He very carefully wrapped the blade of the knife down from the haft, leaving only a few centimeters of the blade exposed.

In Pollsmoor Prison a new recruit to the gangs has to pass an initiation rite. He has to stab a warder. But the stabbing must never be fatal, only deep enough to injure. To ensure this, the gang "doctor," the man who performs a similar function to a medic in a marine platoon, carefully prepares the knife by wrapping it in such a way that the length of the blade is set.

Benny Mongrel had never been a "doctor," but he had stabbed warders and ordered countless terrified young men to do the same. He had supervised the preparation of the blade. His fingers knew precisely what they were doing.

Barnard watched him, his stench filling the room.

Satisfied, Benny Mongrel approached the fat cop. He showed him the knife.

"Where's my son?" asked Burn, standing behind Benny Mongrel.

Barnard shook his head. Benny Mongrel inserted the knife into the flesh of the fat cop's right thigh. It slid in like it was going into prison bully beef. The fat man screamed silently behind the gag.

And so it began.

Disaster Zondi drove the rental BMW up the slope of Signal Hill, the Cape Town map book open on the seat beside him. As he left Sea Point Main Road behind, he slid ever upward into a world of rarefied privilege, each block up the slope a leap into a higher tax bracket. A world of high walls, SUVs, and soccer moms with blonde bobs. A white world.

A phone call to Sea Point police station had resulted in a piece of interesting intelligence: there had been a shooting two nights before at the building site where the red BMW had been found. There might be no connection, but Zondi's hunch was that it was too much of a coincidence.

He found himself at the corner of Mountain Road and brought the car to a stop at the building site. The view was spectacular. He could see tankers lying off Robben Island, yachts catching the wind near Table Bay Harbor, the vista spreading to the Hottentots Holland Mountains in the distance. But Zondi wasn't there for the view.

He shrugged on his jacket, despite the heat that enveloped him as he stepped out of the air-conditioned car. He adjusted his shades and headed toward two men building a wall. One of the men, black, stripped to the waist with the kind of body that no gym can give you, casually tossed bricks up to another man, who straddled the top of the wall, catching them expertly. All the while they were discussing soccer in Xhosa.

Zondi grew up speaking Zulu, a cousin language. That was how he greeted the men. They stared at him with suspicion, this well-dressed black man in his fancy car. He asked who was in charge, and one of them pointed into the site.

Zondi walked through a mess of cement, bricks, and builder's sand. He was careful not to dirty his loafers. He came upon a young white man in shorts and work boots, shirtless, deeply tanned, with blond dreadlocks. A tool belt hung from his waist as he took the span of a doorway with a steel tape measure.

"Afternoon," Zondi said as he approached.

"Hey, hi." The guy gave him a smile. Zondi caught the pungent whiff of recently smoked weed. "You from the architects?"

"No. Special Investigator Zondi." He showed his ID.

The young guy squinted, probably thinking of the nipped joint that was undoubtedly still in his pocket. "There some problem?"

"No. I hear there was a shooting here, the other night?"

The guy relaxed. "Fully. Watchman got plugged." He wiped his hand and stuck it out. "Name's Dave Judd. Site foreman."

Zondi shook the hand. "Would you mind showing me where the shooting took place?"

"No problem." Judd coiled the tape measure and slipped it into the pouch. He led Zondi into the interior of the house, across two planks, toward a stairway. Laborers in overalls were plastering the walls. Judd dodged the men and went nimbly up the stairs, his surfer's balance on display.

He pointed to the stairs leading to the uncompleted top floor. "Happened right here. Guy's pooch got taken out, shame."

"His dog?"

"Ja. Absolutely. Right here. Can still see the bullet holes, hey."

He pointed to the wall, and Zondi went closer. One of the slugs was embedded in the unplastered wall. "You mind if I borrow a screwdriver?"

"No prob."

Judd freed a screwdriver from his tool belt and handed it over, handle first. Zondi dug into the hole and unearthed the slug. He removed an evidence bag from his pocket and eased the slug inside, then sealed it.

He handed the screwdriver back. "Thanks."

"Sure thing."

"All right if I wander around a bit?"

"Hey, whatever. I'll be downstairs if you need me, okay?"

Zondi nodded and watched as the surfer boy bounced back down the stairs, probably counting the minutes until he could get into his wet-suit and go catch some waves. Zondi went up to the top floor, the roof open to the sky.

He was alone up there. He walked to the edge of an unfinished balcony, saw a small pile of cigarette butts. Roll-your-owns. He was prepared to bet that this was where the watchman and his dog had hung out. He wanted to talk to that watchman.

Zondi looked down onto the deck of the house next door. Another one of those high-walled boxes with big glass windows. A man stood on the deck, staring down over Cape Town, the breeze flicking his hair.

Zondi turned and walked back toward the stairs.

It had become too much for Burn. The watchman betrayed no emotion, focused on his task with single-minded determination. He applied the blade with precision to the body of the fat man, stabbing into the blubber, drawing blood that flowed down onto the garbage bags and the newspapers. He worked his way up the legs, then began on the massive torso.

Barnard, shirtless, his immense body streaked with blood, strained in the chair, the veins on his forehead popping out like cords. Sweat and blood coursed off him. He had pissed and shit himself, which, mixed with his fetid body odor and the smell of blood, made the room stink like a charnel house.

Every few minutes the watchman would remove the gag, and Burn would repeat the question. "Where is my son?"

And the fat cop would shake his head, his fringe wet and dangling, and spit two words through his bleeding lips. "Fuck youse."

The watchman would shove the gag back in and tape it up. Then he would wipe the blade down and start his work again, inserting the knife into the body of the fat man deep enough to cause agony but not deep enough to cause death.

"I'm going upstairs. For some air," Burn told the watchman, who merely nodded as he inserted the blade into Barnard's shoulder. A keening noise rose from somewhere within the cop's chest, and tears and sweat dripped from his face. His body bulged against the ropes.

Burn headed for the kitchen, where he splashed his face and drank a long draft of water. Was this fat bastard ever going to break? The longer this continued, the more remote the likelihood that he would ever see his son alive again.

Burn stepped out onto the deck and sucked air. Even the smoky breeze, still heavy with the charred smell of the fire, was sweet after the foul atmosphere of the torture chamber that was now his garage. It was hard to believe, looking out at this scene of quiet beauty, that the world went on, untroubled by the universe of pain and corruption that he had somehow stumbled into. Then he looked beyond the city and the ocean, out to where the land was flat, covered in a haze of smog and smoke.

Burn had taken Matt on a helicopter ride before Christmas. The chopper had done the usual tourist things, gone around Table Mountain, along the coast; then it had banked over the Cape Flats on its way to land, and Burn had looked down at the endless sprawl of box houses and ghetto apartment blocks dumped on the scrubland like forgotten toys in a sandpit. As he stood on the deck, he had a memory of that sprawl. He knew his son was out there somewhere.

Burn had no idea how long he stood there, the wind cooling the sweat on his body, before he heard the voice calling to him. He looked down to the street and saw a black man in a very well-cut dark suit, designer shades, staring up at him.

"Excuse me," the man said for maybe the fifth time.

Burn stepped toward the railing of the deck. "Yes. Hi, sorry."

"I'd like to have a word with you, if you don't mind." The man was holding something toward him.

Burn focused. It was some kind of official ID. He almost wanted to laugh. Not again. Not now.

CHAPTER 27

A voice inside Burn's head told him to open the street door, to extend his wrists in supplication toward this black cop and ask for the handcuffs. Lead him toward the garage that now doubled as a DIY torture chamber. Beg him to find his boy.

But Burn opened the door and did something with his facial muscles that resembled a smile. "Afternoon. Can I help you?"

The black man, his shaven dome gleaming in the sunlight, offered the ID document for Burn to view. "Special Investigator Zondi. Ministry of Safety and Security."

Burn nodded, making no move to open the door any wider.

"Can I have your name, please, sir?"

"Hill. John Hill."

"You're American?"

"Yes, I am." Burn made a point of looking at his watch. "I'm in kind of a hurry . . ."

"My apologies. Do you know anything about a red BMW that was parked next door to your house a few nights ago? Outside the building site?"

Burn shook his head. "No."

The black cop thought for a moment before he spoke. "Was there maybe another officer here, asking questions?"

Burn was tempted to lie. But what if there was some record of Barnard having been here? He told a version of the truth. "Yeah. There was. A few days back."

"Is that a fact? This officer, was he by any chance Inspector Barnard?"

Burn made a show of looking uncertain, playing the dumb foreigner. "These South African names kinda confuse me. He was a big guy, pretty heavy."

"Sounds like him. He asked you about the car?"

"That's right. Wanted to know if I had seen anybody. Heard anything. I told him what I told you."

"Do you live here alone, Mr. Hill?"

"Well, at the moment, yes. My wife and son are away." He was stepping back. "If that's all, I've got to get down to Sea Point. To the bank."

"Just one more thing."

The man reached into his well-cut jacket pocket and came out with a neatly folded sheet of paper. He unfolded it with his perfectly manicured fingers and held it up to Burn. "Do you know this woman?" He was showing him a printout of Susan's mug shots, from ten years ago.

Somehow Burn managed a laugh. "Glad to say I don't. She looks like trouble."

The black man flashed a row of very white teeth. "Well, thank you, Mr. Hill."

"Sure. My pleasure."

Burn closed the door, leaned against it for a second while he tried to convince his heart not to hammer its way out of his chest.

Zondi walked back to his car, pressed the remote, and the lights flashed and the doors clicked open. He removed his jacket and folded it carefully. He slid into the car and reached back, hanging the jacket from a hook in the rear. He shut the door, started the engine, and sat with his eyes closed, the aircon at its maximum.

An American. Coincidence? There were a lot of Americans in Cape Town this time of the year, escaping blizzards and, for all he knew, the War on Terror. The man, Hill, hadn't shown anything in his eyes when he looked at the mug shots of the American woman. He'd even cracked a joke. So either he was on the level or he was a practiced liar. And his shoes, top-of-the-line Reeboks, were those flecks of blood around the toe caps or mud from watering his garden, maybe?

Zondi led his mind to a place of stillness for a minute, feeling the aircon chilling the sweat on his body. Zondi, to his credit, knew that he was an obsessive. He knew enough Buddhism to understand that his quest for order and control was ultimately useless in the face of the cosmic joke called life.

He opened his eyes. What the hell? Maybe he should succumb to Cape Town's charms while he killed time until his flight. The wind had died, and the sun was shining on the ocean. Why didn't he cruise down to Camps Bay, sit at one of those sidewalk cafés, and sip something with an umbrella on top while he watched the girls go by?

Or he could take the used condom and the slug he'd dug out of the wall down to the police lab.

He started the car. The police lab won.

Burn was in the kitchen, drinking a glass of iced water from the fridge. He knew he was delaying the walk down the steps to the garage. He was scared of what he might find.

What if the watchman had taken the opportunity to kill Barnard? That aerial image of the sprawling Cape Flats came to Burn's mind once more, and he imagined Matt lost out there, in the second day of this nightmare. He felt the boy's terror. What if the one voice that could tell him where to find his son had been silenced?

Burn put down the glass and walked across to the stairs.

When he emerged in the garage below, he paused, taking in the scene before him. Barnard was motionless, slumped forward, prevented from falling by the ropes that tied him to the chair. His many chins were compressed down onto his bloody chest, and his hair hung over his eyes, wet with sweat and blood. His naked torso was cross-hatched with cuts, some fresh and bleeding freely, others fringed by darker blood already coagulating.

He's dead, thought Burn. He has to be.

The watchman squatted in front of the fat cop, lighting a cigarette. He didn't look up at Burn. He inhaled deeply and blew out a plume of smoke toward the ceiling; then he leaned forward and gently, almost delicately, placed the cigarette between Barnard's lips. For a while it dangled there; then Burn saw the end glow as Barnard inhaled. He was alive.

Finally, the watchman looked up at Burn.

"Well?" Burn asked.

The watchman nodded. "He has spoke."

The kid woke her, tugging at her arm. Carmen groaned and opened her eyes, immediately feeling the throb in her cheek where the fat bastard had hit her. She ignored the kid, who was whining about his mommy, got out of bed naked, and went across to what was left of her mirror. Jesus, her face looked like shit. The cheek was swollen, with enough colors to make a rainbow look anemic.

She didn't know what was worse, the throbbing cheek or the spiders that crawled across her skin. She scratched herself, hard enough to draw blood with her chipped fingernails. She needed to score, and fast. But she didn't have a fucken cent. All of Gatsby's money was gone, and he had fucked off without leaving her more.

She dressed, trying to tune out the whining of the kid. When she couldn't stand it anymore, the crying and moaning grating on her frayed nerves, she crushed up half a Mogadon in a teaspoon. She poured what was left of a milk carton into a glass, added the powder, and stirred it until it dissolved.

She handed the glass to the boy. "Drink this."

He shook his head, his eyes swollen from crying. She got down on her knees, her face level with his. "Matt, you drink it, and I take you to your mommy, okay?"

He looked at her suspiciously. "You promise?"

"Cross my heart." She made the sign of the cross on her chest, God forgive her, and the kid took a sip of the milk. He grimaced. It was sour. "Only if you drink it all up."

He forced the rest of the milk down, leaving a mustache of white above his upper lip. Within a minute he was looking woozy. She lay him down on her bed and attacked her wild hair with a brush. Soon she heard the child snoring softly.

Now she had to score.

On her way to the door she passed Uncle Fatty, who was in his usual place on the sofa, communing with a bag of wine, dressed only in his foul underwear.

"I'm coming back now, okay?"

He nodded, staring into space.

She went on the hunt for tik, begging, cajoling, absorbing rejection and insult until she found the retard Conway. She told him more stupid lies about getting him to deal for Rikki, and he eventually made her a globe.

She sucked the smoke into her lungs and found peace. At least for the moment.

As she hurried back toward the ghetto block, Carmen tried to work out how long she'd been gone. She had no idea. What if the fat bastard had come back and taken the kid without leaving her more money? She broke into a run, the tik giving her a burst of raw energy.

She ran up the stairs, unlocked the front door, and went inside. The sofa was empty. She walked through to the bedroom and stopped in the doorway. It took a few moments for her to comprehend what she was seeing.

The American kid lay on the bed, passed out on his back. Uncle Fatty was crouched over him, busy loosening the boy's pajama pants. His dentures lay on the bed beside the child. The old man turned and looked up at her, a necklace of drool dangling from his toothless gums.

Carmen grabbed the first thing that came to hand, a plaster statuette of the Virgin Mary. She brought the Virgin down on Uncle Fatty's head, again and again and again, blood spraying across her face and her white T-shirt.

The dead were speaking to Barnard. Whispering to him, a choir of unearthly voices. They were calling his name. He had to fight hard to pull himself away from them, to open his crusted eyes. A blur. Hard sunlight lasered his eyes. He blinked, forced his eyes to focus, and saw the Cape Flats moving by him.

He was in a car. His car. The Ford. In the rear seat, his face pressed up against the side window. Even though the sun was shining and he was covered by a blanket, he was still freezing, shivering. He felt his loose fat shaking like jelly. And he was in agony, every square inch of his body screaming in pain and anguish. His mouth was dry, and his tongue felt as swollen as meat left to rot in the sun.

He tried to move his head. Unspeakable pain burned through his nerve ends as he managed to turn his head and look forward. He heard a voice, the American, speaking from far away, as if through a very long tube.

"He's awake."

Barnard looked into that nightmare face, the missing eye, the snakelike scar. The half-breed watchman, staring at him from the front seat. The watchman reached an arm over and forced him back down on the seat. Barnard heard an animal wailing and then realized it was him, a sound of pure agony tearing itself loose from his body.

The half-breed pulled the blanket over his face, and Rudi Barnard could see nothing but the dead.

CHAPTER 28

There was not a day that Fingers Morkel woke without excruciating pain in his missing digits. The fingers that Benny Mongrel had cut off with his knife. As he lay in bed, Fingers lifted his two scarred stumps up to eye level to make certain—yet again—that his fingers really were gone. They were, but they still hurt like fucken hell. Doctors had told him that he was suffering from phantom limb syndrome. That he was experiencing phantom pain.

They made all sorts of smart-ass suggestions: apply heat to the stumps, flex what was left of his hands to improve the circulation. Some white fucker had even told him to imagine that he was exercising the missing fingers. Fingers had imagined he was raising the middle digit of each hand to the asshole doctor, but that hadn't got rid of the pain or his anger.

The way Fingers dealt with this whole sorry mess was to shove as many drugs down his throat as he could. And to imagine killing Benny Mongrel.

By removing his fingers, Benny Mongrel had deprived him of many pleasures. No longer could he put a gun to some motherfucker's head, feel his index finger curling around the trigger as he blew him away. No longer could he wrap his hands around some bitch's throat until he half killed her before he screwed her.

And then there were his monkey nuts. He loved the fucken things so much that he'd previously been known as Peanuts. A nickname he much preferred to the present one that reminded him constantly of what had been inflicted upon him and by whom. He had refused to eat the nuts unshelled. The pleasure had been in cracking open the shell, letting his fingers find the two nuts inside, each in its own little compartment, and bringing them to his lips.

Now if he wanted to eat monkey nuts, he had to get one of his guys to break the shells open for him, and put them in a little pile on a paper plate, so he could grab the plate between his two thumbs and pour the nuts into his mouth. It was humiliating. He was sure his guys laughed about it behind his back, so he had stopped eating monkey nuts.

Benny Mongrel. The way the ugly bastard had walked into the Lotus River tavern last night and sat and stared at him, as if daring him to do something. Like he still had the power he'd had in Pollsmoor. He was nothing on the outside. Fuck all. The only reason Fingers hadn't had him killed there and then, in the tavern, was out of respect for Llewellyn Hector. He didn't want to make a mess on Hector's doorstep.

But that was then. This was a new day.

When he was finished inspecting his stumps, Fingers sat up in bed. The sun baked down on the tin roof of his small house, and he was parched.

"Rashied," he yelled. After a few seconds a tattooed Mongrel with buzz-cut hair stuck his head into the bedroom. "Bring me some Coke. The whole bottle."

Rashied went to do his bidding, and Fingers trapped his cell phone with his left thumb, using the right thumb to speed-dial for his messages. He hit speakerphone and listened. There were a couple of messages from girls, which he skipped over, and a message from Leroy, the little punk who sold tik for him, which made him sit up. Something about Gatsby. And Benny Mongrel.

Fingers played it again.

Then he went through the laborious process of dialing Leroy's number with his thumb. Leroy was small-time; he didn't rate a speed dial. He got Leroy's voice mail, some smart-ass message with LL Cool J jawing away in the background. Fingers killed the call with a jab of his thumb.

By the time Rashied came back with the bottle of Coke, Fingers was busy with the clumsy business of dressing.

Burn drove the Ford through the sprawl of the Cape Flats, the endless monotony of poverty stretching in every direction. It was a good thing he'd been forced to leave his Jeep at the Waterfront. The only people who drove Cherokees on the Flats were drug dealers. Way too visible.

Burn had flown over the Flats and skirted past on the freeway, but he had never ventured down these mean streets. The small houses huddled together, their foundations unsure in the sandy ground. The watchman's curt navigation led them past rows of soulless ghetto blocks, where the relentless wind danced washing on lines strung across concrete walkways. They passed sandy, open patches, trading spots where young men huddled behind concrete walls scarred by gang graffiti.

Burn had taken the Mossberg shotgun from Barnard's bag in the trunk of the Ford and shoved it next to his seat. He'd used a Mossberg in the military and welcomed its added firepower. He found himself touching it, for some kind of reassurance.

Burn slowed at a stop sign. A small boy, around Matt's age, stood on the corner in front of a faded blue mosque. He twirled a homemade toy, a piece of string with a rock tied to the end, his nose glued to his face by unwiped snot. He stared at Burn in blank fascination.

As he pulled away, Burn checked his rearview mirror. The fat cop was barely visible under the blanket.

"Is he still alive?" Burn asked.

The watchman reached over and lifted the blanket, nodded, then stared straight ahead. Burn needed the fat man to live until he found his son. Then the watchman could do whatever he needed to do.

They were heading deeper into the Flats, moving into the cloud of sand the wind threw over the maze of small houses and narrow streets.

Sometimes Zondi wished that he smoked, to give him something to do at times like these. He was at the police lab, watching as a technician worked a comparison microscope, trying to identify similarities between the slug Zondi had dug from the wall at the building site and the one that had killed Ronnie September.

The technician was a startlingly beautiful woman with burnished copper skin. Her hair, black as squid ink, fell across her face as she leaned forward, peering into the microscope. Zondi had an image of that black hair spread like seaweed over a white pillow.

He was relieved when his phone chirped in his pocket. He walked out into the corridor as he took the call. He listened to the cop at Sea Point station, nodded, asked a couple of questions, and wrote a phone number down in his notebook. He killed the call and found himself at the end of the corridor, staring out a dirty window at the city below.

When he'd driven away from Mountain Road, he'd called the Sea Point police and asked them to check if anything linked back to the American. Hill. It was a long shot, a trial balloon. He knew he was an anal-retentive control freak covering all bases. Even imaginary ones.

But it had produced a hit.

A woman, a domestic worker, had been found murdered the day before on the steps in Greenpoint. Her name was Adielah Dollie. She worked for a Mr. and Mrs. Hill at Thirty-six Mountain Road.

"Investigator Zondi?"

He turned to see the technician waving to him from down the corridor. Her long nails were painted a deep red. Zondi pushed away the image of those nails collecting skin samples from his naked back. He walked up the corridor.

"There's a match," said the technician. "The bullet you brought to us is a .38 caliber, the same as the one retrieved from the child's body. The lands and grooves on both of these bullets are identical. They have the same signature."

So Barnard had shot the night watchman. And his dog. What exactly did that tell him? "Thanks. Now, about that condom?"

The technician shrugged. "The DNA testing will take a little longer."

"How much longer?"

"Try three months."

"Is this a joke?"

"No. There's a backlog at the DNA lab."

"So I'll jump the queue. Like I did here."

She gave him a smile. "You won't have the luck with them that you had with me. They're a lot stricter." She was flirting with him, something dancing in her almond eyes. Waiting for him to make a move.

Zondi walked out.

In the lab parking lot he popped the trunk of his car and grabbed his laptop. He slid behind the wheel and got the engine idling, aircon on high. He booted up his laptop while he dialed the dead domestic worker's daughter on his cell.

The conversation was brief. He voiced formulaic words of sympathy; then he asked Leila Dollie if she had ever met Mrs. Hill. Yes, she had met Susan Hill, more than once. Two Susans? The coincidence count was higher than in a cheap paperback.

He wanted to know if she was close to a computer with e-mail. She was. He e-mailed her a JPEG of Susan Ford's mug shots from his laptop. She received and opened the mail while he was still on the line.

"That's Mrs. Hill," said Leila Dollie. She sounded confused. "Does this have something to do with my mother's death?"

Deep in his gut Zondi knew that it did. He just didn't know what.

"No, we're running a background check on the Hills." He was ready to end the call when he tried one more question. "You don't perhaps know where I could find Mrs. Hill, do you?"

"Well, the last I heard she was at Gardens Clinic."

"She's sick?"

"No, she's about to have a baby."

Zondi thanked her and sat there in the car, his mind alive with loose ends like snakes fleeing a mountain fire.

Susan Burn lay on the bed in the delivery room, being prepared for the cesarean section. Her gynecologist, a sandy-haired man in his forties who had worked as hard on his bedside manner as his golf game, was clearly used to dealing with a succession of mothers-to-be for whom the cosmetic risk of the cesarean section was the major issue. In a city of beaches and health clubs, an abdomen that looked like an early Frankenstein movie wasn't desirable.

He started going into detail about how the lower midline abdominal incision—the bikini cut—would heal, leaving nothing but a hairline scar, which, with the diligent application of tissue oil, would disappear completely.

This was the last thing on her mind, but she nodded appreciatively.

Then the anesthetist arrived to do the epidural. Susan had asked to be awake during the cesarean; even though she wasn't going to push the baby out the way she had Matt, she still wanted to witness that first moment of her daughter's life.

The anesthetist was beefy, with hands like a plumber, but he proved to be gentle and reassuring. He asked her to roll onto her side and lifted her smock. He rubbed anesthetic liquid on her lower spine and then inserted a very fine needle. All the while he was humming a tune. Susan eventually recognized it as the old Beatles song "Lucy in the Sky with Diamonds." She almost laughed but stopped herself, frightened that the needle would snap in her spine.

When the anesthetic started to numb her skin, the humming man approached with a much larger and more intimidating needle. Susan closed her eyes, and she allowed herself to remember when her daughter had been conceived.

It had been after the gambling trouble, as it had become known by her and Jack. After he had come clean, fessed up, she'd allowed him to whisk her off for a weekend to a hut in the Sierras. Just the two of them, Matt left behind in the care of her sister.

It had been an idyllic weekend. Hiking during the hot days, lying in front of a fire as the coolness of the night crept into the hut. They had made love in front of the fire. It was corny, cheesily romantic, and she had loved every minute of it. And she'd loved Jack more than she ever had. She'd opened her heart to him again, and that was the night they made this child.

When they went down the mountain, back to the sprawl of L.A. below, she felt a renewed optimism. Okay, so a bad thing had happened. But they had worked it out. They had cut the cancer from their lives and healed their marriage.

All was well.

Of course he had gambled again. And then came Milwaukee and that terrifying phone call when he demanded that she and Matt meet him in Florida. She had heard something in his voice that made it impossible to argue. So she'd dropped the dog off with her sister and driven with her son to the airport.

They never went home again.

Life became a succession of transit lounges and passports doled out like playing cards, the man she'd married becoming as strange as the names that stared up at her from the fake passports.

The anesthetist was trickling the anesthetic into her spine. There was a moment when the catheter touched a nerve and produced a brief tingling sensation down one leg; then she felt a not unpleasant numbness from the waist down.

There was something reassuring in handing herself over to this process, suspending her own volition, letting others chart the course.

She allowed herself to enjoy this lull. She knew that it wouldn't last for long.

~~~~~~~~

They were deep in the Flats now, driving into Paradise Park. Benny Mongrel reached over the back of the seat once again and lifted the blanket off Barnard. His breathing was shallow and labored, but he was still alive.

Benny Mongrel was a connoisseur of pain. As others in the Cape could roll a glass of wine over their tongue and wax lyrical about its provenance and subtlety, so he knew exactly how to appreciate the effects of the pain he was administering.

And he knew that he had caused the fat man more pain than any of his other victims. Even if the results, initially at least, were less dire than some of his previous exercises. The fat cop's limbs were still connected to his torso, his tongue still lay in his mouth, and his organs were still encased by muscle, fat, and skin. But the relentless insertion of the wrapped blade, piercing each layer of epidermis, moving through subcutaneous fat and flesh, finding nerve ends and connective tissue, had built to a greater symphony of pain than he had ever inflicted on any one body.

The fat man had taken it for an extraordinary amount of time. It had amazed Benny Mongrel. Looking at Barnard, he'd made the quick assessment that, stripped of his badge and his gun, he was nothing but an overgrown fat boy with no spine. He'd expected him to talk as soon as he was shown the blade. But each time the duct tape was pulled from his face, the fat cop had repeated the same two words, *fuck youse*, as if they were a prayer.

Then the fat man had seemed to pass over into a world not quite connected with the brutal reality of Burn's garage. He closed his eyes. He spoke a name or two, then gave voice to a babble that sounded to Benny Mongrel like the crap that some of the happy-clappys in prison had produced when talking to their gods.

That's when Benny Mongrel had thought that he had lost him, that whatever information the fat man had about the missing white boy was gone forever. Benny Mongrel had been ready to unwrap the blade and draw it, once and for all, across that fat throat. Let the American do what he liked. But one of those eyes, like a fly in a plate of prison porridge, had flickered open and fixed itself on Benny Mongrel. And the voice had wheezed out of the chest like the last gasp of a cheap accordion.

"You wanna boy?" It took Benny Mongrel a moment to understand. Then he nodded. "Then I'll tell you. Jus' to shut them up."

"Who?"

"The dead fuckers."

Barnard had given him an address in Paradise Park. Benny Mongrel knew the ghetto block; he had once killed a man in one of those cramped apartments on Tulip Street. Remembered it well as Burn stopped the Ford in the shadow of a wall with *thug life* sprayed across it.

Benny Mongrel wasn't completely sure why he'd even agreed to come on this trip. He could've finished things in the garage and walked away. But no, he was here. Maybe this was how things were meant to end. He had started it, and now he had to see it through.

As he was about to get out of the car, Burn passed him the .38. Benny Mongrel shook his head. He had no use for guns. But Burn thrust it at him. "Take it."

Benny Mongrel checked that the safety was on and jammed it into the belt of his jeans. Then he opened the rear door of the Ford and aimed a kick at the shape that lay on the seat like a beached and bloodied whale.

The three men walked up the stairs. The watchman went first, then Barnard, stumbling, still wrapped in the blanket. Burn brought up the rear. He held the Mossberg close to his leg, hiding it as best he could. Barnard was mumbling, delirious, his great body racked by bouts of shivering. His boots left bloody footprints on the stairs that stank of piss.

They came to a corridor, open to the wind, which chose that moment to gust and blind them with a blast of sand. Burn wiped his eyes and stumbled into the back of Barnard. The stench that rose from the man was beyond fetid, and bile scalded Burn's throat.

The watchman stopped at a warped door and nodded at Burn. Burn leveled the Mossberg. The watchman tried the door handle. It was

locked. The watchman stepped back as far as the narrow corridor allowed, lifted his foot, and kicked the door, right up beside the lock. The
door sprang open, banging against the wall inside. Burn rushed in, the
Mossberg raking the interior. The dingy room was empty.

The watchman stepped inside, pushing Barnard in front of him,
and closed the splintered door. Burn passed the empty kitchen, stuck his
head into the bathroom, then went into the bedroom.

A man lay on the bed. Burn leveled the Mossberg, stepped cautiously into the room. The man, old and wrinkled as a tortoise, was naked
except for a pair of stained briefs. He lay in a pool of blood that came
from the gaping wound in the back of his head. His brains had been
beaten in. Burn nudged him with the barrel of the Mossberg. Nothing.
The man was dead.

It was then that Burn saw the pajama top that protruded from beneath the dead man. Burn yanked it free and held it up. A collection of
Disney characters against a blue background, smeared with blood.

Burn had watched Mrs. Dollie slip that pj top over Matt's head two
nights before. The last time he had seen the boy.

His son had been in this apartment.

CHAPTER 29

Burn had Barnard by his greasy forelock, lifting his head up. He slapped the cop through the face with his free hand. "Open your eyes, you fat fuck."

Barnard wheezed, but his eyes and, more important, his mouth stayed shut. Burn let go of the hair, and the cop's chin dropped to his chest, its fall broken by the rolls of fat that hung from his neck. Barnard sat on the torn sofa, listing to the side like a melting snowman.

Burn wiped his hands on his jeans. He looked across at the watchman, who stood near the front door, sucking on a cigarette. "I need you to get him to talk, for Chrissakes. I need him to tell me where my son is."

The watchman shrugged. He seemed to be getting some sort of

perverse pleasure out of the whole scene. Burn lifted the Mossberg and jammed it against the cop's head. The head flopped to the side.

The cop's eyes stayed shut.

Disaster Zondi found himself driving back toward Mountain Road. Okay, he told himself, you're obsessing. He could've hung around the crime lab and flirted with that forensic tech, whose almond eyes hinted at knowledge beyond comparison microscopes and bullet fingerprints.

Instead he had driven across town to Salt River, to Sniper Security. Wanted to talk to the night watchman, Benny Niemand. Nobody had seen the watchman since the night of the shooting when he had walked out of Somerset Hospital and disappeared. Zondi had found out that he was an ex-con, once a high-ranking member of the Mongrel gang. A 28.

So why had Barnard shot him? The men in the red BMW were gangsters, Zondi was sure of that. And this watchman was another. Was this a drug deal gone bad? And why had it played itself out against the unlikely backdrop of an elite suburb in white Cape Town? And what was the American's role in all of this?

He swung into Mountain Road and parked outside the American's house. He wanted to ask him a simple question: why had he lied when he'd looked at his wife's mug shots? Maybe the answer to that question would join a few of these disconnected dots.

Zondi, out of force of habit, shrugged on his jacket as he stepped into the furnace that was late afternoon in Cape Town. He rang the buzzer. Nothing. He rang it again.

He took a few steps back and looked up at the deck, where he had seen the man, Hill, earlier. The deck was empty, except for a hawk perched on the railing, forced by the fire to leave the mountain to search for prey. The hawk looked down at Zondi; then it unfurled its wings and kicked off, swooping up and catching a thermal. It hung there in a lazy glide.

Zondi went back to the street door, and even though he knew he was wasting his time, he rang the buzzer again. Nothing. He turned and headed back to his car. As he passed the garage, his eyes were drawn to a tread mark, printed cleanly on the short cement slope that joined the road. Zondi knelt and rubbed the tire tread with the index finger of his right hand; then he inspected his fingertip. It was smudged red.

He was looking at blood.

Burn took a piss in the squalid bathroom, the Mossberg lying on the cistern. Where was his son? If the old man had been brutally murdered, what had happened to Matt? Burn flashed on the bloody pajama top lying on the bed, and his imagination spun away from him; he had to fight it to reel it in.

The fat cop knew. Burn had to make him talk. It was as simple as that. He finished, rinsed the cop's hair grease from his hands, grabbed the Mossberg, and walked.

As he stepped out of the bathroom, he saw the splintered front door swing open and three men come in. One of them, a big brown man with his hair cropped to his scarred skull, looked at him in amazement; then he raised a .45 and shot a hole in the wall next to Burn's head.

Burn let go with the Mossberg, and the force of the blast lifted the gunman off his feet and slapped him against the wall next to the door. He slid to the floor, leaving a wet smear on the wall.

As the door eased open, Benny Mongrel saw Fingers Morkel step into the room followed by two of his men. A .45 boomed and the shotgun replied, and Benny Mongrel saw one of the men lift up like washing on a line and smack the wall. The other man dived toward the sofa, out of range of Burn's shotgun. The barrel of the man's chrome .357 was looking straight at Benny Mongrel.

Benny Mongrel remembered Burn had slipped him the .38. He brought it from his waistband and shot the man between the eyes. The man gave him a stupid look and dropped behind the sofa like emptied trash.

That left Fingers, who was standing open-mouthed, his scarred stumps moving in the air, his thumbs twitching like he wished to hell he could hitch a ride out of there.

Benny Mongrel felt the knife in his palm.

No guns for Fingers.

Rudi Barnard was in communion with the dead. He heard their voices; he saw their faces. They were calling his name, inviting him to join their number. He was fighting harder than he had ever fought in his life, fighting the tide that dragged him down.

The roars blasted his eyes open, and he saw the half-breeds before him, explosions of red reaching from their gaping mouths. Reaching toward him, trying to take him with them to join the legion of the damned.

Barnard found some last reserve of energy. He sprang from the sofa and hurtled headlong toward the living room window, and in an explosion of blood, glass, and fat he burst out into that bright, terrible light.

Silence. Burn realized that the weapons discharging in the confined space had momentarily deafened him.

He saw the fat cop leap from the sofa and smash through the

glass, disappearing from view. He saw the watchman kick the legs from under the surviving member of the trio who seemed to be attempting a prayer for mercy without the benefit of fingers. He saw the watchman's blade catch a perfectly angled beam of sunlight as it rose.

"Wait." Burn's voice sounded muffled to his own ears. He held the Mossberg like an extension of his arm, pointed at the watchman. The blade halted in midair.

Burn went to the kneeling, fingerless man and applied the Mossberg barrel to the side of his head. "Where is my son?"

The man stared at him blankly. He shook his head. Burn took the barrel back and smashed the man in the face, seeing thin beads of blood hang in space before they hit the dirty wooden floor.

He took the barrel back for another swing. He felt the watchman's hand on his arm. "He don't know nothing."

He looked at the watchman. "Then what's he doing here?"

"He come here so I can kill him. Old business."

Burn believed him. For some reason this seemed a perfectly rational and satisfactory explanation. But the question of his son's whereabouts remained. And the man who held the answer had just hurled himself out of a closed window.

Burn ran toward the door.

Benny Mongrel looked down into the eyes of Fingers Morkel and realized that a great tiredness had enveloped him. It was all he could do to hold the knife in his hand. But he knew, one last time, that there was something he must do.

He took Fingers by the chin and, with the precision of an executioner, lifted his head to bare the neck and sent the blade across the throat.

"Benny Mongrel say goodnight," he said, and let Fingers slump to the floor.

Then he relaxed his hand and felt the knife slip from his grasp, and, perfectly weighted instrument that it was, it landed blade first in the wooden floor and quivered for a time before, at last, it was still.

By then Benny Mongrel had left the room.

CHAPTER 30

The fat man flew out the window, a trail of blood and glass in his wake, and landed heavily on the sand. As he lay on his back, his great naked chest heaving, the blanket floated down and covered him like a shroud.

People in the street and the adjoining apartments, drawn by the all-too-familiar chatter of small arms, paused when they saw the man plunge. There was a collective gasp when the blanket moved and he sat up. He hauled himself to his feet, and the blanket fell away.

A sharp pair of eyes recognized him beneath the gore, and his name was whispered.

"It's Gatsby."

Wheezing, bleeding, and foaming, the fat cop took off down Tulip Street as if he were being pursued by the devil, massive legs pumping.

The cry grew louder. "It's Gatsby!"

A small boy rolling a bald tire fell in behind Gatsby, following him up the road as women in curlers, hanging over fences, put their gossip on pause as this demonic vision crossed their view.

Farther down Tulip Street, Donovan September lay under a car, parked halfway up on the sidewalk. He was adjusting the exhaust mount, while two of his friends passed him tools and offered advice. He put out his hand for a screwdriver, and it wasn't forthcoming.

Then he heard one of his friends say, "Jesus, Donovan, you better come look at this."

Donovan slid out from under the car. As he stood, he wiped the sweat away from his eyes with the back of his hand, not believing what he was seeing. Gatsby, the cop who had put his little brother in the ground, was running up the road, half naked, bleeding. People were trailing in his wake like pilot fish feeding off a harpooned whale.

Donovan picked up a hammer from the hood of the car and stepped out into Gatsby's path. The fat man didn't see him, ran straight on. Donovan had to sidestep, or the mountain of fat would have rolled right over him. Donovan stuck out a leg and Gatsby stumbled, teetered for a moment, then toppled like a great beast to the sand.

Donovan stood over the felled man, the hammer in his hand. He looked around at the gathering crowd of his neighbors and heard their voice as one. "Do it, Donovan."

He raised the hammer high and brought it down on the fat cop's head.

Carmen Fortune walked back from the taxi toward her apartment, still feeling a buzz even though she knew the tik rush was waning. She knew, also, that she was going to have to face the mess in her bedroom. But she had done good. For once she had done the right thing.

After she had smashed the Virgin on Uncle Fatty's head, she had grabbed the boy, Matt, pulled one of Sheldon's T-shirts over his head, and run with him. She had not stopped to think until she was in a minibus taxi, the blond kid on her lap, watching the streets of Paradise Park slide past her.

The kid was still groggy from the Mogadon, which was a godsend. She hoped that he would have no memory of what Uncle Fatty had tried to do to him. She knew only too well how those memories burned into your consciousness like a hot wire into flesh.

She ignored the stares and whispers of the other passengers. She knew how it looked, a beat-up colored chickie, blood on her T-shirt, with a white kid.

Fuck them.

She stroked the boy's hair, and he lifted his face, trying to focus on her. Then his eyes closed again. Sheldon's T-shirt was too small for him, and it was unwashed, but at least it was better than the pj top with Uncle Fatty's brains all over it.

She knew she had killed the old man, had felt his head all spongy and soft under the Virgin Mary. Served the bastard right. While she was beating him she had flashed back to memories of her own childhood, and there were moments when, what with the tik and all her rage, she wasn't sure if she was hammering Uncle Fatty or her own sick fuck of a father.

The taxi slammed to a stop, and passengers fought their way off, while others clambered in. She grabbed the boy and pushed her way out, past the leering sliding-door operator.

"I see where he got his blue eyes," he said, laughing at her bruises.

She didn't waste her breath on him, just slung Matt over her shoulder and crossed to the community center. The kid weighed her down. He had big bones, the little bugger.

She pushed through the smear of depressed humanity patiently waiting for nursing sisters and social workers and government grants, until she came to the door of Belinda Titus's office.

She banged once on the door and opened it without waiting for a reply. Belinda Titus sat at her desk, fastidiously applying lipstick while she admired herself in a compact mirror. Her freshly painted lips parted like a hooker's thighs when she saw Carmen.

"I beg your pardon, but you can't just march in here!" Belinda Titus, indignant, twisted the lipstick back into itself like she was twisting Carmen's neck.

"I just did," Carmen said, dumping the boy on the chair facing the social worker.

"What is this?" Belinda Titus demanded. "Who is this child?"

"His name is Matt. He's American. I think he was kidnapped." Carmen was on her way out. She stopped as she opened the door. "By the way," she said, rubbing a finger across her mouth, "you got lipstick on your teeth."

She had slammed the door and walked back through the downtrodden and the oppressed, and she had felt better than she had in a long time. She knew it wouldn't last, but what the fuck, she'd enjoy it while it did.

Then, as she came into Tulip Street, she heard the crowd before she saw them. A low animal roar of bloodlust. Carmen pushed her way through the mob and saw a bloody shape lying in the dust. It took her a few moments to recognize Gatsby. Donovan September was hitting him with a hammer, and some of the other boys and men were putting the boot in. The crowd was roaring its approval, calling for revenge.

Carmen, not able to drag her eyes away, was having serious reality issues. At last she convinced herself that what she was seeing was real, not some tik hallucination, and she heard her voice joining in, calling for the blood of the fat boer.

Burn sprinted up the street in time to see the mob form around Barnard and envelop him. Burn dived in, shoved bodies aside, his white skin and American voice surprising people out of his way.

"Stop! Don't kill him!"

The boy with the hammer looked up for a moment, paused. Then he went back to his work, smashing Barnard's head open like a Halloween pumpkin.

Burn tried to level the Mossberg at the boy, but hands in the crowd, like tendrils, took the gun from him. He was jostled, sworn at, and he felt a fist connect with his jaw. Then a rock hit him above the left ear and he dropped to the ground. The crowd became a single organism that lifted him off his feet and moved him to its perimeter, where it dumped him onto the sand.

Berenice September, carrying shopping bags on her way home from work, arrived at the moment when the mob parted and allowed the child to roll his tire to the center.

She saw the unmistakable form of Gatsby lying on the sand. And she saw her son, the serious one she loved so much, crouched over the cop, a bloody hammer in his hand.

"Donovan! No, Donovan!"

Her son looked up at her, and she saw his face as she had never seen it before.

Then the crowd closed again.

Donovan September took the tire that was offered by the solemn child, and he lifted Gatsby's head and slung the tire around his fat neck like a necklace. Then a jerrican of fuel was passed through the crowd, and Donovan doused the fat man's body.

Gatsby was still alive, his ribs pumping, his hands reaching up to the heavens. The mob moved back a few paces, and Donovan September lit a cloth and threw it at the fat man.

Gatsby exploded into flame.

Benny Mongrel stood at the very edge of the crowd and watched as they fell upon the fat cop. Every blow that rained down on that fat body smashed the desire for revenge out of his own.

It was right that this was happening.

It was good.

It was why he had been led here.

Benny Mongrel watched as the flames consumed the man who had killed his dog.

Rudi Barnard was in the lake of fire that his preacher had prophesied. His body was spiderwebbed with black char lines as the flames burned through the layers of his skin. He lifted his arms and welcomed the flames, even though they consumed his flesh with a most terrible agony. This was when he would be granted salvation, the gift of voices, when he would emerge from the fire cleansed of mortal sin and find his reward.

He looked around him in the lake of fire and saw the sinners, the lost souls, damned to burn in this hell for eternity. He tried to lift himself, to take a step forward, toward the light that he knew was ahead of him.

But he could not.

The burning water held him back. The limbs of the damned enfolded him and pulled him deeper and deeper into the inferno. He tried one last time, to drag himself toward the light that grew fainter and fainter as it retreated from him. Then, when the light at last was dimmed forever, Rudi Barnard finally had his answer.

His god was dead.

CHAPTER 31

Susan Burn lay in the operating theater, bisected by the sterile drapes that screened her lower body from her view.

She felt dislocated, detached, a numbness beyond that caused by the epidural anesthetic. She felt alone. Unlike when Matt was born, she had no hand to hold, no familiar presence to give her strength through the pain. No Jack to share the joy when the moment came. The drapes added to the sense of dislocation and alienation. Her doctor and his team were busy beyond the curtain, and Susan was reminded of a puppet show she had seen as a child.

She heard a whirring noise, like a food processor, and the acrid smell of her own body burning reached her nostrils. He's cauterizing your blood vessels, she told herself, trying to pretend that she was narrating something on the Discovery Channel. After the whirring ended, she heard nothing but the muted clink of surgical equipment and the whispers of the doctor and his nurse.

"We have her head here, Susan," she heard the doctor say. "I'm suctioning fluids out of her nose and mouth."

Thank God, she's breathing. That dread, that terrible superstitious premonition, had hung over her the whole day. That some price would have to be paid for the wrong that she and Jack had done. And that price would be the life of her baby.

"Okay, now I'm going in for the rest of her, Susan. I need you to help me, okay?"

She heard herself reply. "Okay. What do I do?"

"Just press your hands into the upper part of your abdomen and push down."

She felt the nurse guide her hands to the spot, and she started pressing. It was nothing like the protracted ordeal of giving birth to Matt, when she had felt as if a part of her body was being torn from her, but at least she was a participant in this drama, no longer a member of the audience. She pushed.

"Okay, we have her," the doctor said.

Then, exactly like in one of those puppet shows, her red and yellow baby, face squashed and furious, was held up above the curtain for her to view. Instinctively, she reached out her hands, but the nurse shook her head.

"She has to go into the warmer. We'll give her to you in a minute."

Susan lay staring up at the lights, listening as another suction did its work. Then the nurse returned with the infant and handed her to Susan. She lay her baby daughter, Lucy, against her breast and felt those tiny lips already sucking at her nipple.

And Susan felt herself crying, really letting go, for the first time since that day in Florida when Jack had told her what he had done to their lives.

✦

Burn wandered, dazed, at the periphery of the mob. His head throbbed, and he could feel sticky blood behind his ear, from where the rock had struck him. The sickly sweet smell of burning human flesh came to his nostrils, and through the shifting mass he saw Barnard's body ablaze.

The crowd, after its initial violent rage, was strangely quiet, as if now that the thing was done, it had to absorb the impact of its actions. People on the outside of the pack started to break away and drift up the street.

Burn moved through the thinning mob until he came to its center. He stood over the charred form of Barnard, the face unrecognizable, the teeth visible in a grimace, the arms stretched upward, blackened claws grasping. Whether this was Barnard's last action or an involuntary muscle contraction caused by the heat, Burn would never know.

But what he did know, with absolute certainty, was that the only man who could take him to his son was dead.

People were dispersing with more urgency. Even those closest to Barnard, the ones who had initiated this act, freed themselves from the mob's grasp. The young man, no more than a teenager, who had beaten Barnard and set him alight, took a last look and turned and wandered into a house nearby. A middle-aged woman stood in the front doorway watching him. They said nothing to each other as the boy went into the house.

Burn realized that he had been listening to the clamor of sirens for at least a minute, and they were getting closer.

He turned and ran back up the road toward the Ford.

He had no idea what he would do next.

Benny Mongrel walked away. It was done. There was nothing more for him here.

On the corner, near the taxi stand, he saw a man around his own age propping up the gate of a cramped yard, smoking, watching the goings-on but keeping his distance. His tattoos and his demeanor were those of a man who knew enough about trouble to give it a wide berth.

"They saying that's Gatsby they got there," he said to Benny Mongrel.

"Ja, it's him."

"He was a fucken bastard."

"Last of his kind." Benny Mongrel saw an opportunity and took it. "You got a smoke for me, brother?"

The man removed a crumpled pack of Luckies from his trouser pocket and held it out. Benny Mongrel took one, slipped it between his lips.

"You know, Gatsby, he shot me once," the man said as he lit Benny Mongrel's cigarette.

"Then how come you still here?"

"He must of been in a good mood." The man laughed sourly and turned and made his way toward the shabby house, dragging one leg as he walked.

Benny Mongrel headed away from the sirens, puffing on the cigarette behind his cupped hand. The wind had died, and the air hung as heavy as a blanket on the Flats.

Carmen Fortune left the mob behind and walked back toward her apartment block. She was relieved that she wouldn't have to deal with Gatsby finding out what she had done with the boy. At least there was that.

She passed a white man getting into a dented brown Ford. Most of the white men you saw on the Flats were cops, but he didn't look like one. He was bleeding from his head, and he looked confused. Lost. When he pulled away, he grated the gears of the car.

She climbed the stairs, and as she got up to the landing she saw her neighbor Whitey Brand come walking out of her apartment with her TV, casual as you please.

"Hey, what the fuck!" Carmen ran up the last few stairs.

Whitey just looked at her and walked on, taking the TV into his place.

When Carmen got to her apartment, she saw the door was standing open. It was splintered like it had been kicked in. Then she saw Whitey's brother Shane bending over some dead guys in her living room—guys she didn't know—ripping off their money and cell phones.

Carmen decided she was experiencing a particularly bad tik crash, that she honest-to-god was starting to lose her mind. She shut her eyes. When she opened them, she saw Shane pushing past her, his hands full. The dead men were still there, bleeding on her floor. And the sirens were slicing through her head like a butcher's saw through bone.

She turned and walked away. There was nothing in that place that she needed anymore.

Disaster Zondi stood and looked down at the charred remains of Rudi Barnard. The smell of burned human flesh reached his nose, a smell both awful and haunting. The clothes had burned into the skin. The hair was gone. The shoes had melted onto the feet. The tire had burned away completely; all that was left were the three steel rings from its inner core circling what had been Barnard's neck and chest.

It had been years, decades, since Zondi had seen a necklacing. The first time had been at the funeral of a youth activist in Soweto in the

mideighties when he'd been sixteen or seventeen. The comrades had attacked a young woman accused of being a police informer. Zondi remembered being drawn into the fervor, chanting freedom songs and
dancing the *toyi-toyi* as the woman was stoned and hacked. A boy
younger than Zondi had shoved a broken bottle up the woman's vagina.
Then she was encircled by a tire and burned to death.

The necklacing, far from being gruesome and terrifying, had been
heady, exciting. Had left him filled with an enormous sense of power, his
own and that of the untold number of kids who were going to bring the
enemy down.

Zondi, a youth of his time, had swapped the Book of Common
Prayer of his mission school childhood for the altogether more appealing
manifesto of Leon Trotsky. Who was he to experience pangs of distaste,
never mind guilt, if they executed their enemies in this way? After all,
the mother of the nation, Winnie Mandela—Nelson's very own wife—
had stood before them and applauded their actions, saying they would
liberate the country with their boxes of matches and tires.

Zondi had participated, at a distance, in a number of other neck-
lacings. He had long since closed the book on those memories and the
thorny questions they sometimes begged. Now, like a lot of men washed
up in the twenty-first century without an easy moral compass, he was de-
fined more by what he didn't believe in than what he did.

But this, he had to concede, had a certain poetry to it.

He overheard two young colored uniforms talking on the other
side of the crime scene tape.

"Shit way to die."

"Ja. I won't be able to eat Kentucky for a week."

They laughed and started talking about South Africa playing Australia in a rugby test match that weekend.

Zondi took a last look at Barnard, successfully fought the urge to
toyi-toyi in his Roberto Cavalli suit and Brunori loafers, and walked over
to the cops.

"He was running away from something, apparently?"

The cops gave him the usual once-over, just a degree away from insolence, before the taller man answered. "Ja, he was in those flats up there. People say he jumped out the window."

"Drive me up there, please, Constable."

Zondi was already walking across to the cop van, getting into the passenger seat. The tall cop exchanged a glance with his colleague, then got in beside Zondi and started the van. They bumped down the sand road, coming to a stop outside the ghetto block branded by the *thug life* graffiti.

Zondi climbed out, looked up at the shattered window. A bloody blanket lay in the dirt directly below. Zondi saw a lace curtain twitch in the apartment above the one with the broken window, and he glimpsed a leathery old face before it disappeared.

Zondi followed the cop up the narrow stairs. His nose wrinkled at the smell of piss. The door to the apartment with the broken window stood ajar. Zondi gave it a push with the toe of his loafer, and it swung open until it stopped against the body of a man. The constable had his service pistol in his hand and followed Zondi into the apartment.

Three dead men. All with that unmistakable look of gangsters. Two of them shot, one probably by a shotgun. The third man, who had at some point in his career had his fingers amputated, lay with his throat cut. Zondi could see bone.

Zondi and the cop walked through to the bedroom. He looked down at the fourth body, an emaciated man in his sixties, wearing only briefs. The dead man's brains were all over the statuette of the Virgin Mary that lay on the floor beside the bed. Zondi saw a child's pajama top, covered in blood and brain matter, lying beside the dead man. He noticed the American label: Big Kmart.

Zondi turned to the cop. "Constable, there's an old woman in the flat above. One of those types who spends her whole day watching at the window. Ask her who lives here and who she saw coming in and out of here today. And ask her about a kid. A boy. A white boy. You got that?"

The cop nodded. "Yes, sir."

He left Zondi to wander around the apartment. Zondi opened a chipped closet in the bedroom and saw a few items of women's clothing. A brush, clogged with dark hair, lay on a dresser beneath a broken mirror. The stinking bathroom didn't tell him much. A few cheap cosmetics and a box of sanitary pads.

Zondi went back into the living room. From the way the bodies lay, the gunshot victims had been met with fire as they entered the apartment. And then the amputee's throat had been slit.

At some point during all the action, Barnard had thrown himself out the window.

The constable was back. "She say a woman lives here. Early twenties, maybe. Carmen something, doesn't know her last name. The old guy is her uncle. An alkie, she say. She saw three guys come in here; one was white. Then another three. Coloreds. Gangsters, she say."

Zondi nodded. "These three."

"She say she saw the woman, Carmen, leave before any of these guys come in. She had a boy with her. He was white with blond hair."

Zondi reached for his phone and called Bellville South HQ. He spoke to a sergeant on duty, wanted an APB put out on this boy.

"Sir," the sergeant said. "The boy. He's sitting right here."

Burn drove through the sprawling ghetto without any sense of direction, just trying to get as much distance as possible between himself and the dead bodies. The wind had come up again, and it drew a gauze of dust across the Flats. The dust hid Table Mountain, the only landmark he could navigate by. He'd given the watchman the .38, and the crowd had taken the Mossberg. He was alone and unarmed in one of the most violent places on the planet.

Burn stopped at an intersection. A taxi drew up beside him, and the passengers stared down at him. He pulled away and almost collided with a beat-up pickup truck. The men inside swore at him. Burn barely noticed.

Maybe he had fled the ghetto block too soon? Maybe there was somebody there who could tell him where Matt was? He could offer money. He still had a million in local currency in the trunk of the car.

Jesus, he told himself, you go back to that place, even if you could find your way back, and you'll be arrested or murdered. And you're the only person who has some vague idea of what happened to your son.

Burn passed a group of youths, who shouted something. One of them threw a beer can, which bounced off the rear window of the Ford. Without the watchman he had no idea of how the hell to get out of this place.

Burn was lost.

CHAPTER 32

When Zondi heard the kid talking American, he didn't doubt for a second that this was the son of the man who'd called himself Hill. He had to be. Just too many coincidences.

The child was sitting on the counter in the charge office, wearing a soiled T-shirt and pajama bottoms. They matched the pj top Zondi had seen in the apartment. The child's hair was matted on one side with something that looked like blood. He was saying, through tears and snot, that he wanted his mommy.

In that unmistakable accent.

A prim-looking woman with tight hair and tighter features stood next to the boy in the charge office. She looked as if she couldn't wait to unload him and get the hell out of there. The constable on duty was taking her statement with painful slowness.

"How did this child get here?" asked Zondi.

The woman looked him up and down, immediately suspicious of this dark stranger. He allowed her a glimpse of his ID before repeating his question.

"My name is Belinda Titus. I'm a social worker. A girl, a former case of mine, brought him in. She refused to say where she had found him."

"Name of Carmen?"

"Yes. Carmen Fortune."

Zondi had no patience with children, but he manufactured a smile as he turned to the boy. "What's your name, son?"

"He says his name is Matt," said the woman.

Zondi's smile frosted over when he turned it on her. "Thank you, but let me handle this."

Zondi took the pen and a piece of paper from the desk cop's hands and slid them to the boy. These American kids were precocious, so he went with a challenge. "Bet you can't write your name."

The kid looked at him through the tears, wiped a grubby hand across his nose. "I can, too."

"Do you like ice cream?" The kid nodded. "Okay, you write me your name and I'll buy you an ice cream. Deal?"

The kid weighed the offer; then he took the pen and concentrated, tongue jutting from his lip, while he applied himself to the paper. His penmanship only a little worse than the desk cop's.

Zondi looked at the paper. "Matt Burn?" The kid nodded.

Zondi reached into his jacket pocket and took out the same mug shot printout he had shown the American. He held it up for the kid to see. "Matt. Who is this?"

"That's my mommy," the kid said, and started to wail again.

Zondi scooped him up off the counter. His suit would need to be cleaned after this. The child stank, and already he had deposited a smear of snot on Zondi's shoulder.

"I'll take this from here," he told the woman.

"This child needs medical attention," she said, anxious that her guest role in this little drama not end without the proper climax.

"I'll take him to hospital, don't worry."

Zondi walked the kid out to his car, set him in the rear, and tried his best to secure him with the seat belts. He retrieved his laptop from the trunk and went online. It took him less than two minutes to find out that Jack and Susan Burn were fugitives from justice.

He didn't know where Jack was, but he had a good idea where he could find Susan.

But first he had to find an ice cream.

>

Susan Burn lay in the recovery room, feeding her baby. A painkiller dripped into the catheter in her spine. She removed Lucy from her breast and lay with her cradled in the crook of her arm. Susan felt blank. Empty. Devoid of volition. Waiting for something to happen.

She became aware of voices outside the recovery room. The nurse's voice, insistent, agitated, and then a man's voice, emphatic. The door opened, and the nurse came in.

"Susan, I'm sorry, but there's a policeman here. And he insists on seeing you."

Susan sat up. The waiting was over. "Okay, bring him in, please."

A tall black man in a dark suit came in. He carried Matt. She saw that her son was filthy, his light hair crusted with dried blood. When Matt saw his mother, he reached for her and started crying. Susan was beyond surprise. She held out her arms for her son.

The man gently placed Matt on the bed beside Susan. She hugged her son, staring at the man over Matt's shoulder. The man turned to the nurse. "Leave us alone, please."

"She's just had a procedure. This is highly irregular."

"I won't be staying long."

The nurse left, reluctantly.

The man showed Susan his ID. "My name is Special Investigator Zondi. Ministry of Safety and Security." She nodded. "Is your name Susan Burn?"

She felt relieved. It was over. Finally. "Yes. Have you come to arrest me?"

"No. That's out of my jurisdiction. I came across your son, and I wanted to return him to you. Get a positive ID on him."

"What happened to him?"

The man was standing. "I'm going to leave you now. I'll ask the nurse to take a look at your son and clean him up."

"Where's my husband?"

"I have no idea, Mrs. Burn."

Susan was staring at him. "That's it? You're just going to leave?"

He nodded. "Yes."

"Wait. Please tell me what happened. Where you found Matt."

He looked at her. "I don't know exactly what happened. My guess, and I could be wrong, you understand, is that your son was kidnapped. And your husband tried to get him back, but the boy was released out on the Cape Flats."

Susan was processing this, through the fog of the painkiller. "Matt was kidnapped?"

"Yes. I believe so."

"And Jack, my husband, tried to handle this on his own?"

"It seems that way, yes."

"My son could have been killed?"

He nodded. "Yes. It was a dangerous situation."

Susan felt Matt crying, his body racked by sobs. Then she felt an enormous and all-consuming anger, like a fire raging inside her. "I'm sorry, I didn't get your name."

"Zondi."

"Mr. Zondi, I want you to help me, please. Help me to put an end to this."

Zondi stared at her. Then he nodded.

Burn had found the distant Table Mountain through the smoke, and that led him to the freeway. He was on his way back into Cape Town. He had made up his mind; he was going to Sea Point police station to report the kidnapping of his son. He knew this almost certainly meant that the truth about who he was would emerge, but he didn't care. He had to find Matt. If it wasn't already too late.

As he came around Hospital Bend, the sprawl of city and harbor below him, his phone rang. When he saw Susan on caller ID, his impulse was to ignore the call. How could he face his wife now? But he answered.

"Susan. How are you?"

"Jack, I'm fine. We're fine."

"So it's done?"

"Yes."

"And she's okay? The baby?"

"She's perfect."

"I'm glad, Susan."

She interrupted him. "Jack, Matt's here."

He thought he was hallucinating. "What did you say?"

"I said Matt's here. A policeman found him out on the Cape Flats."

"My God, Susan, I'm so sorry . . ."

"Shhhhhh, Jack. Don't say any more. Just come here. Come here now."

"Okay." He felt a heady rush of relief. His son was safe. His infant daughter was alive. His wife wanted him to come to their side.

"Jack, you're coming here? To us?"

"Yes."

"You promise?"

"I promise."

CHAPTER 33

Carmen Fortune sat for a long while at the taxi stand, watching the minibuses hurtling in and out, the distinctive cries of "Caaaaape Teeeeeuuuuunnn" as the sliding-door operators urged her to board. She ignored them.

It was still light, only just gone seven, and the sun hammered the Cape Flats.

On impulse she stood and walked a block, until she came to the street where she had grown up. Protea Street. She hesitated, almost turned on her heel, before she gathered the courage to approach the house of her nightmarish childhood. A small, scruffy place surrounded by a sagging wire fence, no different from hundreds around it.

Carmen hadn't been inside, or spoken to her parents, since her mother had thrown her out six years ago. Before she could stop herself, Carmen opened the front gate and walked up the short pathway and banged on the door.

The door opened a crack and she saw her mother's face. She fought the urge to run.

Her mother glared at her, shocked. "What do you want here?"

"I want to see him."

"You're not welcome here. Go back to the street where you belong."

Her mother was closing the door. Carmen pushed the door open, forcing her mother backward. Then she was walking down the corridor toward the main bedroom, her mother's hands clutching at her back.

Carmen swung and faced her. "Is it true that he gonna die?"

Her mother wilted. "Ja. He don't have long."

"Then I have the right to say good-bye."

Her mother said nothing, but she slumped in defeat. Carmen went into the bedroom without knocking.

A skeleton with gray skin and sunken eyes lay under a sheet on the bed. It took her a moment to connect this emaciated thing with the sweating, grunting weight that had pressed down onto her small body night after night.

It was the voice that did it.

"Carmen. You've come." The voice was weaker, but it was still the one that had poured filth into her ears as he raped her. This was her father, okay.

She walked up to him, stood over him, staring down.

He tried to smile, revealing gums set into a mouth like a sinkhole. "Carmie, the good Lord has answered my prayers."

"Ja? Has he?"

"I prayed that you would come to say good-bye to me before I go."

Her father's eyes were filled with self-pity and fear. He was not going easily to his final destination.

A clawlike hand was groping for hers. She slapped the hand away and pressed her face close to his. "Drop this God bullshit, you bastard. You think raping your own child for years, making her pregnant twice, and throwing her out of your house is something God is going to forgive?"

She saw the terror well up in his eyes as his sunken, toothless mouth searched for words. Her mother was hovering in the gloom at the bedroom door. Carmen heard a sharp intake of breath.

"We both know you're going to rot in fucken hell for what you did to me." Carmen laughed in his face and pushed past her mother. "And you'll get yours, you bitch."

Carmen fled the atmosphere of oppression and terror. She stood in the street sucking air, calming herself.

When she walked away, the sky seemed bluer.

Disaster Zondi drove along the freeway toward the airport. The shacks and mean houses of the Cape Flats sprawled on either side of him in the gathering darkness.

So, how did he feel, now that it was over?

He tried out that daytime TV word: *closure*. Was this how it felt? He felt lighter, he had to admit, but at the same time there was an inescapable sense of anticlimax. Was he still yearning for something more acute?

More transcendent?

What he did hear was the creak of the karmic wheel as it turned. For every action, you had better believe there would be a reaction. Like the American, Jack Burn, choosing Cape Town, of all cities, to run to. How different would it have been if he had parachuted his family into the safe, middle-class certainties of a Sydney or Auckland?

The wheel would have turned, no doubt, but probably in a more mundane way.

And as for Rudolphus Arnoldus Barnard getting sent off to the big barbecue in the sky, the punch line of that particular cosmic joke was irresistible.

Zondi laughed.

He found himself whistling as he drove to Domestic Departures. He was experiencing an unexpected feeling, a sensation that he was unfamiliar with. It took Zondi a minute of intense reflection before he decided that, quite possibly, it was happiness.

At dawn Benny Mongrel followed a footpath up the lower slopes of Table Mountain, etched into the scrub like a scar in coarse hair.

When he had walked away from the blackened horror that had once been the fat cop, Benny Mongrel had no desire to return to his cramped shack in Lavender Hill. He'd spent too many years in confined spaces, with the stench and moans and sickness of other men mixed into the foul air he breathed.

So he had come to the mountain.

He had found an overhang of rock that gave him shelter, not far from a stream that hadn't dried up despite the heat. He'd been down a little way now to where large houses clung to the slopes, their back gardens stolen from the mountain. Despite high fences and razor wire, he had come away with a shirt and a pair of jeans off a washing line. He needed no more than that.

As he walked up the path, he saw a movement in the scrub and slowed. He picked up a stone and crept forward, sure that he would find a rock rabbit for his breakfast.

The bush parted, and a puppy with a thick golden coat scampered out. It was too young to fear men, and it wagged its tail and pissed itself with happiness when it saw Benny Mongrel.

He knelt down and scooped the puppy up into his hands. The puppy licked him and wiggled like an uncoiling spring, pawing at him, trying to get to his face with its tongue. The paws were large, and Benny Mongrel knew that this puppy would grow up to be a big dog. The size of Bessie.

He stroked the puppy, feeling the smooth fur on its back. And feeling something that scared him: the thawing of his stone-cold heart.

Gently, he set the dog down. He stood up, gathered his stolen clothes, and walked on up the mountain. He never once looked back as the puppy tried at first to follow him, then stopped and sat down on the pathway and scratched at its ear.

Benny Mongrel was free.

———

Susan lay in the bed in the clinic, feeding her baby. Matt lay on the bed beside her, asleep, clean, dressed in crisp hospital pajamas. When the nurse had brought Lucy in for her early morning feeding, Susan had seen the uniformed policeman still seated outside the door.

Susan knew that the next phase of her life was not going to be easy. A man from the U.S. Consulate had come to see her the night before, a smarmy pretty-boy who looked like he'd been dragged from a game of tennis. He told her she would be escorted back to the States as soon as she was strong enough to travel. Aside from the court appearances and—if she was lucky—a period of probation, there were very real practical issues to face. Like money, or the lack of it.

Their house in Los Angeles had been seized and their bank accounts frozen. Susan was broke. She hadn't worked since she had married Jack Burn, and she knew that facing life as a single parent was going to be tough. That was okay, though; her children were alive and with her. Even if her husband wasn't.

Matt woke up and looked up at her. "You want something to drink, Matty?"

He shook his head, clinging to her hand. He sucked the thumb of his free hand. She gently disengaged the thumb from his mouth. He hadn't spoken since Zondi had brought him to her the evening before. Something had happened to him in those two days out on the Cape Flats. He'd been examined at the hospital, and aside from a bump on his head there was no sign of any physical injury. He'd appeared a little groggy, and a blood test had confirmed that he'd been fed sedatives but not enough to be life threatening.

Susan knew that her son had been injured on a deeper, invisible level. The type of injury that had turned this happy and extroverted child into a frightened shadow.

God damn you, Jack, she heard herself saying. *God damn you wherever you are.*

The tire burst somewhere north of a parched town Burn blew through so fast he couldn't catch the name.

He'd been running since the evening before. Since the call from Susan. When he had told her that last lie, knowing the cops were waiting for him at the clinic. He'd allowed himself a minute to feel relief that Matt was safe, to register that his daughter had been born; then he had turned Barnard's battered Ford north and driven through the night.

The morning found him somewhere in the Kalahari Desert. An endless expanse of red sand, prehistoric trees reaching like clutching hands from the dunes toward the cloudless sky. The road was flat and straight, a length of shimmering black ribbon laid across the sand. Not since he'd been in Iraq had he felt this kind of dry heat. Each breath burned his throat and his lungs.

He was exhausted, but he couldn't stop. He wasn't only running from the cops; he was running from the memories. Images of Susan and Matt and fragile, imaginary snapshots of his new baby girl that threatened to dissolve and disappear. The farther he was away from his family, the better off they would be. Of that he was certain.

A semi swam toward him out of the haze, and the wind of its passing buffeted the Ford, dragging Burn from within himself.

He drank water from a plastic bottle and splashed some on his face. He didn't have a plan, exactly. Knew only that he had to get out of South Africa, cross into neighboring Botswana, and catch the first plane out. It didn't matter where. Just put as much distance as he could between himself and Cape Town. He had the money and the William Morton passport, and he knew that the border between the two countries snaked through the unpatrollable desert. There was a good chance he wouldn't have to trouble immigration officials.

He just had to keep his foot flat. Keep on going.

He heard a tuneless version of "Good Vibrations," and he realized that he was singing. When he caught himself waiting for Matt to join in the chorus, he shut up.

Shut up in time to hear the bang an instant before he felt the Ford veer wildly to the left. He fought the steering, trying to keep the car on the road. But the tires found the gravel on the shoulder, and the car was flying away from him, flipping, cartwheeling, in a dance of torn metal and glass and bloodred sand.

The last thing Jack Burn saw was the sun in his eyes.

Then nothing.

Acknowledgments

Thank you to my editor, Sarah Knight, and my agent, Alice Fried Martell.

About the Author

Roger Smith was born in Johannesburg, South Africa. He is a screenwriter, director, and producer. He is at work on a second stand-alone thriller to be set in and around Cape Town, where he currently lives.